Dec

This book is dedi
Sean, Robert, Benjamin & Daniel
My treasures

Acknowledgements

With my heartfelt thanks to

Clare Orchard for the fantastic book cover
Samantha Parr & Samantha Duffy for proof reading
Rhlanne Statom for her enthusiasm and belief in my characters
Andrew Orchard for his quiet confidence in me
And to the Lord to whom I owe everything

First Published in the USA in 2014 by Create Space

ISBN-13:978-1496043931

List of Chapters

Prologue ~ Denied Escape

"Oh mother of all demons!" Idi cursed under his breath as he swayed slightly on the wet, moss-covered stone. This was the furthest from the village Idi had ever managed to get: he thought that maybe, just maybe, today would be the day he would escape.

The river current flowed fast and the rock he stood on shook slightly. Idi kept his knees bent and his arms out straight hovering in the air helping him keep his balance. The wind blew his hair and he shook his head to move it out of his face. He daren't for a moment take his eyes off *it*.

On the other side of the river was an enormous crow, the same size as Ned's old wolf hound, his claws holding him to the rock whilst his beady black eyes focused on Idi with intent. If Idi hadn't been concentrating so hard on the stepping stones in the river he might have noticed the huge bird arrive. When he did look up and catch sight of the crow he swore. Looking past the crow to the mountains close behind, Idi ground his teeth. *'It isn't fair.'* If he could just get out of this cursed valley he was sure he would find a better life than the one he had now. *'Why is there always something to stop me leaving?'*

The creature, as if sensing the boy's urge to make a run for it, threw open its huge black wings and squawked with piercing menace. Idi wobbled in fright and as he did so his foot slipped on the moss and he went crashing into the river.

The crow stopped his flapping and squawking and seemed to peer with worried, squinting eyes at the water where Idi had fallen. Idi was nowhere to be seen. The crow hopped out onto the first stepping stone and then another until he was on the one where Idi had stood. The boy wasn't in the water there. The bird stretched himself upwards, and strained its neck to peer down the river where he thought he saw something. The bird spread out his wings and flew over the rushing water down the river.

3

Idi, caught in the fast flowing current, was being hurtled down the river, but somehow he managed to get his head above water every now and again to suck in big breaths of air before being dragged back under once more.

The crow realised he wouldn't be able to catch the boy and rose in the air in a flurry before flying off into the woods.

Idi felt the cold current around his body and felt himself relax in resignation to the fact he was going to die. He stopped fighting and trying to reach the surface and simply allowed himself to be swept along. Calm descended on him and he opened his eyes seeing clearly through the bubbling crystal waters to the sky beyond.

'Ma Rose will be looking for me by now; she'd give me a right clip around the ear for being late and for not having all me chores done. I won't miss that. I won't miss anything about me life; if I can't leave this oppressive valley any other way - then river take me!'

Something caught his attention in the sky above. It looked a bit like a huge white bird.

'What is it with giant birds today?' he asked himself as his eyes closed and he drifted into unconsciousness.

Idi came round slowly. He was puzzled. He seemed to be flying? He tried opening his eyes, they flickered for a moment and then closed again. The sensation of flying was confirmed when he felt his body drop onto the grass. He opened his eyes slightly. *'Was that a huge white bird talking with that monstrous crow?'* The white bird's wings seemed to disappear and suddenly a lady's smiling face was in front of him. A gentle hand stroked his forehead. *'I must be dead then!'*

Some time later Idi yawned and stretched. He felt good, like he'd had the best night's sleep ever. He opened his eyes and saw the sky above him instead of the attic roof; he reached out to his sides feeling for his bed. Grass and not a mattress was what his hands touched and he sat up in surprise. He stared at the village in front of him. *'Hell's bells how did I get here and what am I doing in the sodden field?"*

Scratching his head trying to remember, the image of the crow came rushing back. He stood up and turned to look at the stretch of land behind him, taking in the farm lands that lay before him and the mountain range. It had taken half a day to reach the river, how had he got back here to the village when the sun was still in the sky?

"Did I dream it all?" he said shuddering, it hadn't felt like a dream and now he was back here in this nightmare of a place.

Chapter One ~ Oracle's Visit

Marcus's toes curled over the edge of the cliff as he watched the waves crashing far below. Today was his birthday. He was seventy years old and felt ancient and empty.

He had fought all his life to obtain the magic he could now wield, yet now he wondered why he had bothered. He'd not saved a single life, not by use of his oh so limited magic anyway. Adventure and excitement was what he had wished for and instead all he had done was bring the band of Brothers together and teach.

He laughed, bitterness echoing in the hollow sound. No, he was the eldest of the Brothers, and yet the youngest could perform far more magic than he. And the bitterest pill was that he had taught them everything they knew.

Marcus had picked the eleven Brothers to join him after a dream he'd had, many moons ago. One by one he'd found them, seen something within each of them that was good, then brought them here to the edge of the world of Talia; far from the affairs of men and Kings. Here he had become their mentor, teaching them all he knew: inner strength, the ways of the world, all the while constantly searching their hearts for truth. He had watched their actions and deeply searched their motives until; one by one, he had become satisfied that they were men of the light. Then (and only then) he had taught them the power of words and magic. Within ten years they were as powerful as himself, within twenty they had left him far behind. A lesser man might have feared that they would eventually reject him because of his weakness, but he knew within himself, without pride or conceit, that they loved and respected him. He knew, not one of them would try and oust him from the band of Brothers.

Lost in thought and staring out at sea a gust of wind rushed in across the waters hammering his frail body. So powerful was it that he almost fell as he swayed dangerously close to the edge. Uneasy he whirled around searching the surrounding areas for what might have caused the sudden flurry. He could see nothing out of the ordinary, yet a single gust of wind was not natural. Marcus pulled his dark purple cape closer around his thin, wiry body and pulled his hood back over his head. An urge to turn and run filled him, yet his feet seemed heavy and remained stuck to the ground. A breeze brushed against his body and face, pushing back his hood once more. His long white hair billowed in the wind and his clean-shaven angular face felt the touch of the wind as a caress.

He raised his arm to cover his face momentarily afraid as his cloak flew around him, then as quickly as it had arrived, the wind died out. In the stillness that followed he felt the arrival of something.

Slowly he lowered his arm away from his face, becoming aware of a shift of light around him. Something seemed to shimmer, like a reflection from polished metal in the sunlight, and danced in front of him. He watched as the shimmering light slowly stopped moving, and before him Oleanna appeared.

Marcus sucked in his breath in awe. An Oracle – Defender and Guide of Talia - stood before him. He marvelled that a Spirit of the Land should appear to him. Everything about her was light and she seemed to flicker between substance and nothing making it hard for him to focus on her. She hovered momentarily above the ground and then slowly lowered herself down. As her feet touched the ground, she became solid, the fluidity of her anchored into flesh. Her eyes, the palest blue, glistened like crystals, and held Marcus captive. She smiled at him, very slightly, but it was enough to fill him with joy. He wanted desperately to reach out and touch her but he knew he couldn't. As was the way with these Angel like spirits, she spoke into his mind without speaking aloud.

"It is time for you to leave this place Marcus. You must go on a quest of great importance. You will leave today. Evil approaches and you must go with all speed. Head for the village of Clodoth, there you will find a young boy who you are to take on this journey with you."

"Who is this lad?"

"He is to be your ward, he answers to the name of Idi, although this is not his name. He is without parents and is considered the village fool. You will take him, love him and show him the Way. His destiny is vital for the future of the Kingdom, and although he is not 'The One' he will be the person to save 'The One' who is prophesied to come."

Before he could stop it entering his head the thought hit him, *'why couldn't I be the one to save the prophesied one?'*
Oleanna smiled at him. "It is not for you to question this Oracle Marcus, but to hear my words and obey."

"I must have blind faith then?" Marcus responded with a twist of bitterness.

"To each of us is given a gift Marcus, you have many gifts, but by far your greatest is that of teacher. Which of these is more important to your homestead: the roof that keeps the rain from making you wet; the stone walls that keep the wolves from your table, or the foundations that hold everything together? All are important; all make the homestead, without one part the others would not function. You are the foundation Marcus, without you Idi will not reach his full potential, without Idi the prophesied one will not be King. Glory is fleeting Marcus and you shouldn't desire it, seek instead a complete understanding of this deeper magic: Words are containers of power; and no one can release the magic within until they believe in themselves. One must believe magic is within and then must speak the words of power with belief if they are to behold true magic carried into the air. Remember always, that words, spoken in faith, are containers of power."

Marcus felt rebuked, he didn't seek fame; he just wanted to be remembered for doing something wonderful, was that so bad? But even as he thought it he questioned himself. Maybe after all these years he wasn't as pure as he considered himself to be, he felt his spirits falling.

"Which spectrum of magic do you wish me to teach Idi when I bring him back to the homestead?" he asked.

"You are not to return here, instead you are to take the boy with you and find the prophesied one."

"Not return!" Marcus nearly choked, "how can I not return, this is my home, what about the Brothers?"

"The Brothers will remain. I have already sent James to fetch another who will join them. They will continue as before until the time arrives for them to take part in the shaping of Talia."

"But where shall I go and how shall I find the prophesied one?"

"You must travel to a place named Havenshire. Watch the skies closely for it is said there will be a change in the sky on the night the prophesied one is born. You must not be late; you must not for any reason delay in reaching the girl who carries the prophesied one. Her life and the life of her son are in your hands, without your wisdom and protection they will be lost to the darkness. The night creatures are roaming the lands as we speak searching for signs that will lead them to 'The Catalyst'."

"How will I recognise this mother?"

"I saw her once, briefly in a vision. She wore a thin gold band around her head. Her hair was long and the colour of the palest sands, and her eyes as green as the grass."

Oleanna smiled fondly at Marcus. He would not know of it until the end but Marcus was regarded highly amongst the Oracles, he would be the builder upon which the foundations of the New World of Talia would be formed.

Marcus saw a flicker of movement behind Oleanna, and stood in awe as her wings unfolded and opened. They fluttered in the air as if shaking off tiredness, then stretched upwards and outwards, the snowy white feathers unfurling with little movements, like gentle waves hitting the beach floor. She saw him watching her wings and smiled at him with understanding. Slowly the wings lifted her from the floor and once in the air she began to shimmer, flickering in and out of reality.

"Be brave and believe in thy self my noble man," she whispered as she disappeared.

Chapter Two ~ The Quest Begins

For a moment Marcus stood, his heart racing in his chest, his thoughts jumping from one thing to another with all that needed to be done. *'What if I fail her? I have to pack, herbs, books, how much can I take? Triumphant skies I'm going on a quest! Will I find him? I have to, Oleanna is depending on me. ON ME!'*

He started to run, racing with powerful legs, not those of a frail old man as magic flowed through his body. He laughed as he raced across the fields. Pulling on his magic to run faster until the trees and hedges began to blur in his sight, faster and faster until Marcus himself became a blur in the air. There were many things he couldn't do, but there were still plenty of things he could!

As he approached the homestead he slowed down so he could look at his beloved home, absorbing the sights and sounds that meant so much to him. Nestled deep in the valley of the Torrean Mountains the Homestead was a haven in the wildest parts of Talia. Smoke curled softly out of the tall chimney and spiralled into the sky and the smell of roasting pig wafted across the fields.

Caldwin was in the yard; he must have been waiting for Marcus for as soon as he saw him he began ringing the bell in his hand.

With each clang of the bell the brothers began racing into the yard. By the time Marcus reached the clearing in front of the Homestead they were all there. He could see by their faces that they already knew he was leaving. He looked at each brother in turn and his heart began to fill with sadness. He did not know when he would see them again and he had grown to love each one of them as sons. His cloak fell down around his body as he slowed down and by the time he reached the gate he was walking. He pushed the heavy wooden gate open and walked into the cobbled yard. *'My home.'*

The brothers gathered around him, their worried eyes searching Marcus's face for clues as to what was happening.

"Are the rumours true, are you leaving us Marcus?" asked Matthew.

Marcus nodded. "It would seem that I am to go on an adventure!"

"Then I will go pack" said Tanner, half turning to go straight away.

"I must go on my own Tanner, although I would dearly love to take you with me." Tanner turned back to him.

"There is safety in numbers and my magic ...." Tanner stopped himself from finishing the sentence; he didn't want to hurt Marcus by reminding him that Marcus's magic was the weakest of them all.

James came to him and placed his right hand upon Marcus's shoulder, "Before you leave" he said, "please meet the person chosen to replace you

and pass on your blessing as you did for each of us."

Marcus blinked in surprise; they had brought him here already? How long had they known? He nodded at James, afraid to speak lest his voice should not be strong. James turned behind him to the entrance of the kitchens and beckoned to a slim shadow that stood in the doorway. As the figure emerged from the kitchens Marcus's first thought was that this lad must be young indeed for he was so slight, something plainly obvious even with his cloak pulled around him. The lad came to stop in front of Marcus, his head bent and covered by his hood.

"Well if I am to bless you I must first see you" Marcus said and lifted the hood back. Marcus took a step back in shock.

"A girl!" he exclaimed, turning to James, "you have brought a girl to live with the Brothers?" The young girl moved behind James as if afraid and Marcus looked at James his face turning red in his instant anger.

"Well?"

"Her name is Leona, she is without parents, has no home and sleeps in the forest and she has more magic in her than I have ever seen in my life. Oleanna showed me where to find her, but as yet the girl has not spoken." James looked at Marcus his face showing all his emotions, he did not want to upset Marcus but after all it had been the Oracle that had told him to fetch her!

"Come here child" Marcus said, beckoning her to him with his hand. Very slowly she moved from behind James and came to Marcus. He put his hand under her chin and tilted her head back. For a long moment he gazed into her eyes. He was surprised when she held his gaze and did not glance downwards. Her eyes were so speckled with colours that he had no idea how he would ever describe them. The colour was, however, pure, and she looked back at him as an open book. *'No guile here or dark reflections, and if Oleanna wanted her here then she must be special indeed.'* It would, however, raise problems. He turned back to James.

"She will need a protector. Go to the village of Torn across the hills, seek out Joanna, tell her that I ask that she would repay her debt and come to shadow this young girl who must now live amongst the Brothers." James nodded and sighed in relief, Marcus would bless her.

"How do you know she is filled with the magic?" Marcus asked.

"We found her in the forest; two of the boys from the village threw stones at her just as we approached. She turned the stones to flowers Marcus. Not only that but when she turned to leave the clearing the animals moved with her, from the birds to the rabbits but more awesome, three grey wolves. When she saw us she crouched and seemed to speak with them, then they disappeared into the woods." Marcus looked at the girl. *'She can't be more than twelve years old, how can she control that much magic when she is so young and without a mentor?'*

13

"Has someone taught you the Way?" he asked her gently. She shook her head. As Marcus looked at her a passage from one the lost books of Shyne came to him: 'old magic never taught, but passed on through heart and thought'. He had never met anyone with old magic. He had found the Brothers and taught them magic they hadn't even known they had within them before he showed them the way. But here was this child with magic brimming over. For a moment he felt a pang of regret that he wouldn't be the one to show her the Way.
He placed his right hand on her forehead, closed his eyes and sank deep within himself to draw on the depths of his magic. Slowly he felt the heat rise from his inner core up to his heart, and slowly move down his arm, releasing into his hand. A bright blue light poured from his palm and covered Leona's head. She moaned and swayed and Kailin moved to stand behind her lest she fell.

"May the Light always guide your way, may your heart always be pure and may you serve with honour." The light slowly faded and he let his arm drop down to his side. She swayed for just a moment longer and then opened her eyes. Her lips parted slightly as if she wanted to say something but when nothing came out she threw herself forward wrapping her arms around Marcus and laid her head against his chest. For just a moment he hesitated with the feeling of discomfort then slowly he reached up and stroked her hair, as he did so he wondered if life would ever be the same again, life was so drastically changing moment by moment that he feared for the future.

A short time later Marcus was sat upon his horse, his dark purple cloak replaced with an old travelling grey cape, one soaked in oils and magic to make it waterproof and warm. His travelling bags were thrown over the horse that stood ready next to his own. John placed water bags on top of the food box and made sure they were tied tightly to the saddle.
Selwin stroked the mane of Marcus's horse.

"I have been working these horses for twenty-seven moons Marcus. Now magic runs through their veins. They will not tire for weeks on end, even if pushed all day and night. You will see. Their stamina is unmatched, and their speed unequalled. I would wager these fine animals could outrace the wind if challenged. I have also trained them to answer only to your call, no matter the distance between you. Their ears are attuned to the sound of your voice. All you have to do is whisper and they will come. These are the finest I have ever had the pleasure to instruct. I learnt from the best you know". He gave Marcus a quick grin.

Marcus was touched; it was just what he needed to hear that day. All his work had not gone unnoticed. Although he envied Selwin's magic with animals, he was glad of it. It would benefit him on his quest. His long dreamed of adventure.

Marcus pulled on the reins and slowly turned towards the gate of the yard. Each clop on the cobbles echoed loudly in Marcus's ears. Once through the gate he turned the horse back around so that he could see the Brothers one more time.

He could not speak to them, could not offer them some last instruction, some last lesson. Instead he simply nodded towards them as they nodded in return. One last lingering look at the homestead he had built and loved and then he was gone.

Whispers of speed and great need of urgency to the horses was all that was needed. His horse sprang forward and the other was like its shadow. Together they raced into late afternoon and within moments the Brothers were gone from sight. All he could see was a blur of browns and greens as they sped South through the valley, racing to find his new ward Idi, then to journey onwards, to find the one Born to be King.

Chapter Three ~ The King Carrier

Cassandra crept along the narrow dark passages. No-one must recognise her. She kept her soft cloak pulled close around her, her small pale face peeking out from beneath the hood. Mary stumbled hitting her toe and cursed quietly into the early night air.

Cassandra turned, screwing up her face and gave Mary the most annoyed look her delicate face could muster. "Shsssshh" she hissed. They crept along together until they reached the door they were looking for.

"Go back to my room Mary, wait for me there."

"Never Casey, never, I can't be leavin' ya 'ere by ya'self."

"I will be fine, don't worry now. Go back."

"Nope I can't be doin' that, tis enough that I've not told no one bout you dressing up and goin' to the village as if you twas nothin' but a maid, nope am already for the chop I knows that, I won't be leavin' ya to head off into the night alone, nope I won't be. Your father will have me old guts for garters."

Cassandra sighed.

"Well then stay here if you must, but you will not, I repeat *not*, follow me into the maze. I am not going to the village tonight, only to the castle gardens." She looked at Mary for a moment, and leaning forward, placed her hand on Mary's shoulder. "Please Mary, just this once, I won't ask it of you again I promise." Mary's shoulders slumped; she might have looked after Cassandra all of the lass's life but she always found it hard to say no to her. Mary nodded and a smile sprung to Cassandra's face.

"Thank you Mary" she said giving her a big hug, "I will just tell him who I really am, I won't be long I promise, then I will come straight back to you." Mary shook her head; if King Hamish ever found out he would chop her up and throw her body to the pigs for sure for not keeping his daughter under control. But the sailor was so handsome and so well spoken for a seaman, she was sure no harm would come to Casey with him; he seemed like such a nice young man.

Before Mary could change her mind Cassandra slipped out of the door; after one quick look to make sure no one was around she raced across the courtyard and into the gardens. She didn't look back but sped as quickly as she could through the vegetable patches and into the walled Rose garden. Here she slowed her pace; no one would be able to see her now with the walls between her and the castle.

She crept along the wall until she found the gate that would lead out to the open grasses. She paused briefly to check once more that the way was clear and then raced across the grass to the entrance of the maze. She had given Rodanti clear instructions on how to find the centre and she was sure he would already be there, yet her heart raced with fear that he might not have come. She had met Rodanti in town just two moons back on one of her escapades of getting to know the folk of Havenshire. He was with his crew to collect wares for their ship docked over in Hamlyn, and to set up contracts with some of the local traders. They had met up every night since their first meeting, and Cassandra knew that he loved her even as she loved him. That she had known him such a short time did not bother her in the least, he was the one for her, she just knew it. He believed because of the way she had been dressed that she was a maid from the castle. Tonight under her masquerade maid's cape she wore her normal clothes. She would wait for him to tell her how much he loved her, for surely he must, (for he was to leave the next day back to his own lands, Bluedane, far across the seas) - then she would tell him her secret.

She hurried through the maze filled with excitement; maybe he would ask to take her back with him? Even as she thought it she knew she wouldn't be able to go. Not yet anyway because she would have to convince her father first that it would not be the end of the world if she didn't marry one of the many suitors he had lined up for her.

High on one of the castle's turrets was the dark silhouette of Norvora hiding in the shadows of the night.

"Do you see, my ladies?" He lifted a glass orb into the air and over the edge of the turret. "Do you see her? She hastens to her doom." Lights flickered and jumped around inside the glass orb. Three clusters of black smoke flew round, the hues of grey and black swirling them together within the orb. Each cloud of smoke inside was the spirit of three sisters, witches that should be dead, but whose spirits were kept alive by the use of dark magic.

"The witch is coming, it will soon be done, and then the beginning of the end shall dawn. Your freedom from the orb shall come with the death of the 'one'."

Cassandra turned the last juncture of the maze that opened up to the centre, and caught her breath. He had come. She paused for a moment and then ran to him: her cloak, catching on the hedge, came loose and slipped to the ground. The smile on Rodanti's face fell away as he saw the clothes she wore. There was no mistaking that a gown of white, with edgings of gold, belonged to one of royalty. Upon her head she wore a thin gold band. Either she was in great trouble with her mistress for stealing her attire, or she herself was in fact the mistress. She came to stand before him, her green eyes glistening at him with apprehension and love.

"You are of royal blood then?" but even as he asked he knew the answer. She nodded at him.

"Please don't be angry with me, I didn't mean to mislead you - it was just once we had met I wanted to be with you so much, I carried on pretending."

He smiled down at her gently and took her chin in his hand. "It seems neither of us has been extremely honest." Her eyes looked puzzled.

"I will tell you later" he said, "first I have been waiting a long time for this. He slid his right hand behind her neck, cradling her head, whilst his left arm wrapped itself slowly around her waist. He pulled her gently towards him and then lowered his lips to hers. He felt in an instant the shock she felt at the kiss and knew instinctively that it was her first kiss. He would have stopped then, should have pulled back. He knew he should let a single kiss be enough. Yet something was happening to him and he couldn't let her go. His blood raced through his veins, every nerve in his body came alive, and he was caught up in the thrill of passion.

Cassandra had gone weak at the knees and it was only Rodanti's arm that kept her from falling. From the moment he had started to kiss her it felt like her mind had slipped away. She was in a haze of desire and lost in the moment.

Norvora smirked as he watched the Witch do her magic. Unbeknown to Cassandra and Rodanti, the Witch was flying around them. With each circle she flew around them she created an invisible cord that pulled the soon to be lovers closer together. The Witch blew magic filled kisses that flew like blue snakes, at them, whilst the pair remained blissfully unaware of the magic spells that surrounded them. She touched their bodies, causing the heat to flow and surge between them. The magic released grew and grew until the couple, spell-bound, collapsed on the grass. Slowly the Witch pulled back. She observed for a moment checking that all was done, and then, darted high into the air.

The Witch was almost out of Norvora's sight when she spun in the air, and called to him in the cold night.

"The Seed is planted and cursed as you asked. I will come for my reward Norvora, do not fail me." With that she was gone.

Norvora took one last look at the couple lying on the grass. It was time to fetch Hamish.

Hamish was pacing the entire length of his private rooms. He could not explain it but something was amiss, he could feel it in the air, he had not felt this way since the night Cassandra had been born ~ the night his beloved wife had died. The servants had brought him his favourite ale and he had smoked his long pipe and relaxed in his chair by the crackling of the log fire but nothing could take away his irritation. Myles, his most trusted knight, had let him win at Warsomdry but now the game was over he felt his nerves grating. Pacing the floor was the only thing that seemed to make sense.

Just then the huge wooden doors to his private rooms flew open and Hamish spun around to see who had entered without so much as a knock. The breeze from the window met the draught from the corridor and Norvora's cloak billowed in the air like the wings of a bat.

"Greetings your Grace" Norvora said, giving the slightest of bows, "may I join you for a moment? I must be leaving this evening and I wished to pay my respects first."

Hamish gave a curt nod in response and turned back towards the fire. He disliked Norvora intensely but tolerated him for his alliance, for Norvora's dark towers towards the East protected the boundary of the lands of Havenshire.

Norvora moved to the small table by the window, picked up the glass decanter and poured himself a drink. He lifted the glass to his lips and smiled slyly to himself.

"Has your Grace planned his hunting trip yet?" he enquired, moving closer to the window.

"Yes." said Hamish, "We are to venture out seven days from now."

"I hear the pheasant are plentiful this year, I am sure you will have the most enjoyable time." There was something slimy about Norvora's accent, more so than normal and both Hamish and Myles looked at him suspiciously. Aware of their watchful silence, Norvora took another sip of his drink and allowed it to warm him. He savoured not only the drink but the destruction he was about to bring.

"I assume that you will not be taking *little Casey* with you this year, she will probably be spending time with her new lover." There followed two audible sharp intakes of breath. Norvora laughed out loud. In one swift movement Myles had crossed the room and held his dagger against the flesh of Norvora's crinkly neck. Myles pulled Norvora's head back by the hair and pressed the dagger tighter against the skin causing blood to trickle down his thin, bird-like neck, then looked at Hamish for the permission to strike.

"You surely don't think I would utter such *vile words* unless they were true, do you your Grace?"

There was something so blunt in his voice that Hamish knew that this was the reason for the dread he had been feeling all day. He looked at Norvora and let his gaze go to the window. He moved slowly across the room and came to stand in the shadow of the night light. His rooms were at the top of the castle, nothing above his rooms but the battlements. From this vantage point he could see the land in every direction for miles, he could also see into his gardens. Had the previous conversation not just happened he would have shook his head in disapproval at the sight of two people with no control - but as he looked out, he knew the truth of what he saw in his heart. One of the shadowy shapes he saw laying on the grass was his daughter. He stepped away from the window as if in a trance and went to the wall.

In slow motion he raised his arm and took down his favourite crossbow.

Cassandra looked up in a puzzled haze. Although what had just happened was not unpleasant in the least, it should not have happened, she would never have normally let such a thing take place. She felt a panic rising up within her, and in that moment, she raised her eyes and saw her father standing silently in the shadows of the maze hedge.

"Cassandra" she heard his voice break as he whispered her name and then she saw the crossbow.

"No" she choked and lifted her arms wide in protection of Rodanti. But Rodanti had also seen the crossbow, and in one swift movement he flung Cassandra face down on the grass.

Cassandra heard the whizzing sound of the arrow as it shot above her head and like a bang on the drum she heard the thud as it hit Rodanti in the chest. She spun around in shock to face him. He smiled at her. Then his body simply crumpled as he fell to his side and lay on the grass beside her. She looked with horror as blood poured from his chest. Watched as his breath faded and his life slipped from his body. She picked up his head and cradled him to her chest and began to rock slowly from side to side. Slowly a noise went out into the night. People would talk of the sound for many a time to come. It rose and rose in volume. King Hamish heard it as he slowly; trance like; walked back to the castle, tears rolling down his cheeks. The lingering magic within Cassandra turned her wailing into an eerie type of song that carried not only the sound, but the pain, far into the night.

Norvora heard the sound and sucked the night air deeply to embrace the joy of the pain; he settled backwards into his saddle and thought, if he could ever remember what being happy was then *this* was surely it. So many scores settled in one moment, the whole thing was just too perfect. He sat forward and dug his heels into the horse's side. He wanted his towers. As the horse sprang forward Norvora whispered into the night, "I will be back for you Cassandra, and that which you carry, I will take."

Chapter Four ~ A Boy with no name

Marcus sat on his horse on the top of the hill and looked down at the village before him. Clodoth was a small village in the middle of nowhere. *'So this is home to the nameless one. How shall I persuade the boy to come with me, and will anyone try and stop me taking him? No good sitting here thinking about it nought but bum blisters come from sitting still.'* He pushed his knees gently into the horse and set off at a slow trot. *'Better just get on with it.'*

As he rode into the village he was struck by the poverty of the place. Every village and town had its poor quarters, but this entire village seemed to be engulfed by it. He screwed up his nose as the smells of filth rose to greet him. He looked at the children running around bare foot in their dirty rags and wondered what on earth had happened to this place. He trotted slowly into the village square and dismounted. He led the horses to a water trough but after a quick look inside led them away again without letting them drink. He tied them to a sickly looking pale tree, not that they would run, but for appearance's sake, then crossed to the centre of the square to the village well. He was lowering the bucket into the well when a bedraggled overweight woman called out to him,

"'ere mister I wouldn't be drinking that there stuff if I was you's, be sick before the dawn yea would, sick enough to poop for three days at least." The woman nodded away to herself as if confirming the truth of her advice.

Marcus nodded at her, "I am in your debt kind lady" he said tipping his hand to his forehead as a sign of thanks. The woman raised one eyebrow at him and carried on her way. He sat down on the wall of the well and watched the people walking by, all openly starring at him. He smiled at them as he caught their eye but most of them simply dropped their heads and went hurrying by. How on earth was he supposed to find Idi in this place?

A sudden loud bang was followed by angry yells, and Marcus turned to see what was it was happening.

"Ya good for nothing lazy little blighter, ya stupid idiot, ya good for nothing runt, belong with the pigs ya do." A thin wiry woman with a, none too clean, apron on, was hitting a young lad around the head with a cloth.

Some of the village children started laughing, "Ha ha, silly Idi's getting it again." Idi looked up at them from underneath his long scraggly hair that fell over his face as he tried to scramble out of the bad tempered woman's way.

"Get yea back 'ere ya lump of dung, ya be black and blue when I've finished with ya." That last comment seemed to give the lad the strength he needed, and he raced across the square. He stooped to pick up a stone and just as he flew past the laughing children he threw it at them. His aim was good and he hit the largest boy in the shoulder, the targeted boy yelped in sudden pain and then immediately lurched in pursuit of Idi. Idi was too thin for anyone's good health but he moved with speed and so outdistanced himself. As Idi approached the last alley that led to the farm lands he turned to his pursuing rival. The big village boy was out of breath, and knowing from experience that he wouldn't catch Idi in a chase, had stopped. He rested his hands on his knees, and looked down the alley towards Idi.

Idi in mock salute pretended to take a hat from his head, made an elaborate bow and smiled. The village boy simply scowled and turned back to the square, "wait till ya come back ya little lump of dung I'll be waiting." Idi's smile faded as he turned back to the village wall. *'I just might not come back this time'* he said with a twist of his lips. His chin dropped to his chest as he strode away, he would be back, just like every other time he'd tried to run away.

Marcus had seen enough, he untied the horses and slowly went down the alley in pursuit of Idi: *'Nobody here is going to miss the boy; I don't need to be a magician to figure that out. If I had time I would teach them a lesson or two about respecting one another, aargh give me strength not to wipe this miserable, good for nothing place right off the map.'* He hadn't seen one person who showed any pity in their eyes as Idi had been beaten. Marcus could've caught up with Idi in a moment but decided to leave the boy a while to allow his hurts to lessen. The hour glass had almost swung round before Marcus decided it was time to approach Idi.

Idi was sitting on the river bank, his head sunk into his drawn up knees, it was obvious that he had been crying. As Marcus approached several swans went gliding up the river. Idi raised his head to look at them as they swam gracefully by, just as the last one was going by it turned its long slender neck and turned its black round eyes towards Idi and let out a loud squawk, Idi instinctively picked up a stone by his hand and threw it towards the bird. For a moment Marcus froze in anger but the stone hit the water behind the swan sending it squawking and flapping its wings, after its companions. Marcus's felt himself relax, if the boy had meant to hit the bird he surely would have done so.

Idi heard Marcus approaching and jumped instinctively to his feet, ready for battle. Fists clenched tight in the air.

"Easy boy" Marcus said, leaving the horses to roam free. Idi looked at the horses as they wandered off.

"'Ere mister aren't you frightened they will run away from you?" Idi asked, puzzled that someone should let such beautiful horses roam free.

"Firstly I am never frightened, and secondly, you cannot lose that which does not belong to you." Idi's eyebrows rose high in his brow.

"You're a thief?" he said with sudden respect. Marcus looked at the boy sternly, "No of course not, they are free souls and do not belong to anyone but themselves, but choose to accompany me on my journey."

"Now you're just making fun at me, I saw you in the village, they might call me Idi but I'm not as stupid as they think you know." Idi tapped the side of his forehead with two fingers, "I know more than they think you know". He turned and sat back down on the river bank, as if he was closing the conversation. Marcus smiled gently to himself and went to sit next to Idi.

"Is that why you're called Idi then?" he asked softly.

"Yep, old Ma Rose, always says, 'idiot by nature and Idiot by name', I don't know if I ever had a proper name like, but Idi's me name now."

Marcus looked at the cool river rushing by and felt the peace of its sound soothe his soul. He had pondered much, on his way here, as to how he would persuade the village to let the boy go with him, but now he realised all he had to do was to persuade the lad himself. He decided to be direct.

"How would you like to come on an adventure with me boy?" he asked. Idi looked at Marcus side on: distrust plainly written on his face.

"I've heard tales that would make your blood curdle, all sorts of monsters and wizards are out in the kingdom, that's why we hide here, no good thing grows about 'ere really but that's why nobody comes and bothers us like, no I don't think I will go off adventuring with you if you please." Idi's voice was firm and Marcus knew the boy's fears were genuinely felt.

"You would have nothing to fear if you were with me lad, for I fear nothing and would teach you how to be the same." Idi shook his head, "nope don't think so, thanks anyway." He got up and looked

27

down at Marcus, "if I was you I'd be going back to the village and asking for lodgings for the night you don't want to be on these 'ere hills when the dusk falls in, trust me ya don't. Now gud'day to you sire for I'm going back."

"Will you not receive another beating lad?" Idi looked at Marcus as if he was stupid. "Course I will, but better that than the horror of these 'ere hills." He started to march away from the stranger; he could think him an idiot if he liked but Idi had tried to run too often to know that the things that lurked outside the village were real. He wanted to leave, he really did, but something always prevented him from leaving and he knew a frail old man was no match for the creatures he'd seen in these parts.

Marcus looked at the youth as he marched away with his back held straight. The boy appeared to be not very bright to say the least, was bad tempered and looked, with his spotted face and straggly greasy hair, as if the pox was about to take him. For a brief moment he thought the Oracle might have made a mistake, but even as he thought it he knew that Oracles never made mistakes. He called upon his power, throwing his right hand into the air.

"Light" he demanded, and with a flash and a crackle as the power was released, a light appeared in the air above Idi's head. Idi froze as he looked up: an orb of pale blue was emitting a soft light that lit up the evening's paleness. He turned slowly to face Marcus, his mouth open wide in shock.

"Do you think that whatever lurks in the hills would dare to attack the mighty Marcus?" Marcus's voice had risen with each word as if he challenged the very hills themselves. Idi stumbled backwards in sudden fear and Marcus dropped his hand and let light fade away.

"Nothing to fear from me lad: if you will keep me company on my journey I will teach you some magic, so that no-one ever again will dare to call you stupid." Idi's eyes could get no bigger and his mouth would surely any moment now consume the whole of his face if it got any larger.

"Close your mouth lad, or the night moths will begin to take up residence there." Idi's mouth snapped shut but his eyes still remained unnaturally wide. Marcus turned, he did not want to sleep near the river, if indeed there were things in the hills that were none too pleasant he wanted to be somewhere where he could hear them approach; the rustle of the river could mask much mischief. He put his fingers to his lips and whistled softly. Within moments the horses were by his side. He reached up and stroked each of them briefly.

"It is time for us to be gone on our journey once more, if you will carry us we could speed through these lands, which I have on good authority are not safe places to be." He spoke as if to the horses but his words were aimed at Idi. Marcus grabbed hold of the saddle and sprung up onto the horse, then turned to look at the Idi.

"Well?" For just a moment Idi seemed as a statue, then he sprang forward and leapt onto the back of the other horse. The horse neighed and reared high onto her hind legs. "Steady old girl, steady" Marcus said and turned to look at Idi.

"This once you are forgiven. Never again will you mount her without asking her first, never again will you show such disrespect for a living creature, or boy our journey together is over before it has begun."
Idi scowled and looked down at the horse, he had wanted the stranger to be impressed with how agile he was and here he was being rebuked yet again. "Do you hear me lad?" Idi raised his chin high and looked at Marcus.

"I *hear you* Magician," he said sarcastically. Marcus looked at him long and hard. *'What oh what has Oleanna seen in this wretched child?'*

"Let's be gone" he said to the horses and they sprang forward, graceful and strong, building up speed until one hill after the other began to fade behind them.

Chapter Five ~ Into hiding you must go

King Hamish was tired. He had been on horseback for hours and his body was now as weary as his soul, he was not looking forward to seeing Cassandra again. One thing to banish her from her home and leave her without protection, yet another thing to face her and tell her she must now leave her home lands as well. He had no idea where she would go, only that she must leave.

Cassandra had heard the approach of the horses and was waiting in the small cottage garden, Mary by her side, when her father and the Hadrian Knights came into sight. Hamish swung his legs around and dropped to the side of his horse giving the reins to one of the Knights. The Knights all dismounted and tethered their horses to the fence. They waited silently whilst Hamish went in the garden to talk to his daughter.

Cassandra stood straight and tall and held her chin rather high. Hamish's heart tightened for a moment in his chest. She was so like her mother, so beautiful; so fierce; so vulnerable. He stopped in front of her and decided that he could not handle pleasantries and so went straight to the point.

"You must leave here Cassandra, I cannot allow you back to the castle and it would seem my advisers have taken it upon themselves to point the finger of blame upon you for what is about to come. You know how I had great faith in you, that you would one day marry one of the suitors lined up for you, one that would help Havenshire and protect its borders. Now that you have disgraced yourself none of them will have you." The last part was said quietly but his bitterness and disappointment came through very clearly.

"It seems that you have opened a can of worms amongst our neighbours and already they begin to plot and plan our downfall. I cannot take you back to the castle." Hamish paused for a moment. He briefly looked into Cassandra's eyes, if only they had been ordinary people maybe then he would have been able to protect her.

"You are not safe here. You must leave as quickly as possible; all I can say to you is flee." His voice broke on the last word and he stopped for a moment to regain his composure.

"Go northwards Casey, tell no one who you are, leave your finery behind and wear your maids clothes, you have passed yourself off as a peasant before - do so again, for it may be the only thing that will shield you."

They looked at each other, neither flinching, neither moving. Both saying so much with their eyes: which they could not say in words. Hamish so wanted his child back, his little daughter, so wanted her to fling her arms around him as she had done so many times before, but she didn't move. He nodded once, briefly, his acceptance that she would not forgive him, even as he could not forgive her, and turned back to his horse. The Knights waited until their king was by his horse, and then went into the garden to stand in front of Cassandra.

Myles, the oldest knight and unspoken leader, came and stood before Cassandra first. His eyes were full of tears and his heart full of pain. Because it was not war time the Knights did not wear their full armour. The only piece of armour they wore was their cuirass which covered their torsos. The Hadrian Knights were so famed that armourers from all over Talia came to offer their new designs to the Knights. Because of this their armour was beautiful. Made from the lightest of metals melded with gold the suits had a shine that that would reflect the sun and blind the enemy. Although they weren't fully suited there was still no mistaking that they were the Royal guards. Their leggings were the deepest purple and made from the softest velvet, their shirts were white silk with purple edgings to the collars and the cuffs. Their boots were black leather with tops that flopped back down on themselves over the knees. In their full armour the folk of Havenshire would sigh in awe, but even in this less formal wear they commanded respect.

When Cassandra had turned five it had been Myles who had taught her how to fight. He had put her first wooden sword in her hand, her first bow and arrow, her first dagger. All the knights had taught her how to fight and hunt, but Myles loved her the most, the love was returned and Cassandra saw Myles as if he was her grandfather. Myles dropped to one knee before her and raised his eyes up to her. His white curly hair falling around his rugged, weather-beaten face; his blue eyes full of sorrow.

"We are Hadrian Knights Casey, we have pledged our lives to the King above all else, we live to serve him. If we could divide ourselves and go with you, to protect you, we would: but we have all sworn an oath of loyalty till death, to your father." Cassandra nodded and with a very weak voice whispered, "I know."

Myles drew forth the pendant that lay beneath his armour, a circle of gold within which lay a flame and a sword, the crest of the Hadrian Knights, honoured above all other Knights. The crest was held in the highest esteem. Cassandra took a small intake of breath at the shock of seeing that the pendant had been broken. Myles lifted his hand to Cassandra and she looked down to see half the pendant there.

"We have all had them broken in two Casey, it represents that our hearts have been broken. Take this and if ever you need us we will come to you if we can, each of us has pledged to seek you out if ever we are able." Tears were rolling down Cassandra's face; she could not speak; she simply took the broken pendant from Myles and dropped her chin into her chest. One by one the Knights came and knelt before her and gave her their broken pendants. The youngest Knight was Sebastian, the last to kneel before Cassandra, his face was full of anger.

"Tis not right Casey lass" he said, "some of us should be able to go with you, you are the only heir to the throne, if your father should fall, may the Elements prevent, without you to take the throne, chaos will fall. We should be with you to protect you, especially now, now that ..." his words tumbled out quietly. He meant now that she was with child. Eight moons had passed, and although the rest of her was still slim, it was obvious that she was heavy with child.

Cassandra lifted her hand and laid it against the young Knights face. Sebastian was only ten years older than Cassandra and he had been a friend to her always. His straight brown hair lay down to his shoulders, his skin a darker shade than was normal for Havenshire, his eyes a deep warm brown. Cassandra smiled to herself, he should have been married a long time ago; he was far too handsome not to be.

"You are true of heart Sebastian, it would kill you to break your oath to my father, and I would never allow such a thing. I will surely be all right because if ever I was going to die it would have been on that awful night, but here I stand, truly cursed, but still standing."

Mary gave a little whimper into her handkerchief and Cassandra looked at her in surprise, she had forgotten for a moment that Mary was still here.

"Sebastian take Mary back to the castle with you, she does not deserve to be punished for my crimes." Both Mary and Sebastian cried out "No" at the same time, and both started speaking at once.

"Oh no lass, I'll not be leavin' ya, not now, I won't, gosh the wolves will be after ya if I don't stoke the fire, no, I'll be coming with thee." At the same time Sebastian was saying, "No Casey, you need a friend, you will especially need her when your time is due."

"Do I have to give you your pendant back already Sebastian? If you will not take her because I ask it, then I shall demand it." Her voice bore no argument and Sebastian knew if he didn't take Mary back voluntarily then she would hand him back the half pendant and demand his service. Mary took one look at the resignation on Sebastian's face, lifted her longs skirts up to her knees and started running. Sebastian rolled his eyes at Cassandra and lunged after Mary. In a few strides he had caught up with her.

"Oh no ya don't ya little fighting man, I not be goin' with ya I not be." She started battering his shoulders with her fist but he simply turned her around and threw her over his shoulder.

"Let me down ya little boy, let me down ya big oaf, I'll chop ya ears off when you put me down, I'll get the cooks spoon and beat ya black I will, put me down."

Cassandra smiled fondly at Mary as she was carried away, she would miss her and letting her go was hard, but she would not condemn Mary to a pauper's life on the run. When all the Knights were mounted, and Mary flung casually over the saddle of Sebastian's horse, her legs flailing about madly, the King moved off. He did not turn to see his daughter one last time, could not bear to look at her standing there on her own. Instead he stared ahead and set about making his heart cold so that he would not feel the pain. The Knights followed their King as was their duty but it was probably the hardest thing they had ever had to do: no battle would ever inflict such a pain upon them.

Cassandra's bravado fell away and she ran several paces forward, her hand raised as if she would call them back. But she didn't, her hand dropped once more to her side, she stopped and turned back to the cottage. She did not know where she would go or what she would do, so she made a decision that she would stay where she was until a decision was made. '*No point wandering aimlessly*' she told herself.

Myles moved his horse to trot alongside the King and Hamish started talking quietly to him whilst he remained looking firmly ahead.

"The emissary I sent to Bluedane has returned. He brought word that Pedro, King of Bluedane, whose son I have slain, has accepted that the death of Rodanti was an accident. Yet I fear the consequences of this lie, should it ever be found out, will mean war between us."

"Do you think Pedro believed your explanation?" Hamish turned his head and grimaced at Myles.

"I wouldn't if I were him."

"You didn't tell her then?" Myles asked. Hamish shook his head.

"I think knowing the fact that Rodanti was King Pedro's son would not help her, the only shield she has now is the shield of invisibility, if she thinks her child is only a child of a sailor then she may pale into the world of the poor; if she knew her child was the only heir to Bluedane it might tempt her to do something silly." Myles was quiet. "You do not agree with my decision old friend?" Hamish asked.

Myles looked at Hamish, "You, your Grace, are the wisest man I know, if you think it best that your daughter be cast aside without protection, then I am sure you are right." Hamish turned and looked sharply at Myles from under his huge bushy eyebrows; laced with the flattery Myle's obvious disapproval had come sharply through.

"The die is cast Myles, let the colours flow and ebb as they will. She will survive, or not. From this day forth we shall never mention her again. You are to declare that no one is ever to mention her name again; to us she does not exist. Now talk to me of our army, we have much to plan with our neighbours busying themselves with plots of my downfall."

~~~~~~~~~~

Two small children sat on the branch of the old oak that was a stone's throw away from the cottage garden. It was obvious to see that they were twins: for except for the fact that one was a girl and one was a boy, they were identical. Thin white hair laid soft and straight to their shoulders, their ears popping through, with eyes the deepest grass green. Both slender, petite and delicate looking, dressed in soft brown leather leggings and pale green velvet tops, their shoes an unusual pointed shape and deep brown.

"Stop sniffling silly" said the boy. The girl wiped her nose with the back of her hand. "But it's too sad Voltar, she's all on her own, how can they do that?" Voltar put his arm around his sister and gave her a gentle nudge with his head.

"She'll be aright Val she's got us now hasn't she?" Valarie gave a sniffle and looked at her brother, "are we going to take care of her then?"

"Of course we are, we need to go back and tell the Elders what we're doing but then we'll come back." Valarie knocked his arm away, and folded her own arms, looking at him crossly.

"Are you mad? If the Elders knew that we had been ear-wigging their private meetings again we'll be in the most trouble ever."

"But we can't just stay here Val, they'll come looking for us if we don't go back and if they find us here we're in just as much trouble." Both went quiet as they tried to think of the best thing to do, both swinging their legs in unison under the branch.

"We'll have to go back and try and think of a reason to request a visit to Aunt Audrey. After we have been with her for two nights we'll tell her we're going home and then come back to look after the King Carrier." She looked at Voltar to see if he agreed. He nodded.

"Come on then no time to lose, let's just hope she stays here till we get back." They stood up on the branch and reached out for each other's hand.

"Home" Voltar said as they jumped from the branch. If anyone had witnessed their descent they would have been most amazed when the children did not hit the ground, but simply disappeared.

Chapter Six ~ Magician's apprentice

Idi could not stay awake any longer; his chin bounced on his chest making his head snap upwards for the eleventh time.

'Oh stars above' he thought, 'please make him stop.' The horses showed no sign of slowing but Marcus was aware that they had been galloping within the magic for hours now. He reached down and stroked the mane of his horse, "slow now girl" he whispered. Instantly both horses reduced their pace, coming out of magic, and receding to a normal gallop, then slowed down to a trot.

The very first signs of dawn appeared and the dark began to pale as the sun slowly crept into the sky. It was the last thing Idi was aware of as he finally fell asleep and lay over the saddle, his arms draped around his horse's neck. Marcus let the horses walk for a while as he surveyed the land, looking for somewhere safe to rest. Through the blur of magic in which they had come so far he had been unable to see what kinds of lands they had crossed, now he enjoyed being able to look around. Most of the land was moorland, vast and open; barren and bleak. Not a place he would like to call home. There was a small copse of trees not too far in the distance, that at least would offer some protection from the wind that was picking up pace and getting colder by the moment.

The horses turned slightly to the west and moved towards the trees, "slowly now" Marcus whispered, "best be wary before we approach, in case others have also taken refuge here." The copse was not very large and Marcus walked the horses all the way around to make sure no one was hidden within. He checked the land around for recent tracks but could find none other than animals'.

"In we go then" Marcus nudged the horses forward.

Not too far into the trees was a clearing in a slight hollow, it was a perfect place to let Idi sleep awhile. He woke Idi slightly; just enough to get him off his horse and lay him down on a blanket. Idi murmured something that sounded like "Bout bloomin' time" and was instantly asleep again.

The horses took themselves slightly further into the trees to evade the ever increasing wind and Marcus went to gather some sticks and a few old branches. He made a bundle on the ground not too far from Idi.

"Fire" he said snapping his fingers at the branches. Instantly a flame flickered on a twig, within moments the small twigs were all alight and reaching out to the bigger branches. Marcus smiled, normally he would never use his magic for something as trivial as a fire, but this was a new era. He looked at Idi who had curled himself up into a tight ball and was snoring lightly. Marcus shook his head, how was he going to turn this empty headed boy into a magician of great importance? Not for the first time the thought crossed his mind that Oleanna must have made a mistake. He himself saw nothing in the lad except a pitiful boy who was in much need of love. *'But aren't we all in need of love? This boy has had to fight too hard for too long, of course if I had, say twenty years, then I would have a fair chance of moulding his character.'* But they were in search of a young girl about to give birth, and he knew they didn't have long.

'And what happens when we find her?' He had no idea. Marcus took a deep pull on the crisp morning air and wrapped his arms around his body. He hated this, not knowing where he was going, who he was looking for, what he would do. He felt the unknowing tug at his peace, ebbing away; leaving anxiety in its place. He lay down on the moss and pulled a blanket over himself. He looked into the sky as the last stars twinkled merrily before disappearing for the day. "Deep breath Marcus" he said to himself, "it will all come out in the wash." He smiled to himself, it irritated him that he used that saying, but it was something his mother had constantly told him as he grew up. He

39

could see her now, bent over the washing bowl, scrubbing his muddied leggings and top, "tis like life Marcus, all this mud will wash out, just like all your problems will fade away if you give them time."

"I wish I had the time to teach Idi all I know" Marcus said to the stars. *'I would very much like to see him change into the person Oleanna thinks he is.'* With that Marcus let tiredness take over and slipped into dreams of his childhood. As the last star twinkled down on Marcus it whispered a message to the sleeping magician, "Be careful what you wish for."

Idi woke to the smell of cooking mushrooms and dried bacon bits. He sat bolt upright, completely disorientated. He gazed around in shock, and then he saw Marcus knelt over the fire flicking the food with a stick inside the pan. Marcus smiled at him.

"Morning boy." The previous day came flooding back to him, all he knew was left far behind him, and here he was with this bad tempered old fart. Idi yawned and scratched his head. The food smelt good though and he wondered whether the magician would let him eat or would he make him work first? The question was answered for him when Marcus offered him a plate of food.

His eyes nearly popped out of his head when he saw all the food on his plate, he looked at Marcus.

"Is this all for me?" he asked quietly. Marcus nodded and Idi picked up the chunk of bread and bit into it hastily before something could happen to make the magician change his mind.

Marcus looked at him and sighed, there had been no thank you, no manners at all. Idi wolfed the food down like an animal. Marcus kept quiet; he had decided he would teach Idi by example and not by lectures. Marcus sat back, put his plate on his folded legs and raised his arms, "to the Elements that be, I say thanks." Then he picked up his fork and began to eat. Idi watched the old man as if he was mad;

his face screwed up in utter disgrace at the Magician's weird ways: well, at least the food is good, he thought to himself.

After they had packed up their stuff and had buried the remains of their fire they mounted the horses.

"Oh me bloody rhubarb sticks" Idi burst out. Marcus swung in his saddle to look at Idi in concern. "What is it boy?"

"It's me flamin' arse, that's what it is" cried Idi in dismay, "it feels like it's had the worst whipping of its life." Marcus looked at Idi agog; he didn't know whether to be shocked at the boy's choice of words or to laugh.

"After a week or so you'll be used to it."

"A week!" yelled Idi, "you mean I am going to be like this for a week?" Marcus could stand it no longer, he laughed. It started as a normal hearty laugh, but somehow when he looked at Idi's indignant face the laugh grew and grew, until it became a belly laugh that shook his entire body. Idi in response went red and redder which made Marcus laugh louder and harder. A twitch, all of its own accord, happened to the corner of Idi's mouth, the twitch began to jump about, and before Idi knew it he was laughing with Marcus.

~~~~~~~~~~~

"Control it boy" Marcus commanded in his sternest voice, "hold it now, see it in your mind, see the light, and command it to form."

Idi felt his irritation rising again, "I'm trying" he snapped between clenched teeth. Idi held his arms out in front of him, his wrists pressing tightly together his upturned palms forming a bowl in which tiny flickers of light appeared, and as quickly, disappeared again. Marcus was pacing to and fro behind him, his wizards green gown, and his long white hair, flowing in the wind. "Try harder Idi, concentrate harder, see the light, believe the light is there; order it to appear."

"I can't concentrate with you flapping behind me old man" Idi snarled.

"Well I wouldn't be pacing behind you if only you would listen to exactly what I'm telling you *boy!*" snapped Marcus in return.

"Arrrghhhh " yelled Idi in frustration throwing his arms up in the air and letting the last bit of light fade away as he spun around to face Marcus.

"Maybe if I didn't have to wear this stupid dress" he said spreading his hands out in front of him as he looked down at the green gown Marcus had had made for him, "maybe I wouldn't feel like such a girl and maybe I would be able to concentrate!" Marcus was about to retort, when his anger fell away and he sighed in frustration.

"I thought if you dressed like a magician you might feel like a magician Idi; obviously not, take it off, burn it if you wish, it obviously didn't help."

Idi's shoulders drooped in defeat, "give up on me Marcus, I am hopelessly stupid we've been at this for ages now and I still can't do magic, I'm sorry I am not clever enough for you." He turned and walked away, defeat written in every part of his body language. Marcus took several magical steps and was suddenly standing in front of Idi. He put his arms on the boy's shoulders.

"Look at me Idi" he said. Idi raised his head, his eyes pools of water waiting to overflow. Marcus looked at him and sighed. In the months that they had been together now Idi was changed. Long gone were his spots and his greasy hair, he straightened his back when he walked, and except for these lessons, had seemed to have lost his bad temper. Yet still the years of name calling left him beaten and defeated, no matter how hard Marcus tried he could not completely undo the belief that Idi had: that he was in fact, stupid and worthless.

"I can tell you son that I know you are not worthless, I know that you will one day be a great magician – this I know because I believe in the Oracles and because over the months, I have come to believe in you myself, but until you, yourself, believe in you, magic will evade you." A few tears began to roll down Idi's face; no one had ever said anything so wonderful to him before. He threw his arms around Marcus and hugged the tall man's chest. Marcus held him lightly and patted Idi's back. As he held Idi, Marcus looked into the sky.

'Where are you Oleanna' he cried in his heart, *'if this really is the one you want me to teach we could use some help from you for I fear I cannot reach the darkest parts of his heart. If I could ask you anything right now it would be that you would show him a bit of hope, show him that he isn't worthless.'*

No answer came and Marcus sighed, time was running out, they were not too far from Havenshire now and still Idi showed no signs of being able to master the basics of magic.

~~~~~~~~~

Two days later the two of them rode into a small village. It was a pretty little place surrounded by hills with a river running through the centre of it. Cottages were clustered together in little groups and in the centre were several larger houses.

They dismounted at the edge of the village and led the horses in through the cobbled streets. The sun was shining and all sorts of things filled Marcus' senses. The smell of cooking stew: the tweeting of birds; and the barking of a distant dog. A slight breeze rustled through the grass and rocked the tavern's sign gently. It was peaceful and calm and should have been a pleasure as he passed cottage after cottage with flowers growing in baskets; yet something was amiss. Then suddenly it struck him, where were the people? No one was in

43

sight and no voice could be heard. He stopped in his tracks and put his arm out to stop Idi, Idi turned to him and opened his mouth to speak but Marcus put his finger to his lips to hush him. Idi looked at Marcus in surprise but did as he was asked. Marcus handed him the rein of his horse and pointed to a small alley between two cottages. Idi looked at him, questioningly; Marcus said nothing but pointed again, his face stern. Idi shrugged and took the horses down the alley. As he reached the bottom he turned around and Marcus had gone. He was puzzled; Marcus had never acted so mysteriously before. At the bottom of the alley Idi found a gate to a cottage garden, he opened it and led the horses inside; he shut the gate quietly behind him and let the reins of the horses go. The grass of the garden was rather long and he was sure the owner would not mind if the horses made it shorter! He went back to the gate swinging his legs over it to sit atop, as he waited for Marcus to come back.

As soon as Idi had entered the alley Marcus had called upon his magic to move with speed through the streets. At each house he looked in windows and over hedges and opened doors: he could find no one. The sign above the Tavern creaked as it was blown by the wind, and Marcus spun around to face it. He relaxed slowly, just the wind picking up then. Like lightning he reached the end of the village and now alarms were ringing, he sensed them in his every muscle. Something was very amiss. Each house existed as if vacated very recently, people had been in the middle of their various day to day activities, and then suddenly disappeared. Food was still cooking, fires were still burning and the ale in the tankards was still cool. Where had the people gone? Suddenly the sound of the river lapping against the banks caught his attention and he turned.

At first all seemed as it should be, then suddenly he noticed the colour of the water. He took a step towards the river and then another, and then he ran to it. A ribbon of red was mixed with the clear waters and Marcus knew at once it was blood. His heart sank in his chest and his blood raced faster than it had ever done before, he raised his hand in front of him and saw that he shook. Dread made him feel like lead as he walked along the river bank and up towards the source of the red flow.

When he saw the cause of the flow of blood Marcus fell to his knees and cried out loud, "Oh Elements help us." As he looked he felt his body heave in shock. At a small inlay to the river there lay a tiny cove; a place where you might have brought young ones to play in the water in safety. In this inlet there lay a pile of bodies. It appeared to be all the villagers, young and old, male and female alike, all dead. Their bodies were broken. Arms heads legs; all body parts thrown together in a pile of massacred flesh. On the grass bank behind was a pool of blood and Marcus found himself drawn there.

Marcus could smell the blood, could smell the stench of death in the atmosphere. He looked in horror, and wondered why – why was it was there, why did the bodies lay there? He could make out bits of flesh in the crimson pool. Marcus felt his stomach turn again and he found himself asking the same question. What on earth had happened? His forced his eyes back once more to the pile of body parts, made himself look more closely, he didn't know what he was searching for, but all of a sudden he found it. All the torsos had been ripped open, the insides of all these people were on display, and all their hearts were missing.

Suddenly he stood bolt upright; he knew only one thing that did this.

"Idi" he cried and was racing with the wind, calling on his magic so much so that flames flickered from different parts of his body, "Oh Oleanna, don't let me be too late."

Idi sat on the garden gate tapping his fingers impatiently, *'what's happening?'* A faint sound reached his ears and he strained forward.

He leaned forward more into the air trying to determine where the sound came from. At last he heard it clearly and smiled, he jumped off the gate and headed down the back alley. As he walked the sound became sweeter and louder and happiness rushed through him, a smile upon his lips he laughed and started to run towards it.

"I'm coming" he yelled, as he raced towards the hills, "wait for me I'm coming." Marcus in his magic heard the cry of joy from Idi as the boy began to run.

"No!" Marcus screamed into the air, "no Idi wait for me I'm coming, oh Elements please no please, please, let me reach him in time please."

Idi's heart was pounding in his chest, he was so excited, joy was flooding his body, he had to find her, he just had to. Then on the hill he saw a shimmer and he squinted, trying to focus on it. The shimmer flickered and bounced upon the blades of grass for a moment before forming the shape of a woman. Idi knew at once that the woman was his mother. Oh the joy of his heart! His prayers were answered; his mother had found him at last. Tears of joy rolled down his face, "I'm coming mother" he yelled as he ran as fast as he could up the hill. The lady on the hill turned to see the lad racing up the hill towards her.

"Another one" she said slightly surprised, "I thought I had taken all of them?" She looked to the west and seemed unsure for a moment, then paused and looked back at the lad. "I have time for one more if I am quick." She stopped and watched as the lad drew closer to her, a sickly smile on her beautiful face, "hurry to me boy for I cannot retrace my steps, hurry now for I must return quickly."

"I'm coming Mother, I'm coming" then with that thought suddenly something landed on Idi and he fell to the floor crashing his face into the grass. The noise instantly disappeared and he screamed in anguish "No" he fought to push off the thing that had landed on him but could not. Then a bright light appeared and with a crack, like the sound of lightning, a glass dome formed over him and his anguish began to pale and he struggled less and less.

The lady's singing turned into screeches of frustration. From her mouth hues of red and black went flying into the atmosphere all around her. The smoke twirled and spun in the air then dropped like balls of fire upon the dome. Marcus sat on Idi's back, his hands in the air as he willed the dome to remain strong and pure against the rain of fire. The lady's frustration grew as she could not harm the one who had stopped her from another heart. She threw fire ball after fire ball against the dome but it held true and firm. She screamed in utter frustration. Suddenly she jerked and lurched, stumbling backwards as if against her will.

"No" she wailed, "no, give me more time, I will get them, more time I tell you." But still she was pulled backwards and as she went all sight of the lady vanished and that of a golden dragon took her place. She lifted her long neck, thousands of golden scales moving with it and shimmering in the light. Her eyes glistened ruby red and fierce. Horns rose out of her head, one above each eye like elaborate eyebrows.

Her body, from the tip of her head to the end of her tail, was as long as the width of a farm house. Along the length of her back rose spikes. Unlike the rest of her, the spikes did not have scales, but were smooth with the sharpest tips. She had four legs, the back legs being short and stout and her front legs longer and slimmer. Her claws were long and sharp and would have sliced through Marcus with a single blow had she been able to move forward. She was jerked backwards once more, and she raised her head and screamed out in her frustration. The moment the sound faded she turned her fire-filled eyes upon Marcus, throwing flames from her mouth towards him. The flames smashed against the invisible dome but could not penetrate through the magic wall. Once more she was yanked backwards and her temper made her rear high on her back legs. Her wings shot out each side of her as she tried in vain to fight against the force that pulled her. Her wings flapped and crashed around her, splitting open trees and bushes. Still she could not move forward. Finally frustrated and defeated, she let her wings fold back and into her back, turned away and began to walk in the direction in which she was being pulled, her body swaying from side to side with each step. At the top of the hill she paused for a moment and turned her red eyes back to Marcus.

Marcus looked back at her, "You'll not have us today m'lady." And then she was gone. Out of sight, but never again out of Marcus's mind.

Marcus was exhausted and crumbled in a heap on the grass, "Oh Elements, dear Elements, how could this have happened? What is to happen to us now if the Demons of the Depths are able once more to reach the Living?" The Shee-Dragon had returned to the Depths, and knowing they were safe for a while, Marcus let the dome fade. It had been years since he had cried but the dreadful sight of the bodies he had just endured still hung in the air in front of his face, and a fear for the Kingdoms he loved filled him with despair. And so he placed his head in his hands and sobbed.

Marcus was not sure how long he had cried but he became aware that Idi had recovered and was looking completely distressed and so calmed himself down.

"It is okay now Idi, she has gone, we are safe."

"I thought she was my mother Marcus."

"I know lad, she does that. Each one of us will see the one we most desire in her reflection and will race to her with open abandon. She has magical powers so strong; in her singing she sends waves of love through us and blinds us all to reality. And then one by one she would kill us, ripping our hearts from our bodies so that she may feed on them and strengthen her magic."

"But you did not run to her Marcus?"

"No, luckily for us lad I realised she was here and used my magic to close my ears and to be deaf until I opened them again, I have never used the magic to run so fast before and I fear I may now need a new outfit." He looked down at his clothes which were full of scorch burns and large holes. Idi smiled weakly at Marcus, "Thank you" he whispered.

"We need to go back and fetch the horses, and there is also one other thing I must do." The two of them got up and went back to the village. Reaching the cottage garden where the horses still lingered, Marcus put his hand on Idi's shoulder.

"Idi I must do something. I will be as quick as I can, wait here." Idi's shoulders slumped, he did not fancy being on his own right now at, but he nodded in agreement.

"Good lad" said Marcus. Then pulling on his now low resources of magic, Marcus ran through the village. As Marcus literally flew through the village he put out fires and removed pots from ovens. He couldn't bear the thought that the village might catch fire, but he left the worst job for last. When he had finished checking through the village, he went back once more to the pile of broken people. Sadness lay heavy on his shoulders, he knew not how the dragon had managed to sneak out of the Depths, but he knew, if she had done so once, she was sure to do so again. He reached up with his right arm and sent sparks flying from his hands to the pile of bodies.

"Burn" he demanded, and instantly the pile became an eruption of fire. He watched for just a moment to ensure that they would all be cremated and then turned back to the village, time to fetch Idi and to leave this wretched place, before the Shee-Dragon decided to return.

Chapter Seven ~ Katrina Dragon Slayer

Idi didn't mean to wander from the garden; but after scratching his head for nigh on ten minutes he set off not being able to put the feeling away that he needed to do something. *'I won't be long, just walk to the edge of the village.'* The horses followed him and slowly they made their way down the cobbled streets to the far edge of the hamlet. He stood at the village boundary for a while the nagging feeling still strong. He stepped over a small hedgerow and started walking through the field. Reaching the middle of the field he stood, and listened.

'If I don't get back soon Marcus will be worried about me.' He had just decided he had better head back to where Marcus had left him when he heard a sound. He froze, his every muscle tense as he waited for the sound to be repeated. The sound came again and Idi spun around to face the north side of the field. He started to run. As he reached the hedgerow on the other side he slowed down. A wooden stile went over a part of the hedge and not far from the stile something was lying in the grass.

Idi slowly approached the thing on the grass with curiosity. It looked like a cloth of some sort, but the cloth was moving and making an odd sounds. Idi was almost on top of the cloth before he realised what it was.

"And what have we here?" he said bending down. A blanket was wrapped tightly around something small and Idi pulled back the blanket to stare at a baby girl. As soon as the blanket was pulled back the baby's whimpering turned into a full blown wail. *'Hush, hush don't cry little one.'* Carefully he reached forward and picked up the baby. The baby's wailing instantly changed and Idi knew instinctively that the child was in pain. Very, very cautiously he lifted the child close to his chest and began walking back down the field. Just as he reached the bottom of the field Marcus appeared.

"I think she is hurt" Idi said - before Marcus had a chance to scold him, nodding his head as he spoke towards the child.

"Sit down a minute lad let's see." The two of them sat down on the grass and Idi carefully laid the child down in front of them. Marcus very gently ran his hands over the child's body and nodded.

"It seems she has broken her arm Idi, my guess would be that her mother was carrying her when she heard the Demon and in her haste dropped the child as she scrambled over the stile, very lucky for the child."

"Can you fix her Marcus?"

Marcus smiled at Idi. "I have some powers when it comes to healing," he said, "but they are never instant and I normally find the natural healing powers of herbs help greatly. I will go back into the village and see what herbs I can find; I will also look for some milk for her and food for us before it is dark, I very much want to be gone from this place." Marcus stood up and walked back into the village. Idi watched him until he was out of sight, then he looked down at the child who was whimpering in distress. Idi traced his fingers over the baby's forehead.

"I wish I could take your pain away" he whispered to the child. Then as clear as day Idi heard a voice inside his head, which he instantly knew was not his own.

"Draw on your powers Idi, heal the child yourself."

"Pardon?" said Idi in surprise turning around to make sure no one stood behind him. "What do you mean, draw on my own powers? I don't have any." But the voice did not come again. The baby tried to move slightly and began crying again in pain.

"I wish I could heal you little one, but I don't know how. Please don't cry, Marcus will be back soon, he'll help you." But Marcus took his time and the baby's crying grew more and more sorrowful till Idi could bear it no more. He lent down and kissed the baby's head.

"I'll try" he whispered, "I will try my hardest for you." He looked at the child for a moment and pondered: "where to begin?" Light and fire always came from Marcus's hand so maybe that is where healing would come from too? He gently laid his hand on the baby's chest, not wanting to touch her arm and cause more pain.

"Be well" he said in a very shaky voice. The infant continued to cry. Idi felt as if his insides were being crushed and he moaned out loud. "I wish I could heal you" he said again. He closed his eyes and simply started to will his own strength to leave his body and to enter the child. "Be well" he said again but with a firm voice.
Slowly he felt his innards become hot, the feeling of heat in his stomach rose to his chest. "Be well" he commanded: this time with authority, "be well." He felt the heat inside him rising and literally willed it to come down his arm out of his palm and into the baby. And just like that the baby stopped crying. Idi's eyes flicked open instantly.

"Well done lad" Idi looked up to see Marcus watching him.

"I think she might be a bit better" said Idi in a shaky voice.

"Let's have a look." Marcus bent down on the grass besides the child. He ran his hands over her body once more. The child smiled at him. Marcus looked up at Idi's waiting face.

"Amazing! You have completely mended her broken arm; it seems you have at last found the desire to learn magic." Idi threw his head back and laughed, joy was surging through his body, he had helped her and taken away her pain; he wasn't useless after all!

A very short time later Marcus and Idi rode out of the doomed village together. They took the baby with them, wrapped tightly in a blanket that was tied around Idi's body so that she would not be dropped when they hit magic timing and raced away from the sorrowful place.

They travelled for three days without much rest. Marcus was determined to find the next village where they could leave the baby and return once more to the task at hand.

Marcus watched the skies every night and he was convinced that something was happening. Idi could see no change but Marcus was sure there was a change in the air. The time was drawing close he was sure. Urgency seemed to gnaw into his soul and he felt restless, he couldn't let Oleanna down; he must arrive in time.

Marcus sighed, mightily relieved, when at last a village came into sight. He turned to Idi and gave him the briefest of smiles.

"I think we shall stay at an Inn tonight Idi, I grow weary of the earth and desire to feel a mattress once more beneath these old bones, and I very much want a a jug of ale or two." Idi smiled and quietly said,

"And a warm bath."

"What was that lad?" Marcus asked.

"Nothing Marcus" Idi answered and looked down at the baby so Marcus couldn't see that he was smiling.

The village was a homely place, clean and tidy, smells of cooking wafting out of the cottages as the evening light paled, and thankfully on first impression without the tragic sting in the tail of the one before. People were around and seemed to be going about their business in the most everyday fashion, albeit nearing the end of this particular day. At the heart of the village lay the square, and here the Sheep's Inn's orange lights glowed welcomingly through the windows. They tethered the horses and ventured inside. Instantly the lovely smell of local beers; hot stew and mellow tobacco hit them. After a quick look around at the customers Marcus smiled and nodded to himself, this place would do nicely.

A well built stout bald man in a white apron approached them with hasty footsteps.

"Welcome, welcome. Come on in and have the table near the fire, for you must be feeling the cold with the night drawing in." All the time he talked he nodded his head as if agreeing with himself. Idi grinned at him, the Innkeeper's cheeks were ruddy and he didn't stop smiling: Idi had never seen such a cheerful looking fellow! They followed him across the room and after taking off their cloaks sat down at a table near the huge burning logs in the open hearth.

"What shall I get you fine gentlemen?" the Innkeeper asked and Idi had to stifle a laugh by turning it into a cough: *'Gentlemen?'* Marcus gave Idi a quick stern look which spoke volumes and Idi was quickly calmed.

"We will try a pitcher of your best ale my good fellow. We will need some food, and do you have a local woman who would suckle for pay?"

"Oh yes indeed sir we do. I will send young Jim here to fetch our Sally she's not long had young 'uns and she certainly could do with a few spare coppers. As to the ale I shall bring you the best we have, tis mighty mellow, and as for food we have some rabbit stew on the go, would that be fine for you?"

"Indeed it all sounds marvellous, tell me do you also have a room to rent for the night?" The Innkeeper's smile broadened even more, "Finest down mattress in the land, t'will be the best night sleep you've ever had!"

"Excellent, one last thing, after supper and after the lad and baby here have retired, I need to meet with the village officials. The matter is of the greatest importance, would you let them know that I seek an audience?" The smile had faded from the Innkeeper's face and was replaced with a solemn look. "I will see if they are free for a meeting sire."

"Excellent" said Marcus and nodded briefly to confirm their conversation was over.

The ale appeared in two tall thin tankards, quickly followed by the maid Sally who took the baby girl and was shown to the bedroom to feed her. Moments after that, two huge bowls were placed in front of them with steaming oceans of rabbit stew, alongside it were two huge chunks of fresh bread. Idi picked up the bread which was still hot and not long out of the oven and inhaled deeply, he had never smelt anything so good.

For the entire time it took them to eat the stew neither of them uttered a single word. Idi finished first, pushing his bowl away from him slightly and leaning back in the chair with a hugely satisfied sigh. Marcus was soon finished and followed Idi's example with the same sigh leaning back in the tall backed chair in turn.

After a couple of minutes of silence Idi looked at Marcus, "What will you say to the village officials?" Marcus, without moving, looked around the room: no one was close, and all seemed to be deep in their own conversations. "I need to tell them of the Shee-Dragon, I will warn them that they should leave this place before she returns." Idi shivered, "I'll be going to the room then; I want to check the little one is alright anyway." Marcus nodded and beckoned to the Innkeeper who came hurrying over.

"They will see you sir, they have asked that you go to Tafters cottage up the way, me lad here will show you where to go."

"Thank you, Idi here will wait in the room."

"Yes sir, I will show him the way."

"Good, another thing, can you arrange for the horses to be stabled for the night?"

The Innkeeper beamed, "Have already put them in my own stables sir, the lads have brushed them down and fed them some very fine hay." Marcus smiled warmly at the Innkeeper,

"You are indeed an excellent fellow" he said, to which the Innkeeper openly blushed with pleasure. A young lad came over and Marcus stood up, put his cape on and followed the lad out of the inn. Idi was shown to their room by the Innkeeper. In the bed-chamber a young woman was rocking the child in her arms; she smiled shyly at Idi as he walked in.

"She did guzzle well and good sir" she said. Idi smiled back pleased, they had managed to get some milk into the child in the last few days through muslin funnels but he knew she hadn't fed enough.

"I am very grateful, how much do we owe you?"

"Well Simon did say that you would part with two coppers, but honestly sir, one will do." Idi pulled out his pouch, that Marcus had given him earlier, took out two coppers and handed them to her.

"Two is just fine."

"Thank you kindly sir" she answered as she took the money. She gave him a quick smile and left. Idi picked up the sleeping baby and looked down at her. Gently he stroked her head. In the three days, that it had taken them to get here, Idi had fallen completely in love with the little infant. Never before in his life had anyone ever depended on him. Even though she cried from time to time and there was the "smelly job" to take care of, Idi knew he wanted to protect her. He lay down on the bed and sank into the feathered mattress. At first he sighed with the comfort but within a short time he could bear it no more. He got up and dragged the covers onto the floor. He lay on top of them on his side and held the infant close to his chest pulling the cover over them. Marcus had scolded him for sleeping like this, telling Idi that he might roll over in his sleep and crush her, but Idi knew that when he held her he never ever moved a muscle. A smile radiated from his eyes. His tummy was full, he was warm, and for the first time in his life he loved someone, it truly was a wonderful feeling.

"I think we will call you Katrina" Idi whispered kissing her on the head. He had no idea where the name had come from, it had just sprung into his mind and it seemed to suit her.

Idi didn't know then, that Katrina meant 'Pure' and that in years to come Katrina would be known as the purest of all Queens and that she would hold the title of Dragon-Slayer.

Chapter Eight ~ The Protectors

It had taken them four sunrises, but finally they had arrived. Aunt Audrey had been delighted to see her favourite niece and nephew. She made a big fuss of them, offering them all their favourite foods whilst asking them both loads of questions about home. Valarie sat on the comfy sofa, knees pulled up to her chest, her chin resting on them. She smiled softly as she watched her Aunt potter around the room. Her Aunt was so beautiful, famed amongst all the Fairies for her beauty and grace. She had been sought out by all the highest ranking Fairy males, but Audrey had chosen never to marry: something most unusual amongst Fairies.

The average age of Fairies was eight hundred years, so to not choose a mate was very rare indeed. Audrey, in her two hundred and thirty second year, still declared she had not met anyone with whom she wanted to spend the rest of her life. "Shame: shame," the elder Fairies tutted, "such a waste."

Audrey had fire red hair that fell in ringlets down to her waist. Her eyes were possibly the deepest green that a Fairy had ever had, her cheek bones high, her nose perfectly formed, and naturally full and deep red lips gave her a beauty that the Fairy men went weak at the knees for. She was small, yet walked tall, her every move graceful and soft. Her crushed velvet dress had all the colours of the rainbow running through it, and these colours reflected in her delicate wings. Most Fairies let their wings fold into their backs unless they were flying, but Audrey chose to constantly flutter hers behind her. They were almost transparent and when the sunlight caught the colours they seemed to come alive with movement. Valarie sighed - if only she could have been so beautiful.

As soon as possible, without being rude, Valarie and Voltar made their excuses and went to bed.

Alone at last they sat on Valarie's bed to hatch their plan. Both agreed that they had implied; although they hadn't actually stated (because as High Fairies they were forbidden to lie) that they were only there for two nights. On the morning of the third day they would fly back to the King Carrier and make sure she was safe.

"I still don't understand why the Elders won't help her" said Valarie picking at her pillow in frustration.

"I know - I just don't understand them. They are convinced that she carries the One Born to be King, but they won't act. I can't believe that even Nicodemus thinks we shouldn't interfere in the ways of man; I think they're being very narrow minded. I wish I had reached my one hundredth year, if I were on the council of the Elder's I would speak my mind and make them see sense." Valarie smiled fondly at her brother.

"You will be the finest Elder there ever was Voltar." Voltar smiled back,

"I will be won't I?" he said puffing out his chest. Valarie gave him a small smack on his arm.

"I will have to keep your head from getting too big though you vain thing." They chuckled away for a while and then became solemn once more.

"Seriously, how could they ignore her?" Voltar said, "If they let the wizard Norvora get hold of the child the Kingdoms will turn black indeed, sooner or later that blackness will seep into our world, and by that time it will be too late to save them or us."

Valarie nodded in agreement. She couldn't understand why the Elders would abandon the one on which all prophesies pivoted upon. She knew the Fairies believed in letting the Elements turn the wheels of fate, but, she knew sometimes they all needed a little nudge in the right direction. She had been scolded so many times for interfering, but she never saw it that way, she always believed that she knew what was needed, and just helped those along who didn't see quite so clearly! This was no different. She knew the Elders believed in the Prophesies, they knew the Oracles spoke for the Elements, so why would they talk and talk and talk and do nothing to help?

With that thought they said goodnight and Voltar went to his own room. Valarie tossed and turned the night away so she didn't really feel refreshed when she woke in the morning. She yawned, stretched and got out of bed to open the windows. As she pushed open the wooden slats the sun came bursting through and she squinted in the light.

"Lovely day" she said to the world, as she leant out of her round window. Leaning against the edge she gazed out at the grass in front of her. Aunt Audrey always kept an area cut down near the doorway, but all the rest of the house was submerged by the tall blades of grass. She smiled to herself, Audrey was thought of as eccentric, refusing to live in the tree lined valleys like the rest of them; but Valarie loved her Aunt's house out here in the wilds. It felt free and exciting and she knew when she reached 250 years of age and was able to choose her own home, then she would come and live in the Glens with her Aunt. Valarie's door opened slowly and Voltar stuck his head around the corner.

"Good, you're up" he whispered, as he came tiptoeing over to her. Valarie smiled, "What are you up to?" she asked.

"Shssh" said Voltar, "something has happened; I woke because I could hear Aunt Audrey's voice, and she's not pleased about something. She is in the mirror room talking to someone; I think we should go and see what's happening."

"We can't spy on her" said Valarie, slightly cross. Voltar looked at her, puzzled.

"Why not?" he asked, "we spy on everyone else." Valarie dropped her shoulders and pulled a face, she had lost of course. They crept along the corridors till they reached the mirror room. The door to the room was slightly ajar and Valarie bent down on her knees to peek in the crack whilst Voltar stretched to look over her head.

The mirror room was simply a small room with nothing in it, except a huge oval mirror that filled one wall nearly entirely. The mirror was an ancient mirror, created by the Oracles and filled with magic. It allowed those who knew the secrets, to talk to others who had mirrors, wherever they might be.

Audrey was standing in front of the mirror, her hands on her hips and her face red with anger.

"We must warn the girl" she said. Neither Voltar nor Valarie could see the mirror, so they couldn't see who Audrey was talking to, but when the answer came they both recognised Nicodemus's voice immediately.

"No absolutely not. The entire council of Elders has voted; we will not intervene. The Elements are the Gods of Talia and they cast the stones in the beginning; it is not up to us to meddle. Let them sort out their own affairs and fight their own wars."

"But Nicodemus, the Prophesies?"

Voltar was straining to hear Nicodemus's words and so closed his eyes and when he opened them a moment later he was a Fennec fox. His huge ears enabled him to hear, every sound, perfectly.

"The Prophesies will take care of themselves Audrey, despite man's attempt to twist fate to their own will, it always has a way of twisting itself right again."

"But it is said that the "One" will bend one way or the other, nothing about his life is written on the stones, except that the power of light and dark swing on his will. How can you leave his fate in the hands of those who might turn him to the Dark?"

"Let it go Audrey, we have voted, the girl must fend for herself, and her fate and the fate of her child are in her own hands."

"Norvora, that vicious spiteful little man, is on his way to take her Nicodemus. She has no one to protect her, not even one guard has been left with her. If he takes her back to his towers he will kill her the moment the baby is born, and then, *dearest elder*, her blood and her life will be on your hands."

Nicodemus sighed, "Should every human's life be on my hands then? No, I am not an Element, nor even an Oracle; I guide only our kind. In time you will see that I am right. Now it is time for me to go."

"No, Nicodemus please, Norvora is only hours away from Cassandra but if I leave now I can reach her and warn her in time - she is still at the cottage. Please let me go?"

"Audrey the matter is closed, I absolutely forbid you to go to the King Carrier." There was a sound as if glass was cracking and Valarie and Voltar knew that Nicodemus had closed his end of the mirror-way. Both hurried quickly and quietly down the corridor, before Audrey should come out of the room and see them.

Back in Valarie's room Voltar returned to his Fairy form. Valarie's heart was beating frantically fast in her chest.

"What are we going to do Voltar?" Voltar was silent for a moment staring down at the floor lost in a moment's flurry of thoughts.

"We have to get to her before Norvora reaches her" he answered. Valarie nodded fervently in agreement. They didn't say another word, simply opened their wings with a flutter. Both their clothes that morning were a deep purple which sparkled with multitudes of precious stones; however, as they spread their wings they simultaneously changed their clothes to green with speckles of brown, perfect cover as they flew through the woods. Valarie gave a moment's pause to look at the bedroom door, she felt a pang of guilt for not telling their Aunt where they were going, but Voltar had already flown through the window, so with a sigh she followed. They would have to fly fast indeed to reach Cassandra to give her enough time to flee before Norvora reached her.

Like two tiny flickers of light they shot through the blades of grass and then upwards to see the way ahead. They pulled deep on their rich magic, and with endless flight chasing to their advantage, sped off into the morning's light. Audrey stood on her chimney pot high upon the roof.

"Speed, wisdom and strength my little ones, you will need it." She raised her hand and sparkles of gold dust flew from her palm. The dust particles hung in the air before her. "Protection" she said and then blew the particles into the air after Valarie and Voltar. There was a flutter of movement in the air beside her - then Elroy appeared. He was tall and strong, dark skinned, with black hair which stood in spikes all over his head. He wore trousers in green and black stripes, and was shirtless but wore a black waistcoat. He had huge wings, with each side split into four separate sections, in transparent grey with silver speckles through them, entirely edged in black. There was no mistaking he was a Pixie. Elroy reached out his arm and Audrey moved to his side so that he could hold her.

"I can do no more for them. If Norvora catches them..." her voice trailed off in fear and Elroy held her tight.

Chapter Nine ~ The Hunt Begins

Cassandra was nervous. She couldn't shake off this feeling of dread that something awful was about to happen. She paced the room from one wall to the other and back again, over and over, in much the same way that her father did whilst he tried to work out problems. She told herself she was being silly, and that letting her nerves get the better of her was not royal behaviour at all. She stopped her pacing for a moment to lean on the windowsill and gaze into the late afternoon's fading sunlight. What was there to fear out here miles from anywhere? She shivered, then pulled her shawl tightly around her and moved to stand in front of the fire.

Just then she heard a noise behind her and spun around in fear. Valarie and Voltar had changed into the form of children again so as not to frighten her but their sudden appearance was enough to make Cassandra reach down next to the fireplace and pick up the metal poker which she raised in an act of defence.

"Don't be frightened Cassandra, we haven't got time to explain, but we are here to help you. Danger is fast approaching and you must leave this place before it is too late." Valarie had taken a step forward whilst speaking and Cassandra raised the poker high above her head.

"Who are you and how did you get in here?"

"We are your friends Cassandra and we know a little magic but you haven't got any time. You must leave right now." Cassandra took a menacing step forward, her face showing all her fear. Voltar pulled Valarie backwards a step or two and tried to reason with Cassandra.

"You must listen to us, you have to leave, you don't have any time to waste, it may already be too late."

"Get out of here" yelled Cassandra, "Get out before I start to hit you with this poker."

Valarie snorted, "Enough of this" and promptly changed back into a Fairy. Cassandra drew a sharp breath in shock but didn't have time to think, as Valarie set about her. She flew around Cassandra's head and yelled in frustration at her. It was as if a huge fly was attacking her and Cassandra waved her arms around trying to swat the Fairy. Voltar, believing that Valarie was about to get a mighty slap from a 'Large One' changed into a wolf and gave an almighty growl. Cassandra froze at the sight of a huge grey wolf showing its teeth at her and fear made her turn cold. Slowly she lowered her arm back to her side and let the poker fall to the floor. Getting the desired response Voltar changed back into the boy.

"Oh" said Cassandra in relief, and leant back against the mantelpiece for support, her legs shaking. Voltar approached, standing right in front of Cassandra. Valarie now in the form of a girl once more took position behind her brother, hands on hips, and stern faced.

"Cassandra we don't have time to explain everything, Norvora is on his way for you. He plans to take you back to his castle, believe me this will not lead to a happy ending, you have to flee, he's coming now." Cassandra stood up straight.

"Norvora! Well why didn't you say so?" She moved swiftly across the room and pulled a bag off the bed. She went to the wall where her travelling cape hung on a hook, took it down and threw it around her shoulders. As she reached the door she stopped and looked back at the children.

"Thank you" she then pulled the door open and hurried outside. Valarie and Voltar looked at each other in surprise, Valarie shrugged her shoulders and Voltar shook his head then the two of them raced out of the door after Cassandra: changing once more into Fairies.

"Wait" they yelled. As they flew in the air around Cassandra's head she held back the urge to swipe at them and paused to listen to what they were saying.

"You can't go that way" Voltar said, pointing down the path Cassandra had just stepped onto.

"Well I can't go south" Cassandra answered, "I am forbidden to return to Havenshire; so where else in Talia can I go?"

Voltar pointed to the forest in the north. Cassandra laughed as if he had told a joke, but the laugh paled away when Voltar and Valarie continued to hover in front of her face and she could see that they weren't joking.

"I can't go into Tremblin Forest" she whispered, "no one ever comes back from there."

"It is your only chance Cassandra, trust us, we really are here to help you and your baby." Cassandra's hand instantly went to her rather large bump to hold it. She looked at the hovering Fairies for a moment and a tiny smile lit up her face. Everyone told stories about Fairies, but everyone knew they weren't real, and yet here were two in front of her!

The dread she had been feeling all day now had an explanation, and a name, Norvora. This was easier to handle than the unknown. In that moment she decided to trust them, and nodded to acknowledge she would do as they suggested.

Immediately upon her nod of approval Voltar and Valarie flew off in the direction of the forest. Cassandra took the time for one swift look back; as if to see if Norvora was already descending on them, and then as quickly as she could she hurried across the fields that would lead to the Forests and the unknown.

Not too far away Norvora raced his horse and the horses of his men. His black cloak flying in the wind, his thin pinched face set in determination towards the farm he knew held his prize. He had intended to wait until the child was born before moving, he wanted his armies to be ready before the wars began, but the witch Isona had come to warn him that the Fairies were about to intervene to save the girl. He had roused some of his men immediately and set out to fetch her. He would not allow anyone, even interfering Fairies, to stop him now. The plans were becoming a reality at last. Years of plotting, planning and endless tiring waiting, were about to end. It was an era for action, for moving forward, for twisting destiny to his own will. Soon it would be time to release the three Witches from their captivity within the glass orb. He kicked viciously into his horse's side. No, nothing would get in the way now, he was too close.

Villagers finishing a hard day's work on their farm stopped in surprise and stared at the band of men on black horses that sped through their lands, racing with the wind and leaving clouds of smoke behind them. One farmer took his hat off and scratched his head in puzzlement. Nothing used to ever happen in this sleepy place, until recently. Now all sorts of weird things were happening, and for the first time in his life, one spent entirely on this farm, he wished he had somewhere else to go. Dead cows in the fields: missing children; crops dying for no reason and now strange bands of people on the move. He had the feeling this was not a good time to live in this area.

Cassandra was tiring and Voltar knew it, she went at a slow run for only short spells then slowed to a walk. Soon even walking would be hard. He darted high in the air above the trees to look back from where they had come from. As yet there was still no sign of Norvora, but Voltar knew once Norvora had picked up Cassandra's trail it would not take him long to find her. The only chance she had was to get deep within the forest and to let the trees and nightfall hide her. Norvora would probably have to wait until the morning, and with any luck he would have Cassandra safely in the mountains by then. He was just about to fly back down when something caught his eye. In one swift moment he changed himself into an Eagle. He soared higher and higher searching where he thought he had seen something. There it was again. Dust: rising in the air. He couldn't see Norvora but he could see the trail he was leaving behind him. In a flash he was once again a Fairy, flying down to Cassandra, upon landing transforming into a boy as before. Cassandra stopped when she saw him. Huffing and puffing, her chest rising and falling rapidly with the stress of the long run, she took the opportunity for a rest and dropped onto the moss filled grass under a tree, trying to catch her breath.

"He's coming" Voltar said, bending down on his knees beside her. Valarie turned herself into a young lady and came to stand beside Voltar. Cassandra remained silent: she had no breath for talking and no idea what she should say anyway.

"I know you are tired" said Voltar, "but you have to get up. I have a plan to hide you far from this place, a place where even Norvora will not be able to find you, but it is still some way off. We must get you deep into the forest by dark if we are to have any chance of escape." Cassandra slowly got to her feet, her bump looking very obvious and cumbersome and Valarie's heart went out to one bearing such a burden yet carrying on without complaint. She reached down and offered her hand to help pull Cassandra to her feet. Cassandra gave her a small faint smile and accepted the outstretched hand. Valarie decided then that she would stay in the form of a lady for as long as possible, and so instead of letting go of Cassandra's hand she held on. One quick nod at Cassandra to say they were starting and then Valarie was running, at a slow pace albeit, but Valarie pulled Cassandra along with her, using her magic to give Cassandra strength. Voltar, now realising how previously they had not helped her, took Cassandra's bag and threw it over his shoulders.

"Stupid" he muttered to himself, knowing that he should have stopped to think more before flying out in front of Cassandra. The three of them set off as fast as they could towards the trees. It wasn't long before Cassandra cried out that she had to stop.

"I can't go on" she said, "if only my father had left me my horse." Voltar and Valarie looked at each other, both pondering Cassandra's lament.

"I couldn't sustain that transformation for long Voltar" said Valarie. Voltar nodded his understanding. Being high Fairies meant they had strong magic that enabled them to do many things. But the bigger the animal they changed into, the shorter time they could hold that transformation.

"I will see how long I can hold it" said Voltar, and with a deep intake of breath changed himself into a huge shire horse. Immediately he changed back into his Fairy form.

"Too big" he said, then closed his eyes and changed into a pony. Valarie smiled and stroked his mane.

"We don't know how long he can stay like this so let's hurry." Valarie pulled Cassandra up and helped her onto Voltar's back. Cassandra looked at Valarie, her eyes filling with tears at the relief, "I never believed in Fairies" she said.

They had been in the forest for some time now; the trees that had started out being fairly sparse with large open spaces became thicker and denser. It slowed them down, and Voltar in his pony form, was finding the shape shifting harder to hold. The branches of most of the trees grew down to the ground which meant that they had to weave in and out of spaces as opposed to going straight ahead. Voltar felt his own fear rising, this was too slow: Norvora would surely catch up with them before they reached the mountain at this pace.

Valarie transformed into an Eagle and flew through the trees up into the open, now cold and dim air, high above the trees. At first she could see nothing and so decided to fly back in the direction they had come from. She flew for quite some time. Her heart twisted in anguish when she saw that Norvora had reached the edge of the forest already. To her dismay he wasn't setting up camp for the night but had lit several rush torches and Valarie could see the line they made as they began to weave in and out of the trees. There was also a feeling of something else not being right. Valarie searched around for the cause of her unease and finally found herself staring at the Moon. Not long ago it had been a full Moon, brightly shining low in the sky. Now it was only a half Moon and its light was dim. Her heart thudding in fear she flew back to Cassandra and Voltar.

As she came to land on the grass she took the form of the young woman once more. She decided not to mention how close Norvora was or how the Moon seemed to be disappearing.

"I have an idea: I think it will help some." Valarie closed her eyes and when she opened them again she looked exactly like Cassandra. Cassandra let out a soft "oh" in surprise and climbed off Voltar's back. Voltar, relieved of his pony duties, once again resumed the embodiment of his true Fairy self.

"Good plan, we will go northwards, you go to the west. I must fly once more so they cannot see my tracks, with any luck when Voltar reaches this place he will have to split his men between the two tracks. We would not win in a battle against six large ones – but we would have a better chance than if we had to fight the twelve of them."

He turned his head to look at his sister, "Join us as soon as you can, leave a long trail that would take them at least until morning and then come and find us."

Valarie nodded at Voltar, took one quick look at Cassandra – who was now looking extremely pale with beads of perspiration rolling down her face, and started running. Voltar picked up a small branch from the ground. "Kai li in di fornin" he said and the branch started to glow. The soft orange light reflected around the trees and it was only then that Cassandra realised the sun had set and evening was drawing in. Voltar took Cassandra's hand and picking out the easiest paths he could find, led her through the forest.

They had not gone too far when Cassandra was hit with the most tremendous pain in her abdomen. She let out a cry and fell forward to the ground putting her hands out in front of her to brace the fall. Voltar dropped down beside her.

"What is it?" Cassandra was panting heavily as the waves of pain racked her body and could not answer. Voltar knew instinctively that it wasn't just the strenuous run that caused the pain and sat down on the grass in defeat. If the child was coming now they would never be able to escape. Why had they left it so late to come and help the King carrier? Norvora had chosen the dark side a long time ago, his soul knew no mercy, and even if they gave the child willingly to him, Norvora would still kill them to ensure their silence.

Voltar had watched Norvora's dark towers for a long time now. He had seen the witches coming and going, had heard the screams of innocent life being tortured and had grown to fear the amount of magic he could see surrounding the fortress. No, when Norvora found them, as surely he would, they would not have much time to live.

Cassandra's pain began to ebb away and her breathing turned slowly back into a normal rhythm. As soon as she could she began to push herself back up. Voltar instantly stood and helped her. They moved forward together, Cassandra leaning heavily on Voltar's arm. Running was now out of the question, and so was leaving Cassandra to walk by herself, so Voltar did his best to support her and they inched forward painfully slowly.

This was now the third time they had stopped, the third time pains had forced Cassandra to the ground. Voltar was constantly looking back the way they had come, he was sure he could hear

Norvora's men getting ever closer. Each time a branch creaked in the distance he froze, in anticipation of being set upon by the large ones. Just then, Valarie flew through the trees and when she saw them came to them turning herself back into a lady. With her came a bit of hope.

"They split into two groups Voltar. So our plan worked, but Norvora took the path northwards and is ever gaining on us." They both looked at Cassandra. She was exhausted, the birth pains and the pain of the run were taking their toll on her and she looked awful. Completely white, her body beginning to shake with the shock of the pain. Still she looked at them, her chin set firm and determined.

"While there is breath in me I shall flee, never will a princess of Havenshire lay down her life for anyone to simply take. So this piece of moss then - " she indicated the earth below her feet, " this is not the place that I shall lie down and die."

Voltar and Valarie took position either side of her, supporting her. Brave words indeed, but without their help she wouldn't have been able to stand. Slowly they moved forward, Valarie holding her right hand above her head letting a stream of light pour from her hand lighting their way

Voltar glanced at Valarie over Cassandra's head.

'Have you noticed the sky?' Valarie nodded her answer. The Moon had completely disappeared from the sky and had taken with it the last remnants of light. Not even the stars were visible in the blackened sky.

They had not gone far when once more Cassandra was struck with pain. Voltar and Valarie managed to pull her under the hanging branches of a great fir tree that came down and brushed against the forest floor.

Cassandra cried out loud in pain and Valarie lent forward quickly and placed her hand over Cassandra's mouth. "Hush now, they will find us quick enough without your cries of pain." Valarie pushed back the strands of hair from Cassandra's face, now drenched in perspiration. "We will need a blanket Voltar." Voltar looked at his sister. So this was to be the place then. He opened the bag and took out a blanket. They threw the blanket out over the flattest piece of moss they could find and helped Cassandra onto it.

A single thought had been going round and round Voltar's head now for quite some time, he could keep it in his head no more. *"We should kill it."* Cassandra moaned under Valarie's hand as another wave of pain wracked her body. Valarie looked at her brother.

"It is not an `it' *he* is a boy."

"We have to kill him Valarie, if we let Voltar take him and he is `the one' then all the Kingdoms of Talia will suffer. Better to lose `the one' than to leave him in the darkness."

"Life and death are not our decisions to make Voltar: we do not have the power to decide if the baby should live or not."

"But if we leave him with Voltar we may never forgive ourselves, if he ruins the lands and if he grows to kill many – won't that be our fault?" Valarie looked down at Cassandra, the poor girl's body was being wracked with pain and she arched her back so far off the ground Valarie feared for her. "Sssh" she whispered into Cassandra's ear as she stroked her hair, "ssh it will be all right, you'll see." She looked back up at Voltar.

"This decision is not ours to take Voltar, we are of the light: should we step into the darkness – even for a moment, in the aim of doing good? I cannot, my feet are on a path and I don't choose to leave it, not even to agree with you my brother."

"What if it is the wrong path Valarie?"

"But my conscience will always be true for I choose that which I know is light."

"You never see grey areas do you, I wish I had your clarity, but my mind is set for analysis: to work out the best way forward, in doing

73

that I think it would be better if he died rather than grow up in the
dark."

Just then the clear night air brought the sound of a cough, Valarie
instantly put her light out and whispered across to Voltar.

"It looks like your choice then is to kill the King carrier for it
looks like they will be upon us before his birth." The pains were
easing slightly and Cassandra had stopped thrashing about. She
opened her eyes and tried looking at him in the darkness.

"Kill me then Voltar for I am in so much pain I do not wish to
live any longer."

"Hush, hush, you silly thing, the pain will pass eventually and
you will remember it no more." Valarie looked at Voltar, "she doesn't
mean it."

"Oh I do, I do. Kill me: take me from this life of pain. My lover
was killed, my father disowned me, and my Kingdom banished me.
What do I have to live for? Kill me I say and put me out of my
misery." Cassandra started crying, tears of self pity rolled down her
cheeks, all her regal dignity fallen away, she lay there just a young
woman with her hopes and dreams dying in the air around her. Voltar
reached into his right boot and pulled out a dagger. Valarie heard the
knife being drawn.

"Oh Voltar no! This is wrong." Voltar pushed Valarie aside and
moved to kneel over Cassandra. Cassandra stopped crying and
peering into the darkness found Voltar's eyes. He raised his arm to his
shoulder height and lent slightly forward. At that moment Norvora's
voice came to them.

"Spread out slightly men, she must be close now."

Voltar's arm dropped back down to his side. Norvora was the evil
one, not he: he would let the Elements decide the fate of this child. Just
then Aunt Audrey's voice was heard, a single word, loud and clear.

"Protection."

"Aunt?" said Voltar spinning around to look for her. And then they saw the particles of gold dust in the air around them. Valarie came and knelt on the other side of Cassandra and smiled at Voltar, "she has sent a spell."

The tiny gold particles seemed to gather in the air around them, then slowly came down and showered the three of them. From the palest light the sparks gave Cassandra looked at the two fairies with a question in her eyes. Valarie lifted her finger to her lips, warning her to keep quiet lest she should speak. Just then Norvora himself appeared in the trees in front of them, his flaming torch lighting up the forest. He slashed at branches with his sword, each swing of the blade and each footstep bringing him ever closer to the three. Voltar raised his arm, his dagger poised ready to strike at Norvora.

Norvora was now virtually upon them, and slashed at the branches of the tree under which they hid. They all three shrunk back slightly, expecting Norvora to yell in triumph at his find. Instead, to their astonishment and huge relief, after looking around in their direction, he moved on to the next tree. Norvora and his men must have only taken moments to sweep through the area in which they hid, but to the terrified Cassandra, Valarie, and Voltar it felt like an eternity – one in which they held their breath and let fear master their hearts.

As the sound of the men's thrashing and searching began to fade, Cassandra felt the pangs of pain once more, her body instantly tensed to face the onslaught of coming pain. Valarie quickly placed her hand over Cassandra's mouth once more. Her eyes implored Cassandra to be quiet: they might be safe yet. Voltar looked around and found a tiny branch, he showed it to Cassandra and she nodded her understanding. Valarie took her hand from Cassandra's face and then Cassandra bit down on the branch to prevent herself from crying out. Eventually the pains passed once more, and Cassandra, between gasps of breath looking at Voltar said, "No seriously, you can kill me."

This time Voltar smiled. "Not today my lady." By the time the next pains came, Norvora and his men seemed to be gone.

Valarie would have liked the baby to delay its coming by a day, the gold dust and the magic spell of protection had hidden them once but she did not know if it would work again should Norvora hear them and return. But she knew the time was here and the child would not delay. She lit up her torch once more so that it gave out a pale glow.

Cassandra drew up her knees as much as she could and tried to muffle her cries by biting down hard on the branch, would this pain never cease?

"I can see his head" said Voltar in excitement, "he is coming Cassandra ready or not." Cassandra moaned in pain and pushed down with all her might, her entire body felt as if it was being ripped open. Valarie wiped Cassandra's forehead, "you're doing so well Cassandra; it will be over soon." Cassandra moaned, beads of sweat rolled from her forehead and she pushed with every last bit of strength she had. And with that last push, deep in the Tremlin Forest, on a night when the world was plunged into darkness, `The One' came into the world of Talia.

Chapter Ten ~ Interfering Witches

Norvora heard a baby cry.

"Did you hear that men?" "Yes master" replied those close to him.

"It seems to be coming from the river" said one of the soldiers. With that Norvora reached the river's edge within moments; his blood rushing through his veins in his excitement. The torches lit up the river somewhat but Norvora couldn't see far. He looked up at the sky, *'Where is the Moon?'* He needed to see.

"Delfor" he bellowed. A demon arrived as if he slid down a huge invisible slide. He snarled at Norvora and hate poured from his fire red eyes.

"What do you want?" he hissed.

"Take the torch and fly over the river with it." Delfor hissed like a snake.

"No, no, no. *I* don't like the light."

"Take it" commanded Norvora through his clenched teeth. Delfor hopped his way over to Norvora, snatched the torch from him, and with a toad like jump leapt into the air and flew over the river. Once the demon was over the middle of the river Norvora pointed his bony finger at the torch and a thin streak of lightning left his finger and hit the torch. The torch instantly flared into a bright light and Delfor shrieked and covered his eyes with his free hand. Now Norvora could see.

The baby's cry was heard once more.

"There" yelled one of the soldiers pointing down the river. Instantly Norvora could see two women sitting in a boat. One was rowing and the other was holding a bundle from which the crying obviously came.

"How did they find a boat?" Norvora puzzled.

"Master, there are boats just down the river, on the bank." Norvora looked where his soldier was pointing. He didn't stop to answer his own question but sprinted as fast as he could along the river bank. Three rowing boats were moored to a tree. Without hesitation Norvora and his soldiers climbed into the boats and untied the ropes. Norvora could just make out the rowing boat in which Cassandra sat but it was disappearing around a bend in the river, and the high mountain ranges that came down to meet the forest here would block his view very soon.

"Quickly" he ordered, and his men set about with the oars. Around the bend of the river, and out of sight, the two women in the boat looked at each other and started laughing.

"Too easy" said the first one, a lady with long red hair and a face covered in freckles. She stood up in the boat and pointed a stick towards the shore. Of its own accord the boat turned and headed out of the main stream towards the river bank.

"How did Oleanna know exactly where we should wait?" asked the second lady. A slim beautiful woman: with long blond curls and pale skin. Their boat bumped against the bank and they climbed out. They let the boat loose so that it went off on its own once more. "I don't know Sasha" replied the first one, "but we are here, and now is the time, and that is all that matters." As she spoke she waved. Sasha looked up and saw the others standing on the far bank. Six ladies: all strikingly different individuals, except for one thing – they all wore exactly the same dress. A pale orange chiffon outer layer: over layers of deeper orange. The dresses flowed to the floor and rose to their necks, soft folds of material covered their arms, leaving only their heads free of material.

As one, all six raised the sticks they carried and pointed them towards the river. They began to chant quietly, one spell, over and over.

As the words tumbled from their lips the currents of the river began to increase with speed and became fierce and fast.

The three boats holding Norvora and his men came around the bend. Their oars were already lost and the men held onto the sides of the boats as they sped down the river. Norvora knew magic was being used the moment the current picked up, but it had been too late to turn back to shore. Mighty wizard though he was he had never learnt to swim, all his life he had suffered nightmares of drowning; and so had stayed away from water all his life. None of his men would have known fear gripped him, as he thought his nightmare was at last to come true: fear prevented magic from being formed, and so he clung to his boat as much as his men.

He saw them though, as he sailed past, being thrown sideways in the boat as a wave hit them and sent them spinning. Saw the witches on the bank and cursed his eagerness in not recognising that something was not right earlier. He would pay them back - the Earth Clan. Why they should strike out at him he did not know. He had been at war with the Water Clan for years but had always thought the Earth Clan to be uninterested in the affairs of men. His mistake, one he would never make again.

"You will live to regret this, sisters of the Earth, I promise you will."

~~~~~~~~~~

Voltar picked up the baby and held him up for Cassandra to see. All pain instantly gone from her body, Cassandra once more burst into tears, but this time tears of relief and joy. Valarie took the baby, tenderly wrapped him in a cloth and handed him to Cassandra.

They were caught up in a moment of wonder when suddenly Voltar saw something strange through the gap in the branches that

Norvora had made. Lights were finding their way through the trees, and they were not normal lights: they were lights of colour. He crawled to the opening and then gasped in surprise. He turned back to the others.

"Quickly" he said moving to help Cassandra to her knees. Valarie took the child and Voltar helped Cassandra. They came out from under the long branches and stood in the small clearing. Valarie handed the child back to Cassandra and then turned her face towards the skies. Colours filled the air around them. All the colours of the rainbow were there, but most of the colours were different shades of blue. Each colour seemed to have its own river of light: each river moved and swam in the sky. They interlocked with one another and then broke free to reach down to the earth. One by one each river of colour flowed to the forest and wound its way down until it reached the child.

Cassandra held the child to her tightly. Voltar and Valarie stood on either side of her, holding her arms lest she fell. All three of them held their faces up towards the skies. Wonder and awe filled them all. None had ever seen anything like this before. Tears of wonder rolled silently down Valarie's face, she had never felt such peace and joy before. Surely what they were witnessing were the Elements at work? Then, all too quickly, the lights began to pale and fade. Watching them go was like losing the most important thing he had ever owned and Voltar felt the loss heavy in his chest.

The Elements talked to Valarie through the lights, she would tell no one for a long time to come, but they had told her of her importance in the events to follow. She was consumed with sadness at knowing something so painful and yet so important was to happen, she straightened her back, she would not fail them.

Cassandra on the other hand, was filled with the healing power of the lights and the sense of exhaustion from having just given birth was gone, instead she felt like a warrior, mighty and ready for battle.

Chapter Eleven ~ Dark Towers

Marcus stood on the highest point of the hill and looked to the North. The skies were full of colours. Beautiful: magical, breathtaking – and oh so far away. He watched as all the colours began to pale. The last shades of blue swirled around the sky, and then were gone. All that remained was a normal night sky, cloudless with a full moon but filled with eternal darkness broken only by the twinkling of stars. The vibrancy of something special totally gone. In that moment anger consumed him. It was all Idi's fault; he should never have brought the stupid boy with him. He spun around and marched down the hill. His magician's outfit was clear to Idi's watchful eyes as Marcus stomped back down the hill. Today Marcus wore his most precious outfit. Deep purple material with silver signs embroidered into the cloth in a deep panel along the bottom of the gown. Around the outer cloak the silver signs formed a panel that edged the material, swooping around his neckline and the hood. The hood was down and Marcus's long white hair fell around his face. In his hand he held his staff. As if it had a hand, the long piece of twisted wood, held a black stone in its tip. The stone was smooth as marble, felt like ice to touch and was the deepest of blacks: it seemed to catch the moonlight as Marcus marched down the hill and sent sparks of light out into the night. Idi could tell by his every movement that Marcus was furious.

Idi placed Katrina in a basket and then stood to wait for the onslaught of rage that was about to come his way. He knew Marcus would never hurt anyone but he subconsciously moved to stand between the basket and Marcus.

Marcus marched right up to Idi and stood in front of him. The wind was making his cloak flap around but Marcus looked like unmoving stone to Idi. They stood and stared at each other for a few moments and then Idi could bear it no longer.

"We had to stop, she was sick."

"You should have left her at the village like I told you. She would have been looked after. I would have left money to see to it."

"And what if the Shee-Dragon decided to come and have another feast, the villagers were not going to believe you. Was I to leave her to have her heart ripped from her body?"

"It might be a year before the Dragon finds her way to the Kingdoms once more, we could have gone back for the infant later once we had reached The One."

"I couldn't take that risk."

"So now because you demanded we stop for two days we have missed the signs and we are not where we are supposed to be. The One is more important than this infant's life Idi, you were stupid to bring her along and I am the more stupid because I didn't make you leave her behind." Stupid was a word that sent unbridled feelings racing through Idi. His back straightened and he clenched his fists tightly.

"Her name is Katrina and who is to say that another child's life is more important than hers?" Marcus looked at Idi, his anger was fading, it was too late, and they had missed their chance.

"Oleanna did not send us to find this infant Idi, she sent us to find The One, and I have let her down." Marcus shoulders slumped and he sat himself down next to the fire. Idi's hands unclenched and he crouched down opposite Marcus.

"Back in Clodoth when women give birth they take to their beds for several days, surely the same will be for this woman? You said we are only two days away: Katrina is strong enough now, let us fly with the wind and reach the place where the skies turned to colours. We might not have the exact place, but surely when we reach the place there will be people who saw the colours and they will be able to tell us where the colours were strongest?"

Marcus looked at Idi surprised, it was probably the most intelligent thing the lad had ever said, of course the woman would take to her bed; they all did, even with a good healer it was days before any true strength returned. He nodded at Idi.

"Ok lad, let's be gone." Idi smiled and jumped to his feet, he was all ready, bags packed and Katrina warmly wrapped. As one they bent down, Marcus for the bags and Idi for Katrina. Then they swung themselves up and onto the horse's backs. Marcus leant forward and stroked the horse's neck.

"Nearly there" he whispered, and with that the horses shot forward. For two days the horses had rested and Marcus would never know that without that rest they would not have gone much further. Filled with magic though they were, they were still only horses. Now totally refreshed once more it took only moments for them to hit magic timing. The world around Marcus and Idi blurred and faded and became almost as one colour as they sped with their unnatural speed through the countryside.

~~~~~~~~~~~

Norvora was filled with rage. His towers were in sight, but the sight of them and the power they emitted did not soothe him. Six round towers clustered together and joined by blocks, standing high on the hill: pointed turrets and rimmed balconies gave the towers the look of a woven basket full of spears. Everything was black and looked stark against the pale light of dawn breaking over the deep green landscape. The normal eye would not have been able to see, but anyone whose life was filled with magic, would notice the strong currents of magic, swirling in greys and blacks, that enveloped the towers.

The sentinel on the first tower saw Norvora and his men as soon as they came through the mountain pass. He sounded the alarm and men came running from all quarters to lift the moat bridge ready for their master's entrance. Norvora galloped down the sloping hills to the valley surrounding his castles and then slowed to a trot to go up the hill upon which his towers sat. It was a most steep hill and progress up it was slow. They walked their horses across the wooden drawbridge and into the court yard. This was not a palace or even a fortress built for a King: it was his own private world. Norvora had found the four towers built on top of this hill nearly fifty years earlier. They had been abandoned a long time before and were in a state of disrepair. He had set about at first to simply restore the four towers and had built walls in-between them to form an enclosure with only one place of entry. By rights he wasn't really a Lord and had no right to re-build the towers, but Hamish had chosen to allow Norvora to build, determining that the castles would be extra defence for Havenshire.

Over the years as his armies had increased in number he had built a further two towers. Five towers overflowed with his men and his servants. Some of them had wives with them, and a few even had children, but the majority of his soldiers and most of his servants were single men. This suited him perfectly; having no patience for children, and wanting a woman around only occasionally - and then only for one purpose.

Most of his men felt the same way as him, only a few had wives and these because they had been married for years before coming to work at Norvora's dark towers. The majority of the women who came left within a few months anyway, saying the place unnerved them. Norvora smirked as he walked towards the door to his own tower, yes women were definitely only good for one thing. As he approached his tower two sentinels stood to attention and set their spikes to attention to allow Norvora to enter. He didn't acknowledge them as he went in and they quietly shut the door behind him and resumed their position of guard.

Norvora threw his cloak onto a chair and went into his study. Dawn it might be, but he needed a drink. He went to his decanter and poured himself a stiff drink, in one go he downed the glass and then refilled it. He was just about to turn around when he heard the faintest of sounds. Very slowly he placed his glass back down on the table and put his hand on the hilt of his dagger which was in its sheath around his waist.

"Who has come to my private rooms without invitation?" he asked deceptively softly.

"Only I Norvora" answered a woman. Norvora spun around.

"I will chop your head off if you keep sneaking into my rooms Megan."

The woman laughed softly as if his threat was no threat at all, and Norvora was irritated with the witch. Megan had beautiful silky black hair that flowed down to her waist. She had the whitest of skins, clear and unblemished; and beautiful bright blue eyes that twinkled with mischief. Her black gown fitted her body tightly and then flowed in layers to the ground. Her hands lay hidden under tiers of black lace that flowed down her arm under her sleeves. Her low cut dress showed off her femininity provocatively, and she knew it well. She smiled at Norvora.

"You failed then" she stated. Norvora snorted his irritation at her: if she wasn't such an asset to him he would find a way to kill her.

"I lost them in the woods: it would seem that your warning through Isona came too late."

"Still I hear it was but two, quite young, Fairies that came to her aid. They shouldn't have been able to hide her from you." Norvora took another large swig from his glass and turned his beady eyes towards Megan.

"It would seem she had help; not only from them, but also from Misha and her brood." Megan played with her lace cuffs and then looked up smiling.

"Misha would not go to war with me Norvora: she knows my Fire Clan would destroy her, plus she has never been interested in the affairs of men before."

"She is now, I saw her with some of the others, standing on the river bank. They used joint magic to override any that I could muster whilst on my own and unprepared." Megan got up from the sofa and paced around the room. This was bad news indeed. Her fight against Moraine and the Water Clan was going to be hard; but should Misha bring her clan to join with Moraine then she wasn't going to win. She would have to do something, and do it soon. She had come to torment Norvora in his failure but now she had more pressing matters to deal with: she must discover why Misha would interfere like this, and then ensure she wouldn't do it again.

"We made a deal Norvora, the baby is yours: but Cassandra is mine. Fulfil your promise to me before the boy's fifteenth birthday or your life is mine." Before Norvora could answer she had gone. He hated that she could make herself invisible, how was he ever to keep an eye on her?

Chapter Twelve ~ One Destiny, Separate Paths

Marcus and Idi rode quietly into the town square of Havenshire. No guards had stopped their entry at the gate and yet the place had the look of war about it. People were rushing head down, here and there, and no one was stopping to talk. The atmosphere felt tense and Marcus kept a careful watch.

Idi looked about the streets in awe. He had never seen anything so grand in his life. The houses were thrown together in a wonderful way. Not a single house seemed to be the same as another in shape or size. One leant over another and seemed to be resting on it. Another had its middle cut out to form an alleyway for walkers to traverse from one cobbled street to the next. The entire town was encased by a high wall: that turned out to be itself a mass of tiny homes. On top of this huge circular wall were walkways for guards and soldiers. Every so often along the top wall a circular room had been built where the guards could rest between shifts, and where fires burned to offer them warmth at those cold heights. The whole town was a warren of alleyways and stone steps. Every main street was littered with traders: most of them working out of their homes, their front rooms a place to do business; others had wheelbarrows and were calling out the prices of their wares so that all may hear and be tempted to buy.

Idi had not seen such wonderful looking food or clothes or furniture in his life before. The place was alive with colour, smells and sounds: he did not see the scared faces or the mothers rushing by holding their little ones' hands tight to them. He saw only the spectacle and the knights in their grand attire, many riding their horses through the streets so fast that people had to scurry out of the way, lest they fell under the horses hooves.

The city was a stone sculpture and this was made more apparent by small clearings that housed small circular sections from which single trees grew. Idi was completely mesmerised by the beauty of the place.

Marcus had been to Havenshire a few times in his life and he led them through the windy streets to the East of the town. Eastside was neither rich nor poor and he found himself most comfortable here. He headed straight for the Dobbin Inn, which to him, had a feel of a home from home about it.

As they approached a young man sprang up from his seat outside the Inn, "I'll take your horses to the stable for 'ee Marcus." Marcus looked at the young man puzzled. The young man seeing his look laughed. "Tis I Marcus, Martin, Old Thomas's son." Marcus looked at him hard and then the realisation dawned on his face.

"My, I hadn't realised it had been so long since I last visited Havenshire." Marcus had jumped off his horse and put his arm out to shake hands with Martin. After a hearty handshake Marcus shook his head in wonder. "You must have been only so high" he said indicating a small distance off the floor with his hand, "when I last saw you. How have you remembered me so well?"

"My father never tires of telling the entire realm of Havenshire that the greatest of all magicians favours his Inn above all the rest – how could any of us ever forget you?" Marcus burst out laughing, yes coming to the Dobbin Inn was like coming home. He indicated with his head for Idi to follow him and went inside.
Inside Marcus turned his head to gaze all around the Inn, where was Thomas?

He saw him, for a moment the shock hit Marcus and he stood still in sadness. He often forgot that magic kept the Brothers young, but that time was not so kind to normal folk. He crossed the room quickly and came to a table at which sat two old men playing with dice. The men looked up to enquire what the stranger wanted. Slowly recognition crept upon Thomas's old wrinkled face.

"Marcus!" he exclaimed pushing his chair back so to stand on his feet. Marcus took the outstretched hand and shook it warmly. Thomas was a good and honest man: looking into his lined, pale face Marcus was sad that he couldn't find some magic to lengthen the time of his loved ones and friends.

"Pull yourself up a chair Marcus, sit down and tell us of your adventures out in the different Kingdoms of Talia, it has been a mighty long time since we've heard any tales from you or about you: we had begun to wonder if you had left us forever."

Marcus pulled up a chair and sat down.

"How are the Brothers, have you brought any of them with you this time?" Marcus was just about to answer that he hadn't brought any of them with him when he suddenly realised that Idi (although Idi didn't realise it yet) was now one of the Brothers. He turned around to look for Idi. Idi stood near the entrance quietly waiting. Marcus smiled and indicated for Idi to join them. Once Idi was stood next to him Marcus turned to Thomas and his companion.

"May I introduce you to Idi, latest member of the band of Brothers, and – so Oleanna informs me, the greatest magician that Talia will ever see."

There were several intakes of breath around the room and Idi felt his young cheeks begin to flame. The thought of being a magician was still alien to him but the thought of being the greatest magician was just ridiculous: but the emotion that caught him unawares was the one he felt through belonging. Marcus had introduced him as one the Brothers. A feeling of wellbeing was rushing through him and he felt giddy. From this day forward the folk of Havenshire would acknowledge him with respect; it was to start the beginning of change within Idi. The frightened little boy with no self-esteem was beginning to fade. Idi still had no idea who he was, but for the first time in his life he wanted to know.

Marcus had spent endless nights talking to him, telling him that the person he was at the moment did not have to be the person he would always be. He could change; all he had to do was choose to change and then move forward with that change. It must start in his heart, become his desire, and then slowly it would become his reality. As Marcus had talked night after night as Idi had dropped off to sleep Idi began to believe that it was possible. With the healing of Katrina he had discovered that he could do magic, he was still struggling with, what Marcus called, the basic lessons: but now he believed that maybe one day he would master them.

~~~~~~~~~~

They had been walking all day. No one was tired: even Cassandra having just given birth felt strength surging through her. They had drunk from streams, eaten berries from the forest and little else, but they all felt completely strengthened and refreshed.

At last they came to the forest's edge. The trees simply stopped and the scene opened up before them. They had been walking downhill for several hours and once they came into the open Cassandra looked back and realised the forest was itself set on a very steep hill. Before them a fast river snaked its way along the base of the steepest mountain that Cassandra had ever seen. Trees grew on the other side of the river but only in clusters along the river edge. Above the trees shrubs and grasses grew for quite some distance but as you looked the greens soon disappeared to show that the higher you went the more barren it became, stones and boulders formed the structure of this grand mound jutting into the skies.

Voltar followed the edge of the river some way. Soon the river began to narrow significantly as the hill and the mountain came close together, fighting to claim the river that separated them. Just before the river started to widen, there stood a narrow wooden bridge. It rose in an arch high over the water's spray. When Voltar stopped by the bridge Cassandra looked at him in surprise.

"We're not going to go over that mountain surely" she asked. Voltar shook his head.

"No, we're going to go through it." He didn't wait to see her shocked face but headed across the bridge. Cassandra looked back at the forest they had come through. Each footstep was taking her further and further away from her beloved Havenshire; there was no going back. She didn't know why her Father had urged her to flee; and no idea at all why Norvora would want her child, but she did know that she couldn't go back. With a sigh she looked down at the sleeping child against her body, wrapped warmly with the cloth that tied him to her, and nodded. There might be something special about this child of hers that would make Norvora risk going to war with her Father over him, but she wasn't going to wait around to find out what that was. She took a step onto the bridge: the first step of her new life, she told herself. She was no longer Cassandra, princess of Havenshire and most sort after young lady in the Kingdoms of Talia: now she was Casey, mother and nothing more than a maid. Her Father was right; she would find a way to earn her keep and pale away into the Kingdoms: Cassandra would never be heard of again. And in doing so, she would ensure the safety of both of them.

The path they had to take on the other side of the river turned out to be hard going. Small stones were constantly underfoot and many a time Cassandra almost fell as her foot twisted on them. The third time Cassandra twisted her ankle she cursed out loud and Valarie and Voltar turned to look at her, their shock at her choice of words clearly showing on their faces. Cassandra burst out laughing.

"I am getting into character" she laughed. Valarie shook her head and tutted loudly. Voltar simply smiled at her.

Just when Cassandra had definitely had enough of walking this mountain Voltar brought them to a place where the face of the mountain became a sheer cliff. Well we must be lost, she thought to herself, because there was nowhere to go but a straight drop to death. Voltar kept walking and as Cassandra followed her fear began to grow – where were they going? Suddenly it looked like Voltar was walking in the air and Cassandra came to a halt.

"What is it?" asked Valarie.

"I can't fly" Cassandra blurted out. This time it was Valarie's turn to chuckle. "He's not flying Cassandra; he's on a ledge, look closely." Cassandra took a few paces forward, and sure enough a ledge came into view. Still she stopped and shook her head.

"I can't walk on that, if I slip I will fall." She looked down the dizzy heights of the mountain and shuddered. They had been walking and climbing high for most of the day and it was only when she looked down that she realised exactly how high they had come. Voltar disappeared from sight around the edge of the cliff face. Valarie took hold of Cassandra's hand, "I will guide you, trust me you will not fall, and should you slip I promise I won't let you go." When Valarie saw that Cassandra was still unconvinced she leant forward and gave her a hug. "This is the only way to Tamarind for us Cassandra: the only other way is by ship and that is not possible for us now. It is a good place and you will both be safe there." Cassandra looked down at the child she carried and then looked at Valarie, she had no choice. The Fairies had kept her safe so far, she would trust them. She squeezed Valarie's hand and gave a brave smile. No choice but trust.

Traversing the mountain's edge turned out to be the most frightening thing that Cassandra had ever experienced, but somehow she found herself on the other side of it and standing on solid rock once more. She was shaking slightly and her heart was pounding madly in her chest but she managed to smile at Voltar who stood waiting for them.

"When it is time to venture out from this Tamarind, I am most definitely taking a boat!"

They seemed to head downhill again after that and Cassandra was quite surprised, why climb so high to go down again? The answer, if she would have asked, was that the narrow ledge was the only way to cross over to this part of the mountain, down below the rocks were so many and so loose that they simply would have caused a landslide and gone with the rocks crashing to the river. Just when the light was beginning to pale, and Cassandra – even with all the strength the colours had given her, was beginning to think she couldn't go on, Voltar came to a stop.

"We will sleep here for the night" he said pointing to a cave in the mountain, "We'll finish the journey tomorrow."

Once Cassandra and Valarie were settled and seemed comfortable, Voltar changed himself into a Condor. He wanted to make sure no one was following them. He flew high into the cool evening air and soared in circles for a while to make sure that nothing of any danger was nearby that could threaten the resting ladies and the baby below, and then headed out over the forest. His black feathers blended into the night air, only one with sharp sight would be able to see him. He searched for a long time but could find sight of no one. His stomach rumbled and he suddenly fancied something other than berries to eat. Leaving the mountains and the forest behind him he headed out over the farms. He was taking a chance he knew, because if any of the farmers caught sight of him they would likely take a crossbow and try and kill him. Still his growling stomach ensured that on he flew.

He was keeping a keen eye on the land below looking for something that he could eat and also carry back for the others, and so, when a dark shadow flew right in front of him, he was taken by surprise. So much so that he lost his balance and fell some distance in the sky. It only took a moment for him to regain his balance; spreading his wings wide he glided on the wind till he caught his breath. What was that? He circled round searching the skies for the black shadow to see what it had been. After a while when he couldn't find it he decided he must have imagined it and began searching the farms once more for something to eat.

Soon he spotted an apple orchard: that would be perfect. He could eat one and then carry one back in each claw for the girls. As he came under the branches of the apple trees he changed once more into a young man, landing with a quiet bump on the grass. Smiling as he reached up for an apple, he hadn't realised just how hungry he was. He finished the first apple in no time and decided he had plenty of time to eat another. Half way through the second apple, suddenly a black shadow flew right through the orchard. Dropping the apple he instantly took Fairy form. He flew up to a branch and stood behind a cluster of apples, pushing one of the leaves aside so that he could peer down below.

He was a brave warrior Fairy, but he was also wise. He didn't know what it was that was flying around but he felt the hairs on the back of his neck rise and he just knew whatever it was, it was not of the light.

Voltar didn't have to wait long before the shadow flew through the orchard once more. It darted amongst the trees and came to a stop where his half eaten apple lay. The shadow came to rest on the grass and as it did so its true form was revealed.

Voltar got a shock: a demon, what was a demon doing flying around the Kingdoms? The demon reminded Voltar of a pig. He was black with wrinkled leather-like skin; with a few hairs sticking out from it, much like an ailing porcupine. Its eyes were like red beads and its hands looked deformed and claw like. Voltar just wanted the demon to fly away so that he could get back to the girls, suddenly it didn't feel like they were in a safe place at all and he felt a fool for leaving them.

The demon walked around in a small circle and Voltar wondered what it was doing. Then suddenly it seemed to sniff and it's too large head spun around so that its beady eyes looked straight where Voltar was hiding behind the apples. Voltar froze and held his breath: he hoped it hadn't seen him. Suddenly the demon leaped off the grass and threw its vile body straight at the branch where Voltar was. Voltar nearly heaved at the stench that rose from the creature as he leapt from the branch and took to the air.

As the demon left the ground he turned back to black smoke once more and went flying after Voltar. Voltar ducked and dived amongst the apple tree branches and wondered frantically what to do. He was no match for a demon in his Fairy form; if the demon caught him he would destroy him with one blow. No he had to think of something to change into that would be able to combat a demon. His mind raced over all the creatures of Talia that he could remember but he couldn't think of one that would be able to destroy something as strong as a demon. Just then the demon seemed to lunge forward in mid-flight and almost caught him. Voltar, just in time, flew upwards, between several branches, and then back down again. He looked at the open land in front of him, there just didn't seem to be anything that could help him.

Then he remembered. As a child he had watched the Hadrian Knights, he'd marvelled at how wonderful they looked. He made his mind up in a flash and flew downwards. As he approached the open field he changed into a Knight. He was tall and well built, his body dressed in the entire armour of the Knights and in his hand he held a shining sword. He bore a beard and a moustache but if you looked closely at his face you could just make out the face of Voltar the Fairy. The demon seemed to be taken by surprise and came to stop on the grass in front of Voltar, revealing its own form once more.

For a few moments the demon seemed to be sizing Voltar up. He sniffed, and then grunted out loud. Voltar moved his leg so that his legs were parted and bent his knees slightly, ready for the onslaught he knew was about to hit him. Sure enough, the demon leapt at Voltar and would have knocked him over, but Voltar sidestepped quickly: and as he did so he swung his sword round with all his might to slash at the demon as it flew by. The sword caught the demon and it howled in anger into the night air. But it was only a graze and the demon turned back to Voltar snorting steam from his nose furiously.

Once more the demon leapt, and again Voltar sidestepped. This time however, Voltar's sword didn't catch the demon, but the demon's claw caught Voltar's chest as it flew by. The demons claws scratched downward over the breast plate, and even though it couldn't slice through the metal, the sheer power of the force threw Voltar onto the grass. Knowing that lying on his back was the most dangerous place to be, Voltar sprang to his feet. But before he had time to steady himself against the next attack the demon flew at him. The weight of the demon sent him crashing down onto the grass once more. His helmet might have protected him from a deathly blow but the ringing in his ears made him lose all sense of what was happening. Pain suddenly exploded into his side and he realised the demon had found an area free of armour. He swung his arm with all his strength but the sword was too heavy in this position. Another jolt of pain crashed through his body as the demon tore flesh from his side. In that moment he changed the sword into a dagger and so with a second swing was able to bring the dagger crashing down into the demons back. The demon reared up in anguish and growled his pain into the night air. Voltar gave one mighty push and the demon was knocked over onto the grass.

In a flash Voltar pulled out his dagger and stabbed it into the beast again and again.   Voltar wasn't too sure exactly when the beast died but eventually he became aware that the demon was silent and not moving. Panting, Voltar pulled out his knife for the last time and lent back on his heels as he knelt looking at the creature. Suddenly the creature seemed to evaporate. All his weighty flesh that he had thrown at Voltar turned into smoke once more and then simply crumbled away. Where just a moment ago a demon had been; now there lay a pile of black charcoal. The stench of sulphur rose in the air and Voltar hastily got to his feet to move away. He had only taken a few steps when he collapsed on the grass in agony.

Waves of pain washed over him and he felt himself falling into blackness. With the last bit of strength he had he turned back into his Fairy form. Now instead of lying on the grass for all to see, he lay in between the grass, the tall blades hiding him from the world. His last thought was of Valarie as he gave up and let the blackness come and take him.

Chapter Thirteen ~ Dwarf Sanctuary

Valarie suddenly sat bolt upright. She had been drifting in and out of sleep, not quite able to switch off and relax waiting for Voltar to return. Something was wrong she just knew it. She turned into her Fairy form and flew into the night air. She went as far as she could whilst still being able to clearly see Cassandra: where she and the child lay sleeping peacefully. There was no sight of Voltar. She was just about to call out his name when she stopped herself. If something had happened to him, then danger might be close to them also. She flew back to Cassandra and turned into a young woman once more. For a long moment she stood there wondering what she should do when she heard a faint scuffling sound.

Valarie hunched down and listened for the noise again. It came this time slightly closer and she peered into the cave where she was sure the noise was coming from. Yes, there it was again. Suddenly a dagger appeared in her hand, she stood up slowly and then side stepped silently into the cave along the wall's edge.
Whoever it was – was drawing closer and coming out from the mountains heart. She didn't have to wait long before a dwarf came into sight. She sighed in relief and her dagger instantly disappeared. The dwarf came straight to her, even in the dark his eyesight perfect.

"Umm" he said when he was standing in front of her, "are you the lass then?"

"Hush" answered Valarie putting her finger against her lips to enforce her whisper. She nodded with her head towards Cassandra sleeping on the floor.

"Umm" the dwarf said again, "she's the one then?" Valarie looked at him and shook her head in exasperation and indicated for him to follow her out of the cave.

"Turtledoff what are you doing here?" The dwarf looked at her in surprise.

"How do you know my name young lady?" he asked a bit sharply. It was only then that she realised he would not recognise her in this form and turned quickly into her Fairy form. The dwarf peered at her as she hung in the air in front of his face.

"Valarie" he said in surprise, "what are you doing here?" Valarie sighed and turned into a young girl so that she was the same height as Turtledoff.

"It is a long story my friend, but you haven't answered me yet, why are you here?" Turtledoff sat himself down on the grass; he lifted his soft leather hat off and scratched his head.

"I was having a lovely dream, oh I was so comfy in me big feather bed, twas a mighty pleasant dream, when suddenly I was shown the entrance to the mountain and a voice – as clear as day, told me to come here and meet the one. Well you can't answer back at dreams like that can you now, so ups I get and here I am."

"Your timing is perfect Turtledoff. Voltar and I were bringing Cassandra to Tamarind, but Voltar has gone missing and I just know something has happened to him. I couldn't leave her on her own and was just about to call out to Nicodemus for help – something I really didn't want to do, when you showed up."

"And why wouldn't you want to call on your uncle Valarie?" Valarie sighed.

"He would go mad at us if he knew we were helping her, he forbid Aunt Audrey to even help, he thinks we are with Audrey now. I need to find Voltar and go home to the glen before we get into serious trouble. And you are here now," she paused for a moment looking at Cassandra, "well if you could take her home with you I know she would be safe and I could go and find Voltar." She looked at Turtledoff: his brown curly hair fell down to his shoulders and his

100

beard flowed down to his waist. His face showed his old age, lined and wrinkled and weathered brown. The quick march through the mountain had left his chubby cheeks with a ruby glow; all this she saw in one quick look, but it was his big brown eyes under his big bushy eyebrows she sought out. Would he take Cassandra into his care? Turtledoff took off one of his knee high leather boots and shook it upside down so that a small stone could fall out of it, then pulled it back on again.

"You go and find your brother Valarie; she'll be safe with me. That's why I'm here. Now off you go." Valarie bent down and hugged Turtledoff tightly for the briefest of moments.

"Thank you" she said kissing him on the top of his head. Then in a flash she was Valarie the Fairy once more, she hovered for a moment looking down at the King carrier and her little son. She nodded. She would come back for them, she had promised the Elements – she would give her life to defend this tiny boy: this tiny one who would one day rule the Kingdoms of Talia as one. But for now she knew Voltar needed her and she had to find him, so with one last look she flew into the night, down the mountain side, across the river and through the forests: as she went she began to call in Fairy language, "Alish alon ad kailein?" Where are you my brother?

~~~~~~~~~~

"Cassandra." Cassandra moaned. Surely no-one could be calling her now, she hadn't slept enough yet.

"Cassandra." Oh no there it was again. Now someone was shaking her, oh this wasn't fair. Slowly she opened her eyes, moaning again, it wasn't even light yet. Then she caught sight of the person waking her up and instantly she was wide awake.

"Who are you?" she asked.

"Well now, there's no need for you to be a-fearing me now is there? If I had wanted to do you harm lass, I would have done so whilst you slept. My name's Turtledoff and I'm thinking this here cave mouth be not too safe and we had best be getting back to Tamarind before any mischief should happen along."

"Where are Valarie and Voltar?"

"Oh they had to be going, not supposed to be helping you - did you know? Yep they needed to get back: before their trouble got too great. So you coming then for I want to be gone now? Martha will be up an' cooking me breakfast soon, and oh how I hate cold food."

"I don't think it makes good sense to be getting up and going with a stranger" Cassandra answered him churlishly. Turtledoff raised one of his bushy eyebrows at her.

"Well my name be Turtledoff me dear, I've lived in Tamarind all my life and I am sure that the Elements sent me here to take you to safety." He looked at her to see if she was coming, when she didn't move he carried on.

"My wife's name is Martha – best cook in all Tamarind she be: I teach in the school: I love me pipe n' baccy: My favourite colour is purple: My favourite seat is 'old comfy' by the kitchen hearth: My …" before he had a chance to add anything else Cassandra put up her hand.

"Enough" she said, "I think I know you well enough." Turtledoff took his hat off and gave an elaborate bow.

"At your service madam" he said with mock grandeur. Cassandra chuckled and got up. She gave a quick bob of a curtsey back to him.

"Casey" she said. Turtledoff smiled at her, "And who is this young thing?" he asked indicating the baby sleeping on the floor. Cassandra looked down at her son. All of the time she had been carrying she had been planning names: if it was a girl then she would be called Laura; and if a boy then Sebastian. But when the lights had come down they had told her his name. She felt irritated that they should call him something else and wanted to stay with her choice, their choice was so odd. But no matter how irritated she was she knew she would call him as the Elements had said.

"His name is Absalom" she said flatly.

Turtledoff let out a soft "oh" and then knelt down by the child. Cassandra watched him, curious. Turtledoff turned his head and looked at her. "Do you know what Absalom means?" he asked. She shook her head.

"It means 'The Father of Peace'. It is a very special prediction indeed."

"Oh it's not a prediction, it's just a name" said Cassandra hastily, she wanted to hide in obscurity not bring attention to themselves; "maybe I should change his name?" she asked hopefully. Maybe this Dwarf would confirm her thoughts, that Absalom was a stupid name for a baby.

Turtledoff got back up to his feet and shook his chin at Cassandra whilst pulling downwards on his long mangled beard.

"No you mustn't do that, his name states who he is, I think it would be a grave error on your behalf should you change it." Cassandra knelt down, picked up Absalom and hugged him tightly.

"He's just an ordinary child" she said softly.

"Of course he is Casey" Turtledoff answered back softly, "and it is time for all us ordinary folk to be heading home to Martha's breakfast." Cassandra smiled at Turtledoff, she had only just met him but all her instincts told her she liked this little man immensely.

The walk through the mountain was one of the most fascinating things Cassandra had ever done. At the very back of the cave mouth a narrow opening proved to be the beginning of a long and winding tunnel. Turtledoff lit up a torch and its flickering flame was their only light for a long time. The longer they walked the colder it became, and Cassandra stopped to get the blanket out of the bag. She wrapped it round and round Absalom leaving only his face showing and then she cradled him into her.

"We'll walk briskly Casey, that way you will stay warm." He quickened the pace and she almost had to run to keep up with him. After a long spell of travelling through cold, dark, winding tunnels they emerged into a huge cavern. Cassandra drew in her breath in wonder. The ceiling was so high. It was covered in stalactites. In the centre of the cavern was a huge lake, crystal clear and motionless. The whole cavern was awash with wonderful colours: the walls reflecting deep reds and browns; the lake a clear blue and the stalactites and stalagmites oozing yellows and greens. Because they had stopped for a moment for Cassandra to take in the scene the cold had crept upon them. Cassandra suddenly shivered, she had never felt so cold: she felt as if she were standing inside of ice.
All around the cavern were tunnels leading off to who knew where.

"Who made all this?" Cassandra asked with chattering teeth.

"We did" Turtledoff said starting to walk again, "we mined for gold mainly: trading gold with Bluedane kept us very prosperous." Cassandra had started to walk behind Turtledoff, but now she stopped again.

"Bluedane" her voice broke on the word and Turtledoff turned around to look at her. She was looking down at Absalom and tears started to fall down her cheeks.

"What is it?" asked Turtledoff. She wiped the tears away on her sleeve and looked at him.

"I knew someone from Bluedane once" she said, "but he died, the memory of it came back suddenly to me, that's all. I will be alright, but I think we had better go quickly for Absalom's cheeks feel like ice."

Turtledoff looked at her, he knew that some things were too painful to talk about, so he simply nodded and headed off once more.

The sun had been up for some time when they finally exited the last tunnel and stepped into the daylight. Cassandra stood, taking in the sight and felt her chest rise in appreciation of the immense beauty that lay before her. Still fairly high on the mountain they were able to see the whole of Tamarind. The vibrancy of the colours and the textured layers of the valley lay before them - like a basket full of precious stones: and beyond that, the sun bounced sparks off the crest of waves that came from afar to pummel the shores of this magical place.

Absalom gave a whimper and Cassandra stroked him cheek.

"It is time to feed him."

"Can you wait a short while longer - we are not far from home now?" As if he had understood the words, Absalom suddenly started to cry.

"I think I had best feed him now".

"Very well, but walk with me for just a few minutes - I know a place the sun will have reached and it will be warmer than sitting here in the shade." She nodded and they set off once more. It wasn't long before they rounded a corner and came into a place where the sun peeked over the mountain and showered down on a small glen. Turtledoff motioned with his head that the middle of the glen would be a good place for Cassandra to sit and then took himself off to sit on the outskirts; leaning back against one of the most beautiful trees that Cassandra had ever seen. It had huge knobbly branches, extremely deep green leaves and the most beautiful white flowers. She unwrapped Absalom – who was now crying quite loudly, and started to feed him.

Turtledoff observed her from a distance. Such a young thing: and all on her own with a child. He wondered what had happened to her to make her leave the safety of her home. His dream had been true again. He had not had a truth dream for a long time and wondered why the Elements should speak to him now after such a long gap. The child was obviously the one they had mentioned. "Father of Peace eh?" he said to himself as he took his pipe out from inside his jacket, "*I wonder if he is the one that is prophesied to come? Umm - interesting, legends unfolding and there was me thinking all my adventuring days were over.*" With that thought he lit his long thin pipe and drew heavily upon it.

Chapter Fourteen ~ From Boy to Magician

Idi burst out laughing and rolled on the grass. Katrina took one last wobbly step and fell on top of him, chuckling away. Marcus couldn't help but smile and turned quickly to walk into the cottage before Idi should see it. For ten months now they had set up home here a short distance away from the city of Havenshire. He picked up his pipe and banged it heavily against the hearth, trying to summon up his feelings of anger and frustration. He paused: the feelings did not come. Marcus let out a big sigh, with the anger and frustration finally going he had to admit that he had at last given up all hope of finding *the one*.

He was a failure. Oleanna had asked him to find *the one* and he had let her down. He squabbled with himself day after day, part of him repenting being a failure and the other part defending himself with all sorts of reasons: the main one being that it had been Oleanna herself who had made him fetch this street urchin in the first place. Katrina let out a burst of hysterical laughter as Idi tickled her to bits. Marcus shook his head but he chuckled along with her; her laughter was one of the merriest sounds he had ever heard and it was completely infectious. The ten months that they had been living in this cottage had been a mix of frustration and moments of pleasure.

He had questioned anyone who would talk with him when they first arrived, but nobody had the answer he wanted. Marcus and Idi searched every part of Havenshire but didn't find a trace of a young woman with a child born that dark night. No one seemed to know of a woman that had been pregnant and then suddenly disappeared either, Marcus was at a loss to know who this lady had been and more importantly – where she had gone.

The only other mysterious thing he found out was that no one was allowed to talk about Princess Cassandra anymore. At first he had jumped to the conclusion that she must be the woman he was looking for, but the people of Havenshire were all adamant: she had disappeared a long time before the dark night and that she wasn't married. The rumours were that she had gone mad and that the King had had to lock her away in a secret tower, he was so saddened by it that he had forbidden anyone to mention her name again.

Marcus had searched all the neighbouring villages one by one, but it seemed all the babies he could find were either too old or only just born. His frustration had made him turn bitter inside as he fought against feelings of failure. He tried not to take it out on Idi but he seldom talked to the lad anymore. He kept a silent eye over him and the child but had stopped teaching Idi magic, telling him he had no time, as he had to search for the baby that *he* had made them miss due to the constant baby stops.

Idi had spent the ten months looking after Katrina. He talked to her constantly, and as she got older he played with her, in every spare moment he had. When Marcus watched them together he was reminded that Idi was nothing more than a boy himself. Yet playing with Katrina was the only time you would know he was a boy, the rest of the time he was a man. He constantly filled his day with work. He cut down trees and chopped them into logs to heat their cottage and to sell in the streets of Havenshire for a bit of money which he always gave to Marcus to go towards the food. Marcus knew Idi worked extra hard, trying to make up for letting him down, and trying to win back his friendship. But for the first time in his life he held a grudge and hadn't wanted to give it up. He knew it was doing no good to either of them but he wanted Idi to pay for making him fail.

If it is Idi's fault then I am not to blame.

Marcus walked up to the wall and gently knocked his head against it.

What's the matter with me? He gave the wall another gentle tap with his head. *Enough is enough!*

Marcus went to the door, "Idi."

Idi stopped playing with Katrina and jumped to his feet, "Yes Marcus."

"I need you to fetch me some things from the city" Marcus paused for a moment; normally he would just bark his request at Idi. "Would you be able to go for me?" he asked. Idi looked down at Katrina to hide the smile that itched to appear on his face. Straight faced, he looked back up at Marcus.

"Yes Marcus I will be able to go for you." He bent down and picked up Katrina and swung her in circles in the air before bringing her into the cottage.

As Idi set off down the track he felt lightness in his spirit. Marcus was talking to him again! It had taken a long time but he had always known in his heart that Marcus would eventually forgive him and be his friend once more.

Since the day they had first arrived in Havenshire Idi had been longing for Marcus to teach him magic again. The desire had slowly crept up on him from the moment Marcus had introduced him as one of the brothers. He wanted to earn that right to be one of them and for the first time since he had met Marcus he wanted to make magic simply to please the old humbug.

But this new urge to learn had been squashed by Marcus's bad mood and his decision to put the lessons on hold. Maybe now Marcus would start to teach him again, maybe even go back to his night lessons on life as well: for some strange reason Idi really missed those. Happiness bubbled inside of him and he laughed aloud, running down the track.

Half way to town three farm lads got up from the grass were they had been sitting and stood in the track watching as Idi approached. Idi's joy began to fade and he slowed his pace to a walk. He knew these lads, they were brothers from a farm across the way: but if he hadn't of known them, he would have known their intent from their stance: his years of abuse from village children had taught him to recognise the moment he was in trouble.

He squared his shoulders; he would not run from these three – even though they were taller and most definitely more well built than him. He had told himself from the moment he healed Katrina that his running days were over.

He sidestepped slightly to walk on the field so that he could walk around the youths, but the tallest one immediately stepped onto the field in front him.

"Where do you think you are going - weird one?" the youth said, screwing up his nose as if even talking to Idi itself was insulting.

"I'm just going to the city John. Marcus needs some things." Idi had hoped that the mention of Marcus's name might intimidate the lads somewhat, but unfortunately not.

"You're a girl" snarled one of the other brothers coming to stand close to Idi. "Yeah" laughed the third brother also coming to stand in front of Idi. "We've watched you with that baby; you're a right girl. Girl, girl stupid girl," and with the last declaration the lad poked Idi in the chest. Idi took two steps backwards; all his instincts were telling him to run away but something inside snapped. All the years of being pushed around came rushing back to him and anger and hate flooded his body. Before he realised what he was doing he swung his arm and lunged forward punching the brother who had poked him full on the face. The lad staggered backwards yelling out in pain and put his hands up to his face. After the briefest of moments he pulled his hands away and they were covered in blood.

"The bugger has broken me bloody nose" he yelled, somewhat in surprise. That was the cue the other brothers needed and they pummelled Idi to the floor, thumping his face with all their might. Idi waved his arms around frantically trying to knock them away. But he was no match for them and the two brothers landed on the floor next to him punching him again and again.

Suddenly a white light appeared inside of Idi's mind. It started as a small speck but grew and grew until it consumed his entire consciousness. He couldn't stand the light, it frightened him, and so, somehow, he threw it out of his mind. There was a crack of noise like thunder from a long way away and then yells and screams. Idi did not know what had happened but he knew that suddenly he was free of the onslaught. He turned to his side so that he could get up and moaned with the pain; slowly he sat up and managed to open one of his eyes. The youngest brother was screaming and running across the fields towards their farm. Idi looked slowly about him, the other two brothers lay a good distance from him. Both lay on their backs their arms and legs wide, neither were moving. Idi forced himself to crawl over to them. They were covered in black and it looked like they had been burnt. All the hair on their heads, including their eyebrows had been burnt off. Their clothes were black and singed. What had happened to them? Idi knelt down by the oldest brother and gave him a shake.

"What happened, wake up, what happened?" For a moment there was no response and suddenly Idi began to panic that they were dead. He realised, that even though he didn't know how it had happened, he had done this to them. Panic flooded his body, they couldn't be dead; they mustn't be dead. John moaned and Idi felt himself breathe once more. He moved over to the other brother and shook him, and sighed in relief when he also moaned. Idi got slowly to his feet, pain was crashing through his body and sparks started to fly around in front of his face.

"Marcus" he whispered as he passed out.

It was a strange smell that woke Idi. It was none too pleasant and he started at the intrusiveness of it.

"That's it lad, come on now, fight the darkness - it is time to wake up." Very slowly Idi's head cleared and in a rush all his last memories came flooding back to him and he groaned. Slowly he tried to open his eyes but found them closed too tight.

"I can't open my eyes Marcus" he croaked.

"I know lad, they are heavily swollen. I have bathed you in herbs and, believe it or not, my magic has been working on you for some time. But now it is up to you: heal yourself Idi."

"I don't know how" Idi whispered back, "besides everything hurts too much."

"Imagine yourself in a dark room Idi; there is nothing in the room except you," Marcus waited a moment then said, "are you there yet Idi?"

"Yes but everything hurts."

"I know. What is your favourite colour Idi?"

"Blue, light blue – like the sky."

"Good, now I want you to imagine a light blue ladder in front of you. There should be nothing in your thoughts, just you and the light blue ladder. Everything else must be black. Is it there yet?"

"Yes."

"Good lad: now I want you to start climbing the ladder, take one rung in your hand and then start to climb. Are you climbing the ladder Idi?"

"Hmm."

"Now as you climb the ladder I want you to leave the pain far below you. All the pain is to stay at the bottom of the ladder. Now climb and as you go realise that you are leaving the pain far behind you. Have you left the pain behind?"

"It's chasing me up the blooming ladder."

"You can climb the ladder faster than the pain Idi, climb the ladder and leave the pain behind." Marcus watched the features of Idi's pain filled face begin to soften and knew he was mastering the pain. He waited a little while until he was sure Idi was free from pain.

"Now lad you must heal yourself, search for your power." Idi's mind began searching his body for his power.

"I can't find it" he said.

"It's there Idi, you have used it before. What did you see just before you healed Katrina?" Idi instantly started searching for the white light. In his mind, he ran around rooms but they were all dark, some had doors he couldn't open, others had doors he could open but they only opened up into more dark rooms.

"I can't find it" he said in despair.

"Alright Idi; never mind looking for it then: try calling it to you instead." Idi stood still in the dark room, he looked around for it one last time but when nothing appeared he called out to it. Nothing happened. He called again and again: nothing happened. The pain was beginning to creep back onto Idi's bruised and swollen face and Marcus knew they were running out of time: soon Idi would become too tired to try any more.

"Idi believe in yourself. You have great power: you know that. Believe it, accept it. Acknowledge who you are." Marcus placed his hand on Idi's chest and sent the power of healing that he had into him. Idi felt the heat surge through his body and felt the strength that Marcus was sending him. He called upon the power once more, and this time he felt his heart swell with the feelings of acceptance and with the power from Marcus: and there it was – the light.

It came at first as a tiny speck and hovered in front of Idi. "Oh" whispered Idi to the speck, "you're beautiful." As if appreciating the compliment the speck swelled into a ball. Panic suddenly shot through Idi as he remembered the last time the light had swelled and he shut

113

his imaginary eyes to hide from it. After a moment he opened his eyes again, the light was still there, sparkling and pure and Idi knew instinctively that the light was waiting for him to speak.

Can you heal me light? Idi asked inside his dark room. The light did not answer. Idi's mind raced back to the time when he had healed Katrina. Heal me, he demanded. The light instantly shot around his darkened room leaving behind trails of paler light; then it came back into a ball and hung in the air in front of Idi. Idi looked at the light. Why had it come back? Then Idi slowly let his mind wander over his body and he realised all the pain was gone. Idi's eyes shot open and there was Marcus smiling down at him.

"That is one of the most amazing things I have ever witnessed" he said and reached out to touch Idi's face, which was now completely back to normal. Idi moved slowly, expecting pain to come, but when none did he swung his legs around and sat on the edge of the bed.

"How long was I asleep?" he asked.

"Not very long Idi. I brought you back and tried healing you myself, when I realised you were hurt so badly I decided you had better wake up and heal yourself!"

"How did you find me and are the lads alright?"

"I heard you call my name Idi, and no the lads aren't alright, they're alive but badly burnt." Idi hung his head.

"I didn't mean to hurt them Marcus, but" he paused for a moment and looked up at Marcus, "but they were going to beat me to death so I defended myself." The last part of the sentence had been said with anger and venom and Marcus looked at the lad with sorrow in his eyes: had all his work been to no avail?

"We must go to the farm Idi and heal those lads before one of them dies."

"Heal them, why should I heal them? They don't deserve to be healed." Marcus moved away from Idi and started putting his potion bottles back into their leather box; when he had finished he turned back to Idi.

"You do not have a choice. You have been given a gift; you are not allowed to choose who you bestow your gift upon, you must give to him who asks, and their father has already been here to plead on their behalf." Marcus placed his hand on Idi's shoulder and in a very soft voice said, "If you do not do this Idi you will lose your gift."

Idi knew that Marcus was sincere but there was anger in his heart, and he did not want to heal them. Marcus went to the door, opened it and turned back to Idi, "we need to go." He didn't wait to see if Idi followed him, just started walking, and as he did so, in his heart, cried out to Oleanna for her to help them all.

Idi hesitated a moment and then he heard Katrina chatting to herself in her crib. He got off the bed and walked over to her. As soon as she saw him looking down at her she reached her arms out to him so that he should pick her up. He bent down and picked her up and literally felt his heart breaking. He hugged Katrina close to him and she nuzzled her cheek into his neck. He raised his hand and stroked the back of her head.

"Ok Katrina, I'll do it for you."

Marcus didn't need to look behind him, '*Thank you*' he whispered at the sky, as he heard Idi running to catch him up.

A short while later the three of them were on the porch of the McFein's farm. Ma McFein had been watching for them coming and pulled open the door. She was a small, rather rotund woman with fading ginger hair which had curls like wire hooks. She was rubbing a towel over her face and she had obviously been crying very hard.

"Take the child woman" Marcus said and walked into the house. Idi handed Katrina over to Ma McFein and followed Marcus into the farmhouse. The father had heard their voices and came running down the stairs.

"Oh thank the Elements, please hurry: the Soothers are here from the city but they say there isn't anything they can do for them and that the morning will see them dead." The mother let out a wail and her two daughters rushed to her side, one of them took Katrina and the other guided the mother to a chair by the huge kitchen hearth.

Marcus and Idi hurried up the stairs behind farmer McFein. Inside the bedroom the lads were laying on two beds: the two Soothers were spreading some kind of ointment on the forehead of each of the lads.

Marcus stood back to allow Idi to come beside the first bed. At that moment the youngest son came rushing into the room.

"Don't let him touch them, he will kill them," he would have rushed at Idi to fight him but his father grabbed the lad by the cuff of his shirt.

"Go downstairs lad and wait with the women" he growled at his son.

"But" the lad wailed. The farmer didn't answer but pointed at the door with a face that would brook no argument; the lad slumped his shoulders and went from the room throwing Idi the most murderous look he could muster. Idi turned his attention to John who lay before him. Whatever it was that had caused the burns had obviously continued burning after Idi had seen them for they were in a terrible state now. The large farm boy lay inert on the bed and his very stillness spoke of death. Idi shivered and then pulled on all his reserves: he didn't like these lads but if he could help it he wouldn't let them die because of him.

Idi laid his hand very gently over the boy's chest, he didn't quite touch it because the body was so severely burnt that the skin had mostly gone and was exposing open flesh. His hand hovered over the boy and he called to the light. It came instantly.

"Heal" Idi commanded in a husky voice. The light would help him, it must. To be sure Idi demanded again. "Heal."

Idi felt heat surge through his arm and down to his hand. A bright light poured from his palm and covered John's body. John's body jerked and the lad let out a blood curdling scream. The mother hearing the scream jumped up from her chair, threw her apron over her head and started running around the room. The eldest daughter made a grab for her just as she was about to hit the fireplace and brought her back to the chair. The youngest brother went running up the stairs two at a time, but when he reached the bedroom door he stopped.

John's body was still jerking but his screaming had ebbed to soft moans. The entire room watched as his skin began to grow and cover his body. One of the Soothers fell to her knees and hid her face in her hands, muttering the same cry for help to the Elements over and over. The other Soother stood with her back against the bedroom wall, frozen to the spot. Soon John looked like himself once more, his body had stopped jerking and he had stopped moaning. When Idi finally took his hand away from the body, and the light disappeared, the entire room let out a sigh as one.

Idi moved around the bed to the other brother and the healing process was repeated. When Idi had finished this time he wobbled on his feet and Marcus rushed to support him.

"It took much" whispered Idi leaning against Marcus. "I know lad, I know. Let's go home now." Marcus supported Idi as they walked towards the door. Everyone stood aside to let them pass. No one spoke. No one thanked him.

With Katrina in one arm and Idi leaning on his other arm Marcus knew getting home would be difficult. He called to the horses and as one they came galloping across the fields to stop in front of Marcus.

"Thank you" Marcus said to them as he helped Idi climb into the saddle.

As they went back across the fields on the two horses the McFein family and the two Soothers stood on the porch and watched them. It wasn't until they were completely out of sight that instant chatter began. The McFein family ran up the stairs and crowded around the two brothers, touching them in awe asking them questions of how they felt and what had it been like. The two Soothers flung their capes around their shoulders and headed back to the city as fast as their legs could carry them – boy did they have a story to tell this night!

And so the legend of Idi the Magician began. Stories of how he could raise the dead and command animals to obey him began to spread across the lands. In years to come it was threats of calling on Idi the Magician that would send young children scurrying to their beds; and it was stories of his power that would start every adventurous young man's heart beating with the desire to learn magic.

Chapter Fifteen ~ Witches at War

In the far North West of Havenshire on the border with the bleak Northlands, deep in the forest-covered mountains, Megan had built her home. She had taken over an old deserted hunting lodge, and the Sisterhood had camped around her. Eventually a small village had been formed. Because they were on the side of a mountain, cabins had been built wherever a flat piece of land could be found, so there was no structure or format to the place. The only thing she commanded when they asked to build the cabins was that none were to be built higher than her lodge. So as she stood on her wooden veranda and leant against the pillar, she looked down on everyone. She only half observed them today, going about their daily chores, because her mind was on the Earth Witch they'd caught; and whether Isona had made her talk.

Megan shuddered slightly. Sometimes she thought Isona was a little too dark, even for her liking. Still, she and Isona had grown up together and Isona had packed her bags the moment she heard Megan was leaving home. She had never asked where they were going or why - she had simply wanted to be with her, and so Megan felt a bond with her first "follower".

As they'd travelled through the lands of Talia, Megan had been astonished when women simply started following them. She had no idea why they came, they just did. It wasn't too long before she realised that they all had one thing in common: magic. Every woman and girl who followed her had been born with the ability to do magic. Most of them lived in places where magic was either forbidden or not believed to exist; and Megan guessed they came to be with others who were like themselves. She had no idea how they knew she was a witch: she had never practised her witchcraft in public, nor spoke of it to anyone except Isona.

No one had ever asked her where she was going or what she was looking for, and she was glad of that, because until she had entered Havenshire, she hadn't known the answer. Now, here in these mountains, she knew a part of the answer: she had been looking for 'home'. As soon as she crossed the river Tamara and entered Havenshire she had felt a thrill flood through her spirit, she didn't know why or how, she just simply knew she had come home.

It soon became apparent that her band of now one hundred and six ladies were not welcomed in most towns – and definitely not in the cities, and so when she'd found this hunting lodge she knew it was perfect place for them.

Just then Kylie came rushing along the well-worn path to Megan's lodge. Megan turned when she heard her footsteps; she half smiled when she saw tiny Kylie rushing towards her. Kylie had been only twelve years old when she'd joined the Sisterhood. Four years later she was still a tiny, frail thing who constantly looked puzzled about everything. Today was no exception - her head down, her long black skirt hitched up with both hands to aid her haste: if she could've run she would have, but Megan had forbidden running. And so she came at the quickest walk anyone could muster. Megan made sure her smile had gone by the time Kylie finally looked up at her.

"Isona says it is time for you to come Megan" Kylie gave a slight bob of a curtsey, and Megan sighed: she had told them all to stop curtseying; the older ladies had compromised by simply nodding their heads at her when they approached, but the young ones would not be told.

Megan reached down to the balustrade and picked up her stick, she tapped it lightly against her other hand and Kylie took a step backwards. Megan was not looking forward to what was about to happen but it needed to be done. She squared her shoulders and lifted her chin high and started up the path to the cabin where only a few of her witches ever went. She was aware that a hush had fallen over her small village. She knew, without looking, that they had all stopped what they were doing to watch her go to 'that' cabin; some would smile with mirth, others would look sad: but, she felt every last one of them had to be aware that she knew what she was doing, she was in control, or else she would lose their respect. She had never set out to form a band of followers, had never wanted to be their head, never imagined forming a band of Witches – and where their name of "The Fire Clan" had come from she had no idea. But here she was, and here, she had discovered, was where she wanted to stay.

Isona looked up as the wooden door creaked open. Her pale face conveyed a mix of glee and frustration, and Megan knew in an instant that she had brought the Earth Clan Witch close to the point of no return - but had not got her to talk yet. She moved her eyes away from Isona and looked at the captured Witch. She steeled her resolve so as not to show the distaste on her face. The Witch was shackled to metal hoops in the ceiling. Only the shackles kept her upright. Her head hung limp on her chest, her limbs with no strength left; she literally hung by her arms. Her orange dress fell in strips around her body. Isona had been cracking her whip again and the marks were deep and harsh across the young girl's body.

"She put up a good fight; I don't think I would have been able to break her magic if Kylie here hadn't blocked her thoughts." Kylie fidgeted in the corner and Megan knew that she did not like helping Isona like this.

"Has she told you anything?" Megan asked.

"phwffff" Isona spat out, "she won't even tell me her name! I have done all I can, with Kylie blocking her mind I couldn't use mind tricks and all the pain I inflicted on her brought no response." Megan looked at the young Witch hanging from the shackles with admiration, none before had withstood Isona's whip and magic, but she wished she had given in to Isona because Megan hated using her own magic for this purpose.

She lifted her hand and pointed her stick at the girl.

"Wake" she commanded and a streak of light shot from the stick and struck the girl. The Witch gasped and her head jerked upwards immediately. Her eyes were wide and full of terror. Megan hardened her heart.

"What is your name?" The girl remained silent.

"Your name" snapped Megan as another shot of lightning flew from her stick and stung the girl.

"Shona, my name is Shona." Megan smiled. She felt her power rushing through her veins. Why she was such a powerful Witch she didn't know, and although she taught the others all she knew, none of them came close to holding the same amount of power as she.

"Why did Misha stop Norvora from getting the child?"

"I don't know what you're talking about" Shona whimpered.

"Why" snapped Megan, as another bolt of lightning hit the girl.

"It was the Oracle Oleanna, she told Misha where to go and what to do, Misha was just returning a favour. She doesn't know you are interested Megan, honest she doesn't."

"Liar" snapped Megan and threw three bolts of lightning at the girl in quick succession. The girl's body nearly snapped: it jolted so hard with the pain. Streams of sweat were pouring from the girl's forehead and her eyes were wild with fear.

"Why does Misha interfere now, she has not joined in before?" Megan walked over to the girl whose head had dropped back down to her chest. She reached up and lifted the girl's head so she could stare into her eyes.

Like a rabbit caught in the light the girl stared back at Megan and all the fight left her body: she knew she would not live another day and that until Megan had what she wanted she would suffer.

"Oleanna told her that you and Norvora had joined forces. She hates Norvora with a vengeance." Megan was taken by surprise.

"Why?"

"Because he is plotting to release the First Witches."

"But why would Norvora do that? That makes no sense the First Three would destroy everything."

"Ask him about the Three. Oleanna says the Three are poisoning his mind and that he is no longer himself, but lives through their thoughts. They want to be free and they are using him to release the dark. If he succeeds, the Demons of the Depth will roam the lands once more and the Earth Element will die." Megan had heard enough. She stepped back from the girl and with a matter of fact nod of the head, flicked her stick at her. The bolt of lightning that hit the girl this time killed her instantly. Isona rushed over to the girl, glee all over her face.

"Can I have her body?" she asked looking at Megan as Megan walked towards the door. Megan didn't look back but shook her head.

"Burn the body Isona." The girl had suffered enough; it was time to release her spirit.

Without looking at Kylie Megan began to talk as they walked back.

"I couldn't let the Witch go back to Misha and tell her where we live. Part of our security is in the fact that no one knows where we are. We must keep this place safe at all costs. Battle is about strategy Kylie, we must know our enemy and not let them know us: this way we will always have the element of surprise on our side. If we have to go to war with the other clans I want to win, and I want to do so with as few Fire Clan deaths as possible." Megan was slightly irritated for feeling that she had to explain herself to Kylie, but she needed Kylie to understand and to keep Kylie's faith in her.

Kylie was quiet for a moment, but as they came to stop outside Megan's lodge Kylie looked up at her.

"Do you not know why we follow you Megan?" Megan was completely taken by surprise by the question, she was about to snap an answer at Kylie but instead she stopped herself and simply shook her head.

"There is an aura around you that we can all see. It is sometimes silver and sometimes grey, depending on your mood, but it is always there. The power that flows from you is so intoxicating that we are drawn to you like bees to pollen. We strive to learn from you and to be like you, but within the heart of every woman here, is the desire to serve you. Something new is coming to the lands of Talia, change is in the winds; we all feel it. The very air carries the expectancy of what is to come. We believe that you will lead us to a new life Megan, a new world: somewhere where we can be Witches without fear or shame."

Megan stared at Kylie in amazement. She had no idea this is what they thought; she had been simply looking for home, somewhere to rest and belong. She opened her mouth and then closed it again; she had no idea what to say. Kylie gave a curtsey and went off down the path to the village. Megan watched her go; then went to the balustrade, leaning on it to watch the girl walk down the path.

She realised there was still a hush over the village and let her eyes wander around. Every witch stood still and tall and looked up to where Megan was standing. One by one they curtseyed to her. Megan felt her spirit stir. As the women had gathered to her she had at first begrudged their intrusion on her world, but slowly a sense of responsibility towards them had grown within her. She needed to build them a world where they would be free to wield their magic and not fear death or imprisonment because they were special. As she looked at the women, all dressed in black, dotted around the mountainside, a new sense of purpose and direction filled her. She would lead them to a new world, even if it was this world turned upside down.

"Margot" she called out.

"Yes Megan." Megan spun around in surprise to see Margot behind her. Then she shook her head and smiled, it seemed sometimes that Margot knew that she was needed even before Megan knew she needed her.

"We have plans to make. I will not let Misha get away with her interference. I want a potion that will kill her slowly but surely. I need a potion there will never be a cure for." Margot nodded,

"We shall get to work straight away Megan."

Chapter Sixteen ~ Lost & Found

Valarie sat high on a branch of her favourite tree in the apple orchard. She did not know why but she kept being drawn here. She had searched every last inch of the place and could find no trace of Voltar. She had flown in different directions many times but constantly felt the pull to return to this spot. The sun was now high in the sky and fear for her brother gripped her heart. She needed help. She raised her head tilting it to face the sky.

"Audrey" she sang, "Audrey shea alai mai". The words lifted into the air and disappeared. If Audrey heard her she would know instantly that Valarie was in trouble. Valarie curled herself up on a broad branch, under a group of leaves for shade, and although she wanted to stay awake and watch for either Voltar or Audrey, she was soon asleep.

The sun was beginning to set when Valarie was woken by someone touching her face. She jumped in fear; awake in an instant, when she saw it was Audrey who had woken her, Valarie threw her arms around her aunt at the same time started pouring out the whole tale of events that led up to her calling aunt for help.

"Hush" Audrey said, hugging her niece tightly to her, "it's alright. We'll find him."

"We'll have to hurry Audrey, the sun will set soon and the light will fade." Valarie looked up in surprise when she heard the voice, she hadn't realised anyone else was with them.

"Oh" she said softly in surprise. By her aunt's side stood a Pixie. He was much taller than her aunt, but it was his pointed ears that showed that he was a Pixie and not a Fairy. Behind him stood a smaller; slim; female Pixie. Her hair was also black, but hung in soft waves down to her shoulders and was not in spikes like the male. Audrey smiled at Valarie's surprise.

"These are my friends, Elroy and Losia." Fairies did not mix with Pixies: Pixies were uncouth and aggressive; everyone knew that: yet if Audrey had two friends that were Pixies then either their reputation was unjust or Audrey had met two exceptions to the rule. Whichever it was, it was enough for Valarie that they were her aunt's friends.

"Pleased to meet you" she said with a slight nod of her head. Elroy beamed back at her, Losia gave a brief smile.

"You are drawn to this place then Valarie?" Audrey asked.

"Yes, but I don't know why, I have searched the whole orchard, I cannot find him anywhere."

"Yet you are drawn here. I believe the pull between you and your brother is strong Valarie, I think he is here somewhere and he is pulling you to him." Valarie stood up and looked around. In the distance was a farmhouse, but mostly all that could be seen was crop fields. If Voltar was lying hurt somewhere in the field they might never find him.

"Only magic will do, I will need your help my dear" Audrey held out her hand and Valarie put her small hand in it.

"Close your eyes Valarie, I know you do not know magic besides shape shifting, but all the Higher Fairies have magic deep within them. I want you to concentrate on your brother and I will do the rest."

Valarie closed her eyes to concentrate; and so didn't see Audrey lift her hand where a white orb formed and sparkled. Within a few moments the orb darted off Audrey's hand and shot out across the fields. Quick as a flash Elroy and Losia flew after the light, their black edged wings fluttering so fast they were almost a blur.

The orb flew straight for a while and then simply stopped and fell to the earth. In an instant Elroy and Losia stood where the orb had disappeared.

"He's here" yelled Elroy and Valarie's eyes popped open, and filled with hope. She flew with Audrey to where the others stood amongst the tall blades of grass.

Losia was kneeling over Voltar feeling his forehead. Panic accelerated Valarie's heartbeat, and it thudded in her chest fast and faster still. He wasn't moving and she could see by Losia's face that Voltar was in trouble. Valarie gasped as she saw the open wound in her brother's side and panic rose within her, as if choking her. Audrey knelt beside Voltar, put her head down and laid her ear over his heart. After a moment she looked up.

"The good news is we have found him, but the bad news is I don't know if we found him soon enough. We have to get him back as quickly as we can."

Valarie let out a little sob and Losia stood and put her arms around her.

"We will take him back to the Glen Valarie, Sheiline has very special powers I am sure she will heal him." Valarie searched inside herself for the best thing to do then nodded.

"Yes I think that is the best, our Soothers are wonderful, but I think old Sheiline is the best soother I have ever met."

"Let me take him" said Elroy bending down and picking up Voltar carefully in his arms. Voltar moaned and the sound was bittersweet to Valarie because although the movement caused him pain, his moans at least meant he was alive.

Chapter Seventeen ~ Born to be King

Turtledoff and Cassandra soon arrived at a stone cottage set far back into the large flat valley. As they approached Cassandra could hear someone humming and bashing pots in harmony. She smiled; it was such a homely sound and went so well with the idyllic cottage covered in climbing roses.

Whoever was inside had obviously heard the creak of the old wooden gate between the picket fencing, for the cottage door flew open. With great gusto a small rotund women came flying down the path; wooden spoon held high in the air in her right hand. But as the grey haired woman, with round spectacles perched on the end of her nose saw Cassandra she ground to a faulty halt.

Turtledoff went up to his wife and gave her a brief kiss on the cheek,

"Hello my dove, this is Casey, she'll be stopping with us for a while: you don't mind do you my sweet?" and with that he marched off into the house in search of his much belated breakfast, and left Cassandra and Martha to introduce themselves.

Martha looked Cassandra up and down from top to toe, and then for a long moment at Absalom; then nodded to herself as if her inspection had turned out a satisfactory conclusion.

"Come inside petal, are you hungry? Breakfast has been ready a long time past now, but will still be good enough to eat." She gave Cassandra a big welcoming smile (that lit up her eyes making them sparkle) and Cassandra liked her instantly. She smiled back and followed Martha into the cottage.

Turtledoff was already sitting at the head of huge oak table, in an ornate high backed wooden chair. Martha pulled out a chair for Cassandra and went over to the log-burning stove. Cassandra sat down rather gingerly on the chair; fearing her size might be a bit too much for the chair built for Dwarfs, and wondering why Martha hadn't led her to the much larger chair on the other side of the table: but the chair she sat on was sturdily built and took her weight easily enough.

She cradled Absalom in her arms as she looked around the room. The stone walls were very thick and the indent for the windows was deep enough to allow you to sit on the sill in comfort. The paned windows were not very big but there seemed to be lots of them lining the front of the cottage which allowed the early morning sunshine to come pouring in, illuminating the interior of the quaint home.

"Porridge?" asked Martha, holding a bowl full of the steaming oats.

"Yes please" Cassandra answered, shifting Absalom into her left arm so she could take the bowl from Martha.

"I won't be a while lass and then I'll take the babe from you for a bit whilst you break your fast." She scurried around the room and in moments the table was laden with hot bread, butter and a variety of jams, hams of various kinds and a huge chunk of the most wonderful smelling cheese. Martha caught Cassandra sniffing the delightful smell, and smiled.

"Make it myself I do, full of herbs and shallots, gives it a nice full flavour." Martha finished the table by placing a jug of cold milk in the middle and then sat herself down next to Cassandra.

"Can I hold him for you then?" she asked, and Cassandra passed Absalom over to Martha so that she could tuck into the feast before her. Cassandra had never tasted such sweet porridge before: she would learn later that it was Tamerind honey that made it so sweet. She had just finished her porridge as Turtledoff cut her a thick wedge of bread; when the door opened.

"Arr here you are at last Rubin, was beginning to wonder if you were coming today," Turtledoff nodded his greeting as a tall sturdy looking man bent his head and entered the cottage. Rubin grinned in return.

"Been down to the town to sell me runner beans Turtle they went a right treat they did." He reached down and removed his big muddy boots before going over to the sink to wash his hands. It was only when he turned around to join them at the table that he became aware of Cassandra. His sudden shyness was obvious to all, as his ease and comfort with his friends suddenly seemed to disappear and he simply looked awkward. He hovered over the table looking like a giant and didn't seem to know what to do.

"Sit ya'self down Rubin and eat ya porridge before it gets cold," prompted Martha. Rubin sat down abruptly and without speaking picked up his spoon and started shuffling large spoonfuls into his mouth.

Martha chuckled leant over and gave him a playful slap on the back of his head, "Slow down before ya choke." Rubin did as he was told and slowed down a bit but it didn't take long at all before his bowl was empty. When he had finished he looked up and Turtledoff shook his head at him.

"Rubin, your manners are terrible, was your hunger so great that you had to settle it before you could greet our new family member?" Both Rubin and Cassandra looked at Turtledoff, Rubin going red with embarrassment and Cassandra looked at him in surprise at his declaration of her new position with them.

Rubin looked down at his hands and then rubbed them vigorously against his trousers before shoving his right hand out and across the table.

"Pleased to meet you" he said with a forced overly large smile. Cassandra smiled back genuinely and took his hand.

"Pleased to meet you to" she said. That done Rubin snatched back his hand and leant across the table to the loaf. He cut the hugest piece of bread off and Martha could stand it no more and burst out laughing.

"Ar lad tis hungry you are today then?"

"Tis hungry he is every day my dove, only today he seems to have no manners holding his hunger pangs in check." Rubin looked up in dismay, his large deep brown eyes conveying his alarm at the situation. Cassandra couldn't help but smile but looked down at her bread as she lifted it to her mouth so Rubin shouldn't think she was laughing at him.

"Tis a long walk to the town and back again Martha" Rubin stammered. Martha leant over and patted his hand, "Tis alright lad, we only jest with you: eat now, tis a pleasure to see someone enjoying my humble food so much."

"Oh give over wife, tis nothing humble about your food and you know it well" laughed Turtledoff. Martha's smile went almost from ear to ear, her pleasure at his compliment plain to see.

His breakfast finished, Rubin pushed back his chair and stood up.

"Going over to far fields today Turtle, need to start turning the earth there: anything you need doing before I go?" Turtledoff shook his head, "No lad, nothing today, but tomorrow would be mighty pleased if you would stay after breakfast and help me repair the old mushroom shed, the walls are warping and the door won't stay closed."

"Of course. No problem. See you all tomorrow then." Although his words had seemed to include Cassandra he didn't actually look at her and Cassandra observed him without being watched in return.

He was a handsome man. The sun had turned his skin a deep brown and his normally brown hair a sun-kissed blond. By far his best feature though was his warm brown eyes and just for a moment Cassandra found herself wishing that he would look at her so that she could see them again. He didn't though, simply nodded at them all and made a hasty retreat. With the door closed behind him, Martha looked at Cassandra.

"You'll excuse him lass, has a heart of gold does our Rubin but till he knows someone well he is rather shy."

"He seems like a very nice gentle type of fellow," Cassandra answered. Martha smiled and nodded her agreement.

The days that were to follow seemed to melt one into the other. Morning came and not before long it was sunset once more. Each day came and went without much for remembering it by. Cassandra was very soon part of the family; she joined in with the keeping of the cottage with Martha and spent much of her time simply being with Absalom. Whenever he felt like talking, which Cassandra soon discovered – was actually not very often, Turtledoff would fill Cassandra's head with tales of the past Kingdoms. At first he told her all the good stuff, of honourable Kings and brave Knights of how the different segments of the land had naturally formed their own borderlines that had started the growth of the separate Kingdoms. Cassandra already knew that Havenshire was one of the oldest Kingdoms and she could name the past Kings throughout time right back to Hadrian the first King of Havenshire, but she didn't really know much more than that and was fascinated by all that Turtledoff had to tell her.

"How do you know so much about the Kingdoms?" she asked one day after another lengthy session.

"My Father told me, and his Father told him and so on back four generations to my great, great Grandfather."

"And you remember everything you were taught?"

"Just about, it is important that history should be remembered accurately Casey otherwise we forget the lessons we've learnt along the way."

"Yes but say if you forgot or what if you're remembering bits of it wrong?" Turtledoff looked at Cassandra thoughtfully; in his mind he could see the book of Shyne that lay hidden under his bed. The huge leather bound book embossed with gold and wrapped in a black cloth completely inscribed with ancient writings and soaked in magic. For the first time since his Father had passed it down to him he felt an urge to tell someone about it. He raised one eyebrow at the puzzle of this sudden urge to disclose that that had been sworn to secrecy. And then over the image of the book the little face of Absalom appeared, and he knew in a flash what it meant.

In the earlier years of their marriage it had pained both Martha and Turtledoff that they were not blessed with children. Then as the years melted away and their old age crept upon them, they realised they were content and happy with their lot in life. The only pang of regret and worry that Turtledoff had sometimes over the years was that he had no idea who he was to pass the Secret book of Shyne down to. When Rubin's mother had come to live in the valley of Tamarind years back she had been an outsider. The Dwarfs, over the years, had allowed a few of the tall ones to come and live with them but they had had to work hard to receive the Dwarves' trust. Turtledoff had taken an instant liking to Lisa and her young son Rubin and so had taken them under his wing. Once this was done the others soon accepted the husband-less young woman. The mother and son had been happy in a small farmhouse just down the path from Turtledoff: that was until one day when Lisa was taken ill, and never recovered.

Tamarind's heart had gone out to the young giant of a lad and they had taken care of him as if he were one of their own. For a few years Rubin had lived with Turtledoff and Martha but then one day just after his sixteenth birthday he announced he wanted to go home. Martha had cried for hours but when both Turtledoff and Rubin assured her that it was not the end of the world and with Rubin promising to visit everyday, Martha finally stopped crying and immediately set about making his farm a nice place to live once more, doing all those little things that only a woman can.

Whilst Rubin had lived with them Turtledoff had wanted several times to tell the lad about the book. Surely after all, this was to be the son he had never had? But something always held him back. Now as he looked at Cassandra he knew why. He would tell her about the book one day, but the book was to be passed down to Absalom: he knew that with complete certainty. Absalom was the One, he would be the catalyst in determining the new Talia.

Chapter Eighteen ~ Darkness Approaching

Seven years had passed and Cassandra and Absalom were a part of Tamarind. Her hands, that had been soft and white when she arrived, were now brown and wrinkled with all the work that she did helping out at both the cottage and Rubin's farm.

Turtledoff was watching her as she finished kneading the dough and after she put it in the cupboard next to the hearth to rise he beckoned to her.

"Come, walk with me a while before dinner." Cassandra smiled up at him and brushing down her skirts, knocking off the flour that had fallen on her, she smiled and asked.

"Where are we going?"

"We are going to delve deeper into Talia's history." Cassandra was instantly intrigued, and as they began to walk Turtledoff went as far back in the origins of the world that he could.

"In the beginning Talia was one land, one Kingdom." Cassandra looked at Turtledoff side-on, she couldn't imagine a time when the other Kingdoms hadn't existed.

After walking for a little while Turtledoff sat down on a fallen log and lit up his long willow pipe. He pondered for a moment on how much he should tell her. He decided to tell her all except the darkest secrets and the sources of old magic.

"In the beginning magic roamed the lands and no one was afraid of it. Then along came the witches. Three sisters whose combined magic was so powerful they could control the demons of the deep. They called the demons to the surface and used them to do great evil. The Elements began to fear for the land they had created so they called upon their Oracles to stop the witches. Being unable to kill, the Oracles captured the witches and imprisoned their spirits inside a magic glass orb."

Cassandra was fascinated; she had never heard this tale before.

"What happened to the orb?" she asked. Turtledoff drew heavily on his pipe and then let the smoke out slowly.

"No one knows. The Oracles hid the orb so that no one would ever find it."

"So if the witches were caught how did Talia become separate Kingdoms?"

"When the witches called the demons forth there was much bloodshed and villages were burnt to the ground. It was, however, the Shee-Dragon that caused most of the damage and she blackened vast areas that had once been fertile lands. When the dragon and the demons were sent back to the underworld and the witches were captured in the orb the Elements decided to change things.

They created mountains and valleys, deep forests and huge rivers so as to separate the people of Talia. They hoped the blackness would not come back, but if it did, then maybe parts of Talia would be saved by its borders."

"So now we have the different kingdoms" Cassandra said.

"So history tells us Casey. The Demons have not been seen en masse like that since that time so I guess the Elements' plan has worked. It would take some very powerful magic to find the three witches and release them from the orb. And yet. . . " Turtledoff's voice trailed off.

"What?"

Turtledoff looked at Cassandra as if surprised that he had spoken out loud.

"Nothing. Nothing child. It is just the prophesies and I sometimes dream things; that's all, Martha is always telling me I have an over imaginative mind."

"What have you dreamt?"

Turtledoff sighed, no harm in sharing dreams, he supposed.

"In my dreams I have seen things flying in the night skies. They are dark shadows and they are searching for something but I can never quite see what it is they search for. I also saw a woman once turn into a Dragon, her mouth and hands were covered in blood – it was a dreadful sight." Turtledoff gave a shiver and then shook his head as if trying to shake out the memory.

Coldness had fallen on Cassandra's shoulders and she felt the chill go to her heart. "Yes, but it is only a dream?" She had meant it to be a statement but it had come out like a question. Turtledoff turned to look at her and reached up and touched her arm.

"Yes Casey, tis only a dream."

Cassandra had never been so glad to arrive back at the cottage. She raced inside and straight up the stairs. Absalom was playing in his room; she ran over to him, bent down and flung her arms around him. An overwhelming urge to hold him tight and make sure he was safe had filled her the moment she had gone cold.

Absolom laughed and pushed her backwards, "Mam you're squishing me!" Cassandra laughed and let go of him, then sat back on her heels and smiled at him.

"What's up Mam?" Cassandra shook her head.

"Nothing, I'm just glad to see you." Absolom gave her a puzzled look.

"Dinner" yelled Martha up the stairs.

"I'll race you" challenged Absalom, who was up in a shot and out of the door. Cassandra laughed and chased down the stairs after him as fast as her long skirts would allow. Just as they were scraping back their chairs the door opened and Rubin came in.

"Evening all" he said undoing his laces and kicking off his boots.

"Evening" everyone answered as they began passing the plates around the table. Rubin gave Absalom a gentle nudge with his shoulder as he passed.

"Special day for someone tomorrow?" Absalom looked at Rubin and his face lit up.

"It's my birthday!" Absalom declared.

"Arr so it is now" said Martha, "I had forgotten all about that!"

"No you haven't Martha I saw you baking a cake earlier."

"Oh did you now? Just so happens, that Ma Smithy asked me to bake a cake for her niece, seems Ma Smithy can't bake to save her life, and is awful fond of her niece she is."

"Oh" said Absalom, all dejected now, and everyone laughed. The usual dinnertime banter followed: everyone interjecting, and reflecting on their day's events, what they thought of this and that.

That Rubin was in love with Cassandra was clear for all to see. He looked at her often and longingly; and if love were a hat, then he was constantly attired with conspicuous headgear. Martha sighed very softly to herself when she saw him looking lovingly at Cassandra and wished with all her heart; as she already had countless times; that Cassandra could love him back.

Cassandra saw Rubin as a friend and loved him with affection, but as a brother. She thought him handsome and kind and gentle, all the things that should have made any woman fall in love with him. But for Cassandra there was no spark of excitement, no stirrings of mystery. She saw his honest nature and admired him for it. He would make someone, someday, a wonderful devoted husband. But it wouldn't be Cassandra: she wanted to be swept off her feet and to feel her heart beating madly with passion like it had before when she had been with Rodanti.

When dinner had been devoured and all the plates were empty Turtledoff moved to his favourite old comfy chair by the open hearth. Cassandra and Martha cleared the table and set about washing the dishes.

"As it is the eve of a very special day" said Rubin, "I wonder if you'd like to spend the night with me."

"Oh yes" squealed Absalom in excitement, "can I Mam, can I please?"

Cassandra turned around to look at the excitement on Absalom's face. She normally was pleased when Rubin spent time with Absalom for she knew that growing boys needed male companions, but after the dread she felt this afternoon she was loathe to let him out of her sight.

Absalom saw the doubt appearing on her face and ran to her, looking up with pleading bright blue eyes, and begged.

"Oh please Mam, please." Cassandra reached out and touched his cheek; he was so like his father. She would go long periods not thinking of Rodanti, but then there were moments, like now, when Absalom looked at her with his piercing blue eyes, his straight black hair falling down to his shoulders and often falling over his face, and she would catch her breath, for he was image of his father. She nodded her approval and Absalom whooped and cheered and ran up the stairs to fetch his things. She stood staring after him, lost in her thoughts, worried for him. Turtledoff, Martha and Rubin could all see Cassandra's obvious concern.

"I'll not take the lad if you wish Casey." Cassandra turned her head to look at Rubin and her features softened.

"No it's alright Rubin take him, he loves spending the night with you."

"If you're sure then?" Cassandra nodded and turned back to the sink.

"You alright lass?" asked Martha. Cassandra was suddenly choked up, a hard lump had formed in her throat and she couldn't talk so she nodded back at Martha and tried to give a small smile. Martha and Turtledoff exchanged glances - they would be talk about this later.

And so with the dawn of the next day Absalom turned another year older. He was slim and tall for his age and was always full of the joy of life. His laughter was heard every day and wherever he went his whistling could be heard echoing through the valleys.

Most of the time Cassandra forgot about her Father and the life she had left behind, but every time Absalom's birthday arrived she felt homesickness pull at her spirit. She wished her Father could see his grandson, she was sure he would be as proud of him as she was. And with the homesick feeling the dread also came. She felt each birthday marked time, and that the time she had left with Absalom grew shorter with each year. Having once shared these feelings with Martha, Martha had assured her they were normal and that every Mother knew a day would come when her child flew the nest. Although she had agreed with Martha, Cassandra had always felt that there was more to her dread than that.

This birthday turned out to be the same as the rest, but with the added fuel of the fear that had crept upon her the day before, Cassandra was anxious.

Rubin brought Absalom home at breakfast time. Absalom came charging into the house brandishing a small wooden sword in the air.

"Look what Rubin made for me, I'm a Knight and I'm going to kill the bad 'uns." Cassandra looked at him in horror and went cold. Rubin saw the look on her face and froze in the doorway.

"Oh tis a mighty fine Knight you are there Absalom, the most dashing Knight I've ever seen" said Martha, giving Absalom an exaggerated curtsey.

"Mam?" said Absalom looking for her approval.

"Yes indeed you are the most handsome Knight that ever lived Absalom."

"Phew" replied Absalom, "I dun wanna be handsome I wanna be fierce."

"I *don't want to* be" corrected Cassandra.

"Yea" yelled Absalom as he charged out of the cottage.

"I'm sorry if I gave the lad the wrong thing Casey" said Rubin, his agitation that he might have upset her clear for all to see.

"It's alright really, it's just he's still a bit young to be learning to fight that's all" Cassandra replied.

"Umm" interjected Turtledoff, "thought you said you were three when the Hadrian Knights started teaching you to fight?"

"Well that's was different" said Cassandra defensively.

"Why?" asked Turtledoff.

"Well I grew up in a castle for one, and I was expected to be able to defend myself."

"You grew up in a castle?" said Absalom coming around the door, his eyes full of wonder, "you never told me. What was it like? Why did you leave? Can we go visit it?"

"Absalom one question at a time how many times have I told you?" Absalom pulled a face and sat down on the stool next to Turtledoff. Everyone looked at Cassandra and she knew she had to give her son an answer. Without telling any lies she managed to tell him briefly that the Knights had taught her how to fight and that she had lived in the castle all her life until she had met Rodanti a sailor from Bluedane. She did not outright lie, but she knew she gave the impression, that she had been a maid there. She also skipped over Rodanti's death simply saying a terrible accident had happened that had killed him before they could marry.

"Mam will you teach me to fight then; like a Knight?"

"No Absalom I don't think so, we live a quiet life here it is not necessary for you to learn to fight."

"Why not Casey?" asked Turtledoff.

"Who's to say that Absalom will spend all his days here in Tamarind: I think it is a good idea that the boy learns how to *defend* himself."

Cassandra looked at Turtledoff and they held each other's gaze, and she knew that he was thinking about his dreams.

"Ok" said Cassandra and Absalom jumped off his stool with another yelp and went charging out of the cottage again.

That very day on Absalom's seventh birthday Cassandra began to teach her son all she knew: from the sword and the spear to the bow and arrow and, when she finally found one, the crossbow. From that moment on Absalom began to grow up quickly, bit by bit his baby ways fell away. Not only was he consumed with becoming the greatest Knight there ever was, he also began to thirst for knowledge and began following Turtledoff around night and day, plying him with question upon question about everything and anything he could think of.

On the surface all looked well and everyone was happy; but over the next few years several things happened that would rob Cassandra of all her joy.

Firstly the rumours that her Father was going mad reached her. His madness was driving him to work his people without pay and to increase the size of his army so much that the careful structure that had been in place for centuries was falling away, and Havenshire was in chaos.

Secondly she heard tell that ships from Bluedane had started coming to Tamarind's port more and more and each time they came it was obvious that they were preparing for war. But the third thing - that frightened her most – was her dreams. At first they were vague and took the form of her hearing a very faint indiscernible far off call. But over time the call turned out to be her name, and as each night came, the calling of her name, became more and more intense. She woke most mornings un-rested and more often than not had large dark circles under her eyes.

Turtledoff and Martha questioned her often to see if something was troubling her, but she always answered that she was fine and eventually they stopped asking. As the nights passed, and the call to her seemed louder and closer, her fear began to consume her. Joy left her completely and she spent hours walking alone. No amount of love and concern from Turtledoff or Martha could reach her, and slowly she sank into a dark depression. Someone was coming for her and Absalom, and she knew it was only a matter of time; there was nothing she could do about it.

Chapter Nineteen ~ Love & Dark Magic

Seven years had passed since the McFein brothers had been burnt near to death and healed again. In his twenty-second year of life Idi was happy.

He sat on the riverbank and watched Katrina, who swam like a fish in the clear waters. She was the reason why he was happy. She filled his life with love and laughter and his heart filled with pride every time he saw her. At seven years old she was adorable. She insisted that Idi regularly chop at her hair - with much argument from both Idi and Marcus; she however, proved to have the stronger personality! And so her hair often stuck out all over the place, the deep brown framing her delicate little face perfectly: and because she was always outside her face was freckled and brown.

Katrina disliked being a girl and refused outright to wear skirts and dresses. One time, when Marcus had removed all her trousers from the house, she had remained in her bedroom for eight sunsets refusing to come out. He had finally relented and brought her back her specially made trousers. Marcus had refused completely to let her wear boy's shirts and so in the end, after much battle, they had shirts made for her that came well down over the tops of her legs, they were made in the softest colours, contrasting with her black trousers. One of the women from the city had crocheted for her a multi-coloured waist coat that Katrina had fallen madly in love with and hardly took off, and so Katrina by her own willpower had become completely unique.

The joy that Katrina brought him, however, wasn't the only reason Idi was happy. Since the healing of the brothers, people had begun travelling to see him seeking their own healing. It was probably fair to say that the only people who didn't take to Idi very well were the Soothers – who were fast losing their standing in the community.

All manner of people came to him from wealthy lords to gutter boys. He never took anything for the healings (on Marcus's advice) and so folk had started leaving gifts. They now had a multitude of chicken and geese and their larder was never empty. If ever they needed anything someone or other would turn up with the desired item and so life, even in these harsh times, was for them, abundant. But for Idi, the most perfect gift he had been given; was respect. It had started the day the two Soothers had fled back to the city and started the tale of Idi the healer: the tale that would soon become a legend.

His thoughts took him back to six moons after the McFein healing, when four witches had turned up at their home, in the middle of a storm filled night.

Marcus had been awake for quite some time that night, the thunder and lightning seemingly not the only thing to keep him awake; he had paced the room waiting for whatever it was that had woken him to arrive. Sure enough, well before the dawn had come, there had been a knock on the door. Marcus had opened the door, and reacting with only a rising of the eyebrows he'd let the witches enter. He hadn't met them before, but their green cloaks over their oranges dresses told him immediately that they were of the Earth Clan. They had pushed back their hoods and stood in line looking at Marcus. Idi closed his eyes for a moment to recall the night's events.

"Welcome ladies" said Marcus with a brief bow, "what can I do for you?" The tallest Witch took a step forward.

"We are in need of a healer; we have heard there is none better than Idi the magician." At that moment Idi came into the room, the voices having woken him. He was surprised to see the four women and wondered why Witches would need a healer as they were renowned for healing themselves.

"Why are you in need of a healer?" he asked. The Witches seemed to bristle and Idi took a step towards Marcus, who in turn looked at Idi with a slight look of amusement.

"We cannot say, but you are badly needed and you will have the Earth Clan forever in your gratitude if you come with us." Idi thought on all the things that he had heard about the Earth Clan, which in comparison with the other two clans; was actually not very much. Still he hadn't actually heard of anything bad that he could think of. They kept themselves to themselves (as the other clans did) and rarely came into Havenshire. From what he had heard, except that everyone knew they could do magic, they were basically farmers.

"I'll get dressed then" he said and disappeared back into his room.

"It's a bit dark in here" said Marcus and threw his hand into the air, "light" he demanded and an orb of light appeared. "You must be cold as well since you are all soaked," he continued. "Burn" he said pointing at the fireplace and instantly the cold logs were aflame, flickering their heat into the room. Then he turned around and looked the tallest Witch in the eye.

"I expect Idi to be returned to me in the same condition that he goes to you. He goes freely, freely he will return. His mind must not be meddled with, and I will know if it has. Do you understand?" The Witch's face stayed as marble, she knew that Marcus's display of power was supposed to warn her that he was a magician of some standing: her estimation of Idi increased; to have a mentor of such power.

"We are in need of his aid; we will not meddle with his mind, even if he should not be able to help us – so long as he tries." Idi returned then and went to the wall to fetch his cape. In a whoosh he flung it around his body and tied it under his chin.

"Shall we go ladies?" he asked.

With a crackle there was an explosion of orange light, and both Marcus and Idi slid to the floor in an instant sleep. One of the Witches drew out from under her cape a webbed cloth. Another came to her aid and they spread it on the floor next to Idi; then they rolled him over until he was in the centre of the cloth. Once he was there, the tall witch waved her hand at the door and it flew open, then as one they reached down and each picked up a corner of the cloth. They walked a few steps outside the house and in unison they lifted into the air, taking the sleeping Idi between them. Idi slept the entire time the Witches flew and so when he woke a few hours later he had no idea how he had got there.

A beautiful fair-haired woman was touching his face when he woke. He jumped, startled and disorientated.

"Drink this" said the woman, "it will help you get back to normal quickly." Idi looked at the glass filled with a pink liquid and shook his head.

"Silly, we need you, we wouldn't harm you. Now drink for I need to take you to her as soon as you're alert." Idi gingerly took the glass, gave the contents one hard look and then knocked the drink back in one go. She had told the truth, he felt the lethargy leave him like a passing shadow.

"See" she said bending down and kissing him briefly on the lips, "I don't lie, Idi, the magician." Idi was in shock over the kiss and his stunned face made her laugh, "My! Don't tell me you've gotten to this age without being kissed?" Idi's face went bright red and he pushed her aside so that he could get off the bed quickly. She giggled.

"Sasha is he awake?" The Witch spun around as another Witch came into the room. She raised her hand and pointed to Idi who stood awkwardly next to her. The tall Witch took in Idi's red cheeks and gave Sasha a disapproving look.

"Come" she said, turned around and went back out of the room. Sasha indicated that Idi should follow her and Idi moved towards the door. As he moved past, Sasha pinched his bum. Idi yelped, startled sending Sasha into fits of giggles. The tall Witch stopped and turned back to Sasha.

"At a time like this, that behaviour is most inappropriate." This time it was Sasha's turn to go red and she hung her head, "sorry Angelica" she mumbled, but the tall Witch was already striding down the hallway.

Angelica led them down a series of narrow, winding corridors. The sun was rising and a pale glow crept in through the windows but torches were still lit along the way to light them up. Now and then they came across Witches huddled together in small groups whispering away. Each time they approached the Witches would go quiet and would openly stare at Idi as he walked by. As soon as they had passed by the whispering would continue again in earnest.

At the end of a particularly long corridor there opened up a large chamber. The chamber was completely filled with Witches and Idi was quite shocked, as he had no idea that there were so many of them; he had always thought of the Clans of a bunch of about twenty to thirty women; now he realised they must be much greater in number.

Angelica went up to a beautifully ornate door, whispered with two Witches standing outside, and then turned around.

"She is inside Idi." Idi wondered who 'she' was but thought she must be someone of some importance for them all to be standing here. "Before you can go in, Melinda needs to access you. It won't hurt but you mustn't fight it." Alarm bells started ringing in Idi's head and he took three steps backwards. Sasha touched his arm and stopped him from going any further.

"I promise it won't hurt Idi, she just has a quick look inside of you that's all." Idi shook his head, a firm no resounding in his mind.

149

He had heard from Marcus (now he remembered!) that some Witches have the power to control your mind and make you do things you don't want to.

A smallish dumpy Witch came and stood in front of him.

"My name is Melinda Idi, and if you don't fight me this will not hurt. But if you resist me then I can't promise that no damage will be done, do you understand?" Idi looked down at her round face and said nothing.

"I will look to see what kind of character you are Idi, it will only take a moment." Idi wondered what would happen if his character was not to her liking.

Melinda reached up her hand and laid it gently on Idi's forehead. Instantly he was surrounded by Witches. They all laid their hands on him, and held his arms and his legs with a collective vice-like grip. He knew he wouldn't be able to move, let alone run away.

At first his natural survival instincts kicked in and he built a wall around his mind to keep her out. But into his mind her soft voice came, like a mother to an infant she soothed and coaxed him, until at last he let the wall fall down. And the instant the wall came crashing down Melinda moved her hand away and it was finished. He was surprised at the sudden removal of her presence in his mind, and alarmed that he should instantly miss it! Melinda smiled at him.

"That is the reason why I must be so quick" she said as if reading his mind still. "If I stayed too long you would not be able to function properly without me." She turned to Angelica, "he will not tell anyone about Misha." The Witches around all seemed to relax and they smiled at him and touched him gently as he was guided to the ornate door. He had heard the name Misha, he was sure that she was the Witche's Head, was it their leader then that was sick?

His question was soon to be answered. The heavy wooden door opened silently, and as one – seemingly floating, the Witches flooded into the darkened room sweeping Idi along with them.

The room was silent and Idi was very aware of the rapid beating of his own heart. A large ornate bed had obviously been pushed away from the wall and stood in the centre of the room. On the bed, under the softest pale green covers, lay a most beautiful woman. Her deep brown hair spread across the pale green pillows like a feathered fan. Her features were delicate and chiselled and her skin pale and unblemished.

Around the bed stood twelve Witches, they touched (but didn't hold) hands, all their eyes were closed and they were so still they might have been statues.

"They are holding her away from death" whispered the tall Witch into his ear. "We have tried everything we know and we cannot wake her. We know that she has been poisoned, and that it was by a very magical potion, but we know no more; and each day holding her above death becomes harder. Without a power outside of our own we will lose Misha within hours."

"Each day" whispered back Idi, "how long has she been ill?"

"Forty nine sunrises have passed."

"I hope you haven't waited too long to fetch me" Idi said softly.

"We have great strength and know much about healing. Some of us would have fetched you a long time back but others said an outsider would never be able to help her. So Idi, the Magician, you are safe today so long as you try to save her, but you are also on trial, do what you can," she paused for a moment and then looked at him, "please". It was a heartfelt plea and Idi knew that Misha must be greatly loved. He took a step forward but the Witch placed her hand on his shoulder to stop him.

"The Witches are holding Misha in a circle of light, the moment you cross into the circle it will break and we will not be able to hold her above death. Must you go next to her to heal her?" Idi nodded.

"I don't know any other way, I need to place my hands on her or within a breath from her, and I don't think I would be able to help from here." Several of the Witches huddled around together and although they whispered, it was obvious that they were disagreeing.

"Branwen, as Misha's closest friend you have the final word." Branwen's face flooded with pain at the responsibility, and her normally pretty and motherly features blurred as she screwed up her face and buried her fists into her eye balls. Angelica gently touched Branwen on the arm, "Branwen?" she asked. Branwen's hands dropped away from her face and she looked at Idi. She had heard such wonderful things about him, Misha herself had mentioned on more than one occasion that she would like to meet him, and that memory made up her mind.

"Let him go to her." Several Witches drew in their breath as one, but they stood back so that a space appeared between them and the twelve around Misha's bed. Idi walked forward. His whole body was trembling: if he failed, she would die. He wasn't afraid for himself, as some of the Witches were thinking, but he feared for Misha, he never wanted anyone to die in his hands, the thought of the death of someone being caused by him made him feel sick to the stomach.

As he took the last step to be next to the bed he felt the warmth coming from the Witches magic, he also felt it begin to pale the moment he stood inside their circle. He reached up his hand and very slowly brought it down to lay upon Misha's chest. He saw Sasha grab another Witches arm, fear all over her face. He took a deep breath and told himself to concentrate.

The moment his hand touched Misha he yelped and pulled it back. The Witches all murmured and their voices rose with their fear that their leader was about to die. Idi turned to look at Branwen.

"She is covered in, in, in" Idi struggled, how could he describe it? "She is covered in thick black liquid, it is oozing from her and it smells foul." Branwen's face clearly showed her surprise as she looked at Misha and saw nothing but her friend, as beautiful as ever. She could see no black stuff, and she couldn't smell anything bad either. Idi took in her look of surprise and knew that this then was something he would have to try to handle himself.

This time before he touched her he called on his magic to cover himself in light, as protection. There was an audible "Oh" as the Witches saw the light appear around him. Branwen nodded to herself, so the stories about him were true then, she had done the right thing.

Idi lowered his hand slowly back down onto Misha's chest. This time he was prepared for the feeling of evil and of death. The black magic made another grab at his life but Idi sent a shock of light down his arm, and as if struck by lightning Misha's body jerked violently as the light hit her. Now the Witches began to mutter in earnest, one look between Branwen and the tall Witch and they turned to the other Witches, pointing to the door. Not one of them moved but they immediately became silent, so Branwen and the tall Witch dropped their arms and turned around once more to Idi.

The evil knew now that Idi was a force of the Light and shrank back from his hand, Idi allowed himself a small smile when he saw it. Now, to find Misha's life force: he raced along with the healing light that was pouring into Misha's body and his soul dived into her body to find her spirit. He knew the evil was reflecting back his healing light and that at the moment it was not reaching her. He needed to find her himself so that he could bring her to the healing light. As soon as he entered her body he felt cold grip him, not a normal cold, but a kiss of death cold. All was dark. He called her name but no answer came. He searched and searched and found himself tiring. Was she dead already? He should have been able to find her.

"Misha", he called, "Misha help me I can't find you". Nothing. Suddenly he felt something slimy crawl over his flesh. He went to pull himself out but instinctively knew that was what the evil wanted, so he forced himself to stay inside her. Misha he cried, in fear that time was running out. Misha where are you? Still no answer came, all around him was cold and black and he waded through it as if trying to walk through deep mud. The slimy thing on his flesh grew bigger and thicker and to all intents and purposes felt like a snake trying to choke him.

Suddenly Idi coughed and blood spurted out of his mouth. The Witches gasped, Sasha looked at Branwen; surely they must make him stop? Branwen purposely turned her attention back to Idi.

Idi was no longer looking for Misha, now he was fighting for his life. He felt the snake contracting around his chest and it was becoming hard to breathe. Oh Marcus what do I do, Idi cried out in his soul. Idi struggled and struggled against the snake but the more he did the more he seemed to be sinking into the oozing black liquid. He knew he was fighting against powerful magic but his training with Marcus (as Marcus put it) was still in its infancy. Idi felt the cold begin to freeze his heart and knew he was fading fast. He began to lose consciousness, starting to lose the desire to fight, he began letting go of his body. The black was calling to him: it felt so calm and quiet and he had a longing to fall into it.

Just at the moment when he was about to relinquish himself to the dark Katrina's face appeared in front of him. Her normal happy laughing face was screwed up and she was crying. It was a jolt to Idi's heart; he instantly blinked and woke himself up. What is it Katie he called? But she was fading and he couldn't see her properly anymore.

"Katie!" he yelled in anguish and dived into the dark after her. Suddenly a sword appeared in his hand and he slashed at the dark like a madman. "Katie" he called again, chopping holes of light into the darkness. Then he saw her, far away, curled up and afraid.

"*Power*" Idi roared with all his might and the Witches took a step back in sudden fear as Idi's body started flooding light into the room. Now the going became easier, the heavy wading-through-mud feeling began to fade, and soon he was charging through Misha's body searching for Katrina.

And then with another mighty thrust of his glowing sword the last of the black ooze slid away and there lying before him, curled up into a ball of fear, was Misha. His sword instantly fell away and he knelt by her side.

"Misha" he whispered gently. Slowly she turned and looked at him.

"You came" she whispered back in a shaky voice, "she said you would." Idi didn't know who 'she' was but he knew he had to get Misha to the healing as quickly as he could, her spirit was faded and bits of her were missing. He reached out his hand and she very slowly reached up and took it. Once he had her standing, and in his arms for support, he led her through the dark and towards the light of his healing power.

He stayed with her for a while to make sure she would recover: and she did. Slowly but surely, her spiritual light came back on and the image of her became firmer. After soaking in Idi's healing Misha wanted to go to sleep, and so Idi let her drift off, watching her to make sure she would stay in the light: after a while he was satisfied the evil had gone and withdrew himself from her body.

The moment he lifted his hand off Misha's chest, Idi collapsed. He was instantly picked up by numerous hands and carried back down the corridor to what was to become known, forever more as, the Magician's room.

It took Misha weeks to fully recover, even with the Witches pouring their magic into her every day. But once recovered, Misha would be fabled to be immortal. From the day she walked out of her bedchambers she would never again be ill, and as the Witches around her became old and died Misha would seem to be ageless and outlive them all: but she was mortal and eventually Fate would bring her to that day. In the meantime a new determination to serve the Earth Element consumed her, and her Earth Clan gathered around her to make sure all her ideas became reality.

The Earth Clan also gathered themselves to Idi. This was much to Idi's embarrassment, Marcus's amusement and Misha's irritation! Misha would forever be grateful to Idi and would have done almost anything for him, but that her Witches should idolise him so riled her. The Earth's Clan first loyalty would always be to Misha, but after that they lived to serve Idi, he only had to mention wanting something and it would appear as if by magic, so much so that he soon became very careful about what he said when any of them where around him!

That Megan had poisoned her Misha was certain, but instead of seeking revenge she poured all her efforts in teaching the Witches greater magic, and for the first time since they had joined themselves to her, Misha began to teach the Earth Clan warfare.

Chapter Twenty ~ Born to Fight

Katrina climbed out of the river and came running over to him. Like a dog she rapidly shook her head from side to side, showering him with water.

"Hey you" he said catching her and encasing her in a wrap. She chuckled and snuggled into his chest for a hug.

"You're the best papa there ever was" she said.

"Nope" answered Idi.

"But I haven't asked for anything" Katrina said most indignantly.

"You're not learning to fight with Knights and that's that."

"You're not being fair" she burst out pushing herself away from him.

"And you're not behaving like a lady" he retorted mimicking her voice.

"They've said they'll teach me, Sebastian says I have great promise!"

"Marcus and I agree, the answer is no."
Katrina pulled a face. Idi had of course played a trump card; for often she could work her way around Idi's objections, but most of the time, she was unable to change Marcus's mind.

"I've told Sebastian that you will come and see him this evening and talk to him about my lessons. If I can't go you must at least tell him so yourself!" Idi raised an eyebrow at Katrina's tone and she quickly dropped it and started getting dressed.

"I'll go see him Katie but I think I will not be best pleased with you when I get home late to the fireside." She couldn't help herself and smiled at the ground as she quickly pulled her shoes on. Sebastian would change Idi's mind. He just had to.
True to his word, after taking Katrina back to the cottage he set off for the city. He was used to walking into the city all the time but these

days it somehow didn't feel safe to be walking on your own. Strange happenings were going on, and unless he was with Marcus, Idi now always felt slightly on edge.

He arrived at the city gates in the late afternoon. He walked slowly over the wooden drawbridge and into the cobbled streets. He remembered his first visit to the city and how excited he had been. It didn't seem like the same city anymore, most of the market stalls had shut and the streets were no longer crowded, people ventured from their homes only when they had to. He shivered. He felt a darkness brooding over the city and wished he could do something about it, but as yet he and Marcus had been unable to find anything definite that they could tackle. He decided that after visiting the garrison he would pop by and see Martin and old Thomas at the Inn in Eastside and see how they were faring.

As he approached the inner castle he could hear a lute-player, his melodic tune drifting down the near empty alleyways. It was an eerie sound and Idi shivered again. His shoes clipped loudly on the stone cobbles and rang in his ears; no, this wasn't a safe time for Katie to be coming to the city: even if he did agree to let her learn to fight – which he wasn't going to.

He walked into the garrison, his eyes searching everywhere for Sebastian. Soldiers were sitting around, some were playing dice, and others were cleaning their weapons. Idi approached a couple who were cleaning their crossbows.

"Could you tell me where I could find Sebastian?" he asked. One of the soldiers merely grunted and carried on cleaning. The other, an extremely young fellow with gentle features, looked up at him.

"You're Katrina's father aren't you?" Idi nodded, he had given up trying to explain that he was just her guardian years ago.

"She's mighty spirited, will make a great warrior one day. You'll find Sebastian on the battlements just above. Glad you're going to let her learn, she'll do you proud one day."

"Oh I don't intend to let her fight. I am here to tell Sebastian she can't come, but many thanks for your help." And with that Idi turned around and went back outside to the stone staircase that led up to the battlements. The soldier who hadn't looked up whilst Idi had been there turned to his companion, "Mark my words lad, he'll let her learn and she'll grow to be one of the greatest warriors Havenshire will ever see, listen you to my words for they'll be true one day, you'll see." And with that he looked down again and started rubbing the tiller vigorously with walnut oil, making the yew wood shine like metal.

Idi took the steps two at a time and soon came to the top. A few Knights were just coming out of the hourd as he came to the last step. They stopped and looked at him. In times gone by the people had been able to roam the castle and its walls for pleasure walks but these days the soldiers were the only ones allowed on the battlements and they looked at Idi with instant distrust; their hands instinctively resting on the hilts of their swords.

"I seek Sebastian, is he here?" Idi asked.

"Aye he's here" said one of the Knights stepping forward, "what's your business with him?"

"I've come to talk about Katrina's lessons." The Knights instantly relaxed and the Knight who had spoken came up to him.

"You her father then?" he asked and Idi smiled and nodded.

"Come on inside, let's have a talk." With that the Knight turned around, and went back inside. Idi followed him into the round room. It was sparsely furnished, with just a table and some chairs in the centre and a huge fire burning at the far side. Besides that, armour lay around in various degrees of repair and Idi could imagine the Knights sitting in here on cold days fixing up their armour and weapons.

"Come sit down, I'm Sebastian by the way" the Knight motioned, sitting down at the table. Idi sat down opposite him. Sebastian picked up a jug of honeyed mead and filled two pewter tankards, he picked one up and nodded at Idi that he should do the same. Idi hesitated for a moment; he normally stayed well clear of the heavier drinks after Marcus had warned him of the effects. But he looked at Sebastian and saw pain in the young Knights face: knowing of Sebastian's reputation but never having spoken to him before Idi was intrigued to know him better, so he picked up his pewter and raised it to Sebastian with a nod, taking a large swig. Idi instantly felt the heat of the drink warm his lungs and gasped at the strength of it. Sebastian laughed, "Tis made by the Monks in the castle, mighty good stuff ay" he chuckled knocking back another large swig.

For a short time they drank and talked small talk, Idi asked him lots of questions about how long he had been a Knight and why he chosen to become one in the first place. Sebastian in good humour answered all the questions openly. How he was just twelve when he had first come to live in the barracks, and why he had, which was slightly harder to explain: something had called at his heart to serve the King and to protect Havenshire at all costs. He laughed bitterly, "I was naïve in those days you understand" he said. Idi looked at the Knight's face; his soft brown hair fell in waves to his shoulders but that was the only thing that was soft about him. He had obviously been good looking not so long ago but now his face was filled with lines and his smile never reached his eyes. Idi didn't stop to think that he was stepping out of line, simply opened his mouth and asked, "Why are you so unhappy Sebastian?"

Sebastian looked at him in surprise but then turned his gaze into his pewter, he swilled the drink around for a short while and then tipped back his head and downed the remains.

"I don't know about being unhappy, worried more like it. What's your name by the way?" Idi smiled, he was rarely asked his name these days.

"I'm Idi" he answered simply. Shock showed on Sebastian's face and he leant back in his chair as if to move slightly further away from Idi. Idi smiled to himself, and that was why he delayed the telling.

"You're a lot younger than I pictured you" Sebastian finally muttered.

"And you're a lot older than I pictured you" Idi answered. The two looked at each other for a moment and then started laughing.

"Another drink" said Sebastian and refilled their pewters. They drank some more in a comfortable silence but eventually Sebastian knew it was time to answer the question.

"Strange things have been happening, started a few years back. At first I didn't think too much of the rumours but then the number of people reporting things simply grew too great to ignore."

"I've heard there have been many strange murders lately" Idi interjected.

"Yes terrible killings have been happening, bodies are being mutilated in the most horrific ways, but still it's not that which frightens me so much." Sebastian sighed and looked inside his empty pewter. Idi let the silence lie; waiting for Sebastian to tell him what was worrying him. Suddenly Sebastian looked up with a forced grin.

"Another drink" he said pouring out the last of the contents of the jug. He took a quick swig of the mead and then looked at Idi full in the eye.

"We could do with your help, Magician" he said, unblinking. Idi leant back in his chair with a soft sigh. He felt the weight of the whole city on his shoulders every day; he saw the expectation in their eyes and the disappointment on their faces – they wanted him and Marcus to rescue them.

"We don't know what to do Sebastian, believe me we have spent many a long hour agonising over the issue, but we feel helpless for there is no visual enemy to fight."

"I meant you could help *us* Idi" Sebastian looked at Idi who looked slightly puzzled. He leant forward on the desk, "the Knights need you Idi, and I fear, more than anyone else in the Kingdom, the King needs you."

"The King?"

Sebastian nodded and sighed heavily.

"We fear a sickness has taken him, either that or" Sebastian paused for a moment before finishing, "or black magic is being worked on him." Sebastian stood up and started pacing around the room.

"You could help us Idi, if it is sickness then who better than you to attend the King? And if it is magic then maybe you and Marcus could rout it out?"

Idi swung round in his chair to watch Sebastian as he paced, "Of course I will come and see the King. We'll come tomorrow."

"No you don't understand. He won't see you. He hardly sees anyone anymore. All the Knights used to have free access to the King. Now we have to request an audience. Tis terrible times man. Myles has already asked the King to let you visit with him but he will hear none of it. The only person these days who is free to come and go around the King is that dog Norvora" Sebastian turned and spat in the spittoon, as if even the name of Norvora made him sick. Sebastian stopped his pacing and leant forward with his hands on the table towards Idi, his face earnest and full of hate.

"The man is evil I tell you. From the moment he started having private counsel with Hamish his mind began to deteriorate, he has been making terrible decisions concerning Havenshire ever since. In this time when we believe others are planning to attack, Hamish has been giving orders followed by counter orders that have put the army, let alone the Knights, in disarray. We should be building up our defences and what are we doing? Building ships!" Sebastian slammed his fist onto the table.

"Ships I tell you, what good would they be to us? We're not sailors, we can't go to sea to do battle, we're land farers and yet Hamish has been convinced that to protect ourselves we must build ships for battle!" Sebastian picked up the empty jug and went to the door. A young boy ran up to him instantly and took the jug away. Sebastian came back to the table and sat down.

"No Idi, to help us you must come and live with us." Idi had not been expecting that request and started thinking instantly of all the reasons why he couldn't come and live with the Knights. The first to pop into his head was of course Katrina.

"We can't come and live here, too many people rely on us; where we are at the moment is easy access for most people. Besides a castle is no place for Katrina, it is full of men."

"There are many children in the castle walls Idi, she would have other children to play with; I believe she has no special friends in her life where you are now." Idi looked at Sebastian his head cocked over to one side looking at him, had Katrina told him she didn't have any friends?

Just then the young boy returned and brought a full jug to the table, Sebastian reached up and ruffled the lad's hair and the boy went away with a big grin on his face.

"Do you know," said Sebastian reaching for the jug and filling their pewters to the top, "that not so long ago Knights were only allowed Mead on their day of rest? Now the Monks have been ordered to keep a constant flow coming to us, don't you think that is a strange thing for a King to order? Of course if I didn't love the Old Fart so much I would say that he was trying to turn his most trusted Knights into drunks! But of course he can't be doing that can he? Because then who would defend him if we were attacked, and all his Knights were so weak and mindless due to the constant flow of Mead?" He looked into the drink, "Golden poison it is Idi" then he raised his pewter and drank heavily from it. Idi picked up his drink and was surprised to find he had the urge to drown it as well. When he had finished taking the longest drink he hiccupped and looked in surprise at Sebastian. Sebastian laughed, "ay mighty pleasing poison it is". He lifted his pewter to Idi and Idi crashed his into it, Mead swilled and spilt over, the sight of the Mead spilling onto the table suddenly seemed to be the funniest thing and the pair of them threw back their heads and laughed until their sides hurt.

There was no conversation after that point that Idi would ever remember, he felt his words slurring together and felt most peculiar, as the wall of the round room seemed to suddenly start moving. He wouldn't remember stumbling and falling down most of the stone steps; he would vaguely remember hugging Sebastian in the biggest hug of his life. This part of the evening would remain a blur.

"Did you see that?" Idi asked looking into the night sky. The pair had staggered laughing through the cobbled streets of Havenshire and now stood on the wooden draw bridge.

"What?" asked Sebastian.

"I don't know what it was; it kind'a looked like a flying pig!" Sebastian looked at Idi who was searching the sky intently for another glimpse of the pig. Sebastian spluttered and nearly choked and started laughing again.

"Arr me lad oh, you know what they say about men who see flying pigs don't you? Wouldn't mention it to anyone else if I was you." Idi chuckled a bit but the flying object concerned him and he felt himself sobering up.

"Get back now Sebastian, your bed's calling to you. I'll bring Marcus in the morning and you can talk to him about your idea." For a moment Sebastian also sobered up and offered his hand to Idi.

"Thank you" he said firmly holding Idi's hand. He looked hard into Idi's eyes. Idi knew he was reaching out to him, along with Marcus, as his last hope. He nodded at him, "I'll see you tomorrow Sebastian." Sebastian nodded back, and they went their separate ways, with a growing feeling of anxiety rising inside Idi.

Chapter Twenty-One ~ Ghosts & Castles

Idi set off down the well-beaten track that led away from the castle. The area around here was all flat farmland with only the odd tree dotted around. The moon was almost full and shone down, lighting the way. Idi shivered again, the light night mist was making his clothes wet already and he wished he had brought his cloak with him.

"Think I'll get home quick" he said to himself and started to run. After about twelve steps he fell flat on his face on the dirt track. He picked himself up and knocked the dust off himself, puzzled. He couldn't do what Marcus called 'magic timing' but he was getting there, each time he attempted it he seemed to get closer and closer to the magic, and yet just now when he had attempted it he had felt himself to be in thick mud. Something was wrong. The thought sobered him up even more.

"Light" he said, throwing his right hand up into the air. A little flicker appeared in front of him and then twinkled itself out. Idi felt a slight panic in his chest, he had mastered the basic of light magic long back, this was a simple spell.

"Light" he said again in a more fierce way. This time the flicker was brighter and lasted longer but it too faded away. Idi felt a tightening in his chest: had he been bad to get drunk – was this his punishment? Suddenly the realisation that magic had become his life entered his head, quickly followed by the complete devastation he felt at the thought of losing it. He couldn't help it, it was a reflex: 'Marcus' he called in his head and started running as fast as he could down the track, and with each step he took he became more and more sober. Soon he had passed the flat fields and entered the coppice where the road split three ways. He took the path that led west towards home. He stopped running as his chest had begun to hurt, but he walked as quickly as he could. As he came out of the coppice he came into another area of flat fields. Soon be home, he thought to himself. The thought was comforting and he slowed his pace slightly.

There was a noise behind him that sounded like someone running through the trees. He spun around, his heart instantly beating faster. He searched the tree line waiting for the sound to emerge but from the moment he had spun around the sound had ceased. He waited a long moment, then, having convinced himself that he must have been hearing things he turned around and started along the path once more. He had only gone a short distance when he heard the sound of someone running in the field alongside him. He whirled around to the field to see who was there but all he could see was swaying grass. His heart was now pounding so fast in his chest he felt it would break his rib cage.

"Light" he demanded. This time a light appeared and did not go out but it was pale and only seemed to magnify the weakness of his magic so he snapped his fingers at it and it flickered out. That would not frighten anyone off. He stopped for a long moment and searched the area. He made his heart beat slower; took deep slow breaths and forced himself to be calm. Fear is the biggest killer Marcus always told him, if not for fear many a good man would still be alive. "I fear no man," Marcus had told him, "and you must do the same."

Satisfied that his imagination and the evils of the golden mead were playing tricks on him; and that there wasn't anyone around; Idi set off again. This time he made himself walk, "I fear no man" he said out loud.

Something soft brushed against his face, like the feel of walking through a spider's web, and he flung his arm up to knock it away. A woman laughed behind him and he spun around.

"Do you fear no man little Idi, how sweet, but you know I am *no* man" the ghost of a woman slunk up to Idi and wrapped herself around him. Her touch was of ice and Idi's teeth instantly started chattering. He went to knock her away but his hands went straight through her. She laughed again chuckling playfully to herself.

"I can touch you my sweet but I am afraid you can only look at me." Idi took a couple of steps away from her and she pouted at him.

"What? Don't you like my touch?" She drifted up to him again and ran her hands over his body. He felt frozen to the bone and felt his muscles cramping with the cold. She traced her hand down his arm and grabbed his wrist tight.

The iciness her touch up shot up his insides to his heart and he gasped at the pain of it.

"Such pleasure my touch don't you think?" Idi knew his life was in danger and sunk deep into himself to find his magic. 'I need you' he called inside his body to his magic. The light ball appeared before him, "Strength" Idi demanded and suddenly his body had warmth flooding through it and light poured from his flesh.

"Ouch" screeched the ghost releasing her hold on Idi, "now that wasn't very nice of you" she said, her appearance taking greater dimension. Idi didn't wait for her to touch him again, turned and started racing for home. He called on the magic timing to come. His pace did increase, but not enough.

The ghost screeched and flung herself onto his back, throwing her arms around him and scratching at his face. Coldness flooded in rivers through and over his body from his face downwards. He tried to knock her off, but he couldn't touch her and he stumbled and fell onto the field. Time seemed to slow and every second felt like an eternity. She laughed as he hit the ground. Once floored, he felt his body begin to freeze; he could no longer move even a finger. She spun webs around him, cocooning him deep in her magic. Leaning over him she licked his face, and his eyelashes blinked – the only part of him still able to move.

"I think sucking the life from you will be very sweet, I don't think I will hand you over to Norvora; I know he will be angry with me but you smell so good I must have you for myself." Idi's eyes closed and no matter how hard he tried he couldn't open them. He felt himself rise in the air, and then as if he had been put on an invisible sleigh he felt himself being pulled away.

He wasn't sure what happened but suddenly he felt himself falling and he landed harshly on the ground. Screaming and screeching from what seemed to be many places all at once rang in his ears, but then there was one almighty screech. Idi then thought he heard the ghost whine, "But he's mine" before the noise diminished. He then drifted in and out of consciousness, but for a moment he thought he heard Marcus calling to him. "I'm here" he called in his soul before falling into sleep.

Marcus let Idi sleep until late the next day, and then finally decided to wake him with a Camomile tea. He gave him a gentle shake and Idi stirred and moaned.

"Is it morning already? I feel like I've only just gone to bed." Idi slowly opened his eyes, yawned and stretched and smiled at Marcus. Marcus smiled back him, his whole body flooded with relief. He had grown to love Idi very much; the earlier resentment he felt towards him about losing the tracks of The One had long faded. Now he enjoyed teaching him, felt thrill after thrill as his lessons sunk in and Idi not only became an outstanding Magician but a good soul, with pure intentions.

"You had an eventful night Idi, time to wake up and discuss it all." Idi looked at Marcus, puzzled for a moment, and started retracing the previous day's activities. Bit by bit it started coming back to him, then when the memory of the ghost came to him he sat up in bed with a start and looked around.

169

"Was it real?" he asked, not knowing whether he would prefer it to have been the effects of Mead or truly a ghost.

"She was very real Idi." Idi shivered and reached across the bed to pull his shirt off the back of the chair. He pulled his baggy white shirt on and then Marcus passed him his black leather waistcoat.

"How did you find me? I have a feeling that I was flying."

"I heard you call to me Idi. I would have reached you sooner but I feared to leave Katrina on her own; so it was awhile before we were ready. Also your call was faint and felt like a long way off so I was confused as to where you were."

"But you found me in time."

"Actually the witches found you first, I helped cast the ghost back to the depths but if the Witches hadn't have been there she would have taken you to her world long before I found you."

"The Witches found me?" Marcus looked at Idi and raised one of his white bushy eyebrows.

"It seems you always have an escort Idi, did you know that?"

"No I didn't, but they can't be with me all the time for I would see them." Marcus shook his head slightly and pulled at his chin.

"It would seem that a few of the Witches know how to make themselves invisible; and apparently from the moment you saved Misha one of them has been trailing you wherever you go."

"No" exclaimed Idi in disbelief, "can't be true I would know if someone was following me."

"Apparently not." Marcus looked at the lads reddening face and felt sorry for him.

"It was a very good job for you that young Elaina was trailing you last night. As soon as she saw the ghost she flew back to the Clan to get help. I saw what at first I thought, was a rushing cloud, but it turned out to be twenty odd Witches flying together. Never seen such a sight in all my years. Strange days these Idi I tell you." Marcus shook his head; then turned back to Idi.

"Katrina and I turned up on the back of Thunder just in time to see you crashing to the ground. I helped the Witches and Katrina ran to you to start pulling the web off you."

"Is she alright, was she very upset by it all?" Marcus smiled and put his hand on Idi's shoulder.

"She is fine, very fierce when someone she loves is in trouble." There was a chuckle then from the door way and they looked up to see Katrina standing there. When she saw Idi smile at her she flew across the room and flung herself into his arms.

"So my Katie is a fierce lady is she?"

"Oh I was so mad when I saw you might be hurt I wanted to strike the ghost across the face but I had to see you were ok first."

"Well thank the Elements for that, what would I do without you? And are you really alright Katie?" Katrina looked up at Idi full of pride and love.

"Yes I am fine," she hesitated for a moment, "well my hands still hurt a bit but I am fine really."

"Your hands, what's wrong with your hands?" Katrina turned her hands over to show Idi her palms, they were raw and blistering as if badly burnt.

"The cold" said Marcus; "she pulled the web off with her hands". "Oh Katie it must have hurt so" whispered Idi. Katrina looked up and squared her shoulders.

"It didn't hurt, not one bit." Idi and Marcus smiled at her.

"Give them to me" said Idi. Katrina lifted up her hands and gave them to Idi. He bent down as if to kiss them but as he lowered his head he blew healing over them so that by the time his lips touched them they were healed. She smiled at him and her chest filled with pride.

171

"You are the best person there ever was" she said and buried her head into his chest. Idi cuddled Katrina tight for a moment.

"Can you go out and play for a while Katie - I need to talk with Marcus for a bit?" Katrina raised herself up, kissed Idi on the cheek and ran outside.

Idi told Marcus about his time with Sebastian and all that was said.

"T'was the mead Idi that dulled the magic, I would advise that you wait until you know you are in a totally safe environment before you partake of so much in one go again." Idi nodded his agreement. He felt a bit ashamed to actually say out loud that he agreed with Marcus.

"If the King will not see us I am not too sure why going to live at the castle would be of any good Idi."

"Yes I know, but their need is great - I can feel it, Marcus, and maybe we could discover something more about this Norvora. Oh. . ." Idi looked at Marcus as he remembered something the ghost had said, "the ghost said she was supposed to hand me over to Norvora."

Marcus got up and started pacing around Idi's room. "I wonder why he would want you, he must know you're a healer but he wouldn't consider you a threat to him I don't think. Our paths have never crossed so far."

Idi pulled on his knee high soft leather boots. "We need to go and talk with Sebastian. I said I would bring you to meet him." Marcus stopped pacing and looked at Idi.

"We will go and live in the castle, start packing - we will go today." Idi looked at Marcus in surprise.

"Are you sure? You haven't met them yet. How do you know we should go?" Marcus had already left Idi's room and gone to the dresser to put all his bottles and potions into his travelling case.

"Katrina" Marcus called loudly, stuffing the bottles into their special holders. Katrina came running from her room, "Yes" she answered.

"Pack your things little one, we're going to live in the castle." Katrina let out a screech of excitement and ran back into her room to pack.

"Marcus?" Idi asked. Marcus stopped his packing and came up to Idi putting his hands on his shoulders.

"It is not safe for Katrina here anymore, with ghosts and demons anything could happen and we can't be with her every moment of every day. She'll be safer at the castle, she will have boundaries and rules that she will have to obey; the discipline will do her good. If we don't know our enemies, we're in trouble. We need to know this Norvora and find out what he is up to. Living under his nose might be safer than hiding out here. As for the King, I don't know if we can help, but if our presence at the castle encourages the Knights, whom I know are honourable men, then we do a good thing. Now go pack!"

Idi went to pack. He stuffed his few belongings into a long soft leather bag and tied the ends with string. He was the first one packed. Katrina was soon packed and jumping up and down with excitement. Lastly Marcus decided to change out of his daily brown shift and into his special purple and silver tunic. They called the horses over, Marcus told them they were going to live at the castle and asked if they would cope with the confines; both horses neighed and nodded their heads elaborately. Marcus was relieved. He would have set them free but he had the feeling he might need their speed again one day. They threw their few bags and pouches over the horse's saddles, and then Marcus went into the cottage one last time.

When he came out his staff was in his hand. Idi had not seen the staff since the first day they had turned up at this deserted cottage, which had become their home over the last years.

Marcus came and stood on the grass beside them and then turned to look at the cottage. He raised his staff in his right hand; the black stone immediately seemed to come alive and sparkled with lights.

"Hidden" Marcus thundered, and crashed the bottom of the staff onto the wooden veranda. There was groaning and creaking and the cottage seemed to shiver slightly, and then, to Idi's and Katrina's amazement brambles, bushes and yew trees grew before their eyes and in the space of a moment the cottage was completely hidden with greenery, and surrounded by trees.

Marcus turned and started walking down the path, "Come" he said and Idi, Katrina and the horses followed. Idi, already on his horse, put his hand out and Katrina grabbed it and swung up on the horse behind him.

"This will always be your home if you need it, just speak the words – hide no more, and the growth will go." Katrina turned to look at the cottage, it was nowhere to be seen, just a group of trees clumped together with heavy undergrowth. She looked up at Marcus, who had swung up onto Thunder, he was like a giant and her heart filled with pride that she was part of this family. She had tried for years to learn magic but had finally come to the decision that she would never be able to perform it: this had made her feel useless and insignificant at first, and often ashamed, like she was letting Idi and Marcus down somehow.

But such was her character; that instead of letting the defeat define who she was, she discovered something she could do – fight. She had punched Harry so hard his nose had bled, but he had never made fun of her clothes again; and from that moment she knew fighting was something she could do. The desire to be the best fighter she could be had made her sneak into the castle many times to watch the Knights when they practiced fighting in the large arena. It was whilst she was watching one day that Sebastian had spotted her.

"Here child" he had called to her and she found herself climbing over the fence and running to him. Sebastian had taken a sword off one of the lads who was having a lesson and passed it to her. She had taken it in awe and touched the blade. It was small in size; and blunt for practising, but it was a sword.

Sebastian hadn't said anything, just taken up the position, sword in right hand, and left his hand on hip, knees bent, waiting. Katrina quickly imitated the stance and then Sebastian had lunged at her. Her reflex was good, and she had jumped out of the way and looked at him in surprise because of the speed of the lunge. He lunged again, and Katrina brought her sword up to take the blow of his sword. Sebastian had lunged at Katrina until she was exhausted.

"Bring your father to me. I would ask him if I could teach you," and with that Sebastian had walked away. The lad who had been watching came and took his sword off Katrina.

"That weren't too bad for a first time, think Sebastian must have been impressed with you to say he would teach you himself." Katrina had flushed with pride and had run all the way back to the cottage. She would be a Knight, strong and fierce and both Idi and Marcus would be so proud of her.

She looked at Marcus now climbing on his horse and squeezed Idi tightly.

"Oh I am the luckiest person alive" she whispered to herself. She was between the love and strength of two great men, she knew they would always love and protect her and she couldn't imagine ever wanting anything more.

They alighted the horses and walked them over the drawbridge into the castle of Havenshire.

There was always an afternoon lull in the castle; even during good times, many people took to their beds to rest before the evenings duties: and so the streets were fairly quiet as they entered over the drawbridge. Still, their arrival was to make a huge impact. Those that spotted the three riding into the castle knew at once that they had come to stay. Besides their horses that followed them with their belongings there was something purposeful about their walk. Their shoulders were square and their backs were straight. Idi looked handsome in his leathers and his light brown hair curled around his face and framed him perfectly, his sharp square features of his face softened by his large lips and soft brown eyes. Katrina wore her multi-coloured waistcoat and britches, her smile lit up her face and made it radiate light in turn

But Marcus, in his purple tunic and matching cape, his staff held tightly in his right hand would be the one all would be speaking of that night. For he had surely entered the castle with the intent of letting everyone know that he was Marcus: the Magician.

Chapter Twenty-Two ~ Shape Shifters

Valarie sat on the broken branch of a tree that lay in the glen. She rested her chin on her drawn up knees, her wings very gently moving in the slight morning breeze. She waited for the sunrise in the East - the day was already becoming light but the actual sunrays could not be seen yet. She loved the sight of the sunrise, just as much as she loved the sunset; the markings of each passing day.

Finally the first rays peeked over the plains and Valarie raised her face to soak in the warmth.

"Oh Elements" she prayed, "help us to make a difference this day." Although the sun had finally come up she shivered and pulled her shawl tighter around herself. Today should have been a glorious day; a day for merriment and laughter; for Voltar was finally to become an Elder. Thinking of Voltar brought emotions to the surface and tears fell slowly down her cheeks.

"I miss you so much my brother" she said aloud. Then the memories of how they had been together in the past choked her and she started to cry in earnest, tears streaming down her cheeks and soaking her dress.

Voltar had recovered from the demons' attack, but he was not the brother she remembered. Wingless, crinkled old Sheiline had saved his life, but not his soul it seemed. It had taken him months to recover and to finally come home. The Elders had questioned her about everything that had happened and she had tried her hardest to persuade them to build up their defences: but the Elders would hear none of it. She was sure that once Voltar recovered he would be able to change their minds. But Voltar was changed. He was sullen and hardly spoke. He would not discuss Cassandra with her or talk about the demon that he had killed.

At first she had gone to see him everyday hoping that this day, he would be himself once more, but he was bad tempered with her and yelled at her to leave him alone with her constant chatter, and so finally she had stopped going to see him.

Although he would not talk to the Elders about reinforcing their boundaries he did take up lessons with sword fighting and spent endless hours training. Younger Fairies who looked up to Voltar decided that if he needed to learn the sword then so should they and it was not before long the old masters had every moment of every day filled with training the young ones.

A hand softly rested on Valarie's shoulder and she looked up to see Audrey. "Come little one, it is time to get ready." Audrey leant down and with a soft white handkerchief brushed away at Valarie's tears.

"It should be a happy day Audrey, why do I feel so sad?"

"You are mourning the brother of your youth, even if he was still the same Voltar you used to know, this day would still see a break in your relationship for he must prove himself to the others now and he would have no time for you anyway. It is life Valarie, nothing ever stays the same all the time: that is why it is so important for us to enjoy every single day for what it is." Valarie gave a little sob and her Aunt wrapped her arms around her and hugged her tight.

"I do have a little surprise for you Valarie and also a favour to ask."

"Oh" said Valarie wiping her own eyes and looking up, "what's that?" Audrey looked behind her and beckoned to something in the air.

A beautiful butterfly came to land silently next to Audrey. The colour of its wings was breathtaking, but as Valarie looked in awe at the butterfly it suddenly shimmered and then was gone and in its place stood Losia.

"I would never have known" said Valarie looking at Audrey, then turning to Losia she said, "the butterfly was beautiful" when suddenly something dawned on her and she turned to her Aunt.

"She's a shape-shifter!" Audrey smiled at Valarie.

"She didn't know she could but one day as she was going into the lake I noticed that she almost became transparent like the water and I realised old magic was in her blood, so after a few lessons she can now shape shift" Audrey paused for a moment and then finished, "like you." Losia and Valarie stared at each other. Pixies were not supposed to be able to shape shift; old magic had gone from their heritage a long time back.

"I need you to do something for me Valarie." Valarie turned back to Audrey.

"What do you need?"

"I need you and Losia to go to Havenshire for me. Once there I want you to shape shift into mice and enter the castle. I need to know what is happening to Hamish. I would fly myself but the castle is encased in a magic bubble and every time I try to enter I feel sick and lose my ability to fly. If I could shape shift I would go myself but that part of magic is not available to me. I think if you change into mice you would be able to enter the castle through the drains underground, I do not think the spell that is over the castle would go into dungeons and tunnels."

Valarie looked at her Aunt in slight wonder and gently shook her head.

"I know tis a great thing that I ask, but I am worried about what is happening in Havenshire, I have my reasons Valarie, will you go for me?"

"But of course, but do we have to go as mice? Can't we simply fly through the tunnels?"

"Yes, probably, but I would feel better if you went as mice. No one would notice a pair of mice scurrying around and I would worry much less about you." Valarie shrugged her shoulders and stood up.

"Then as soon as the ceremony is over we shall go, what do you say Losia?"

"Oh I'm game; I shall meet you at the end of the glen as the sun passes over Celon's peak. Meet me by the lightning tree." With that Losia nodded at Audrey and flew out across the grasses of the glen.

"She is a true soul Valarie; she will be a good friend to you. Now come, we need to get ready for the big day."

The ceremony was grand and noisy and filled with much merriment. Harpists lined the grand hall and their inspiring music drifted out in all directions. The Elders were dressed in their grandest attire and the ladies of the court did their utmost to outshine each other.

When the High Lord laid the wreath of leaves on Voltar's head he seemed to increase in stature, pride obvious in his every movement and Valarie felt herself fill with tears once more, for she knew her brother had longed for this day: she wondered if he still wanted to be the wisest Elder ever known, but somehow she doubted it.

When Voltar had talked to nearly every courtier and received their congratulations he finally found Valarie sitting on a stone bench in the garden and came to join her.

She smiled up at him. "You look wonderful Voltar, truly the handsomest Elder there ever was!" For the first time since his fight with the demon Voltar smiled.

"Everyone is telling me how wise I'll be and what an asset to the Elders I'll be, but you - all you can say is I am handsome, something which I am already well aware of." Valarie drew in her breath at his vanity but then she saw his raised eyebrows and the look he was giving her and she started laughing. After a while she stopped laughing and looked up at her brother whom she loved so dearly.

"You will be the best Elder there ever was Voltar, I have always known that you were destined for great things. If trouble is coming to Talia then only you will be able to protect us: you will be wise and one day you will be a clear leader above all other Elders, regardless of their age. This I know as surely as I know my name is Valarie, Higher Fairy of Hal-Luna-Tania." Voltar looked at his sister in surprise. She mostly brushed off the fact that she was a higher Fairy, but to put her name before her birth right and before the Fairies name for the glen meant that she spoke from her spirit.

"Thank you" it was all he could think of to say. He placed his hand over her hand, which was in her lap. "Will you come dance with me sister?" Valarie's heart warmed, it was the first time he had called her sister in a long time. She smiled up at him happy and content.

"No brother, I will let all the single Fairies fight over you. There are many that will simply *die* if you don't dance with them." They both laughed.

"Then I had better go and start dancing for I surely do not want their death on my hands!"

Valarie watched Voltar go back into the grand hall and then turned to look at the sky. It was time to leave. She walked through the gardens enjoying their spread of vivacious colour and smells, then after checking no one was looking with a nod of her head, she changed her clothes into mottled greens, shook her wings to loosen them for the flight, and took to the air.

Audrey stood on the tip of a boulder and watched her niece fly off.

"You will watch for them?" She turned to Elroy who nodded. His black and silver wings fluttered in the air, the light dancing through them.

"I will watch that no one follows them and then I will wait for them to return out of the tunnels and bring them safe to you." Audrey nodded. It was risky sending them into the castle when so much magic was obviously being weaved there but she wanted to know if Hamish was beyond help.

Elroy took Audrey's face in his hands and kissed her. Her knees felt weak, as they always did when he held her and she smiled up at him as a youngster when he finally let her go.

"Go" she said, shooing him away, "go before you won't be able to catch them up anymore." Elroy gave her a little bow.

"At your command: my gentle lady." With that he turned and flew into the air. She watched him go until he was out of sight and then sighed; she must return to the festivities and pretend that nothing was amiss.

Valarie and Losia came close to the castle just before it began to go dark. Elroy had shown Losia earlier where the castle drains ended, and she led them to the river. They flew over the flowing water for a while until Losia found the round entrance way to the tunnel of the castle drains. They came to land on the ridge of the opening. Water, that smelt none too pleasant, was coming out of the tunnel but it wasn't gushing. They peeked through the bars but it was too dark inside to see much.

"Must we be mice do you think?" asked Losia, "there seems to be a ledge inside, maybe we could just walk along it for a while and turn into mice later?"

"If Audrey thought it was best to enter as mice, much though I don't like it, I think we should do that." Losia pulled a face but in a moment she had changed herself into a full sized field mouse. Valarie quickly followed suit. After a brief look around to check no one was near or had seen them they pushed past the bars and entered the drains.

The ledge felt slimy and the smell inside the drain was much worse than outside. Valarie coughed and put her now mouse-paw over her nose.

"Oh I forgot mice have a good sense of smell this is just awful" she moaned. Losia got the giggles. She stood on her hind legs and waved her front paws around her.

"You look so funny! If someone could see a field mouse holding her nose like that they would surely wonder if they were seeing things."

"Well you don't look so mouse like yourself waving your paws around like that; anyway if anyone should hear us talking I think our game would be up!" Losia calmed down.

"Yes suppose we had better get going, don't know how long it will take us to reach the castle, I hope it doesn't take too long." With that she turned to start along the ledge once more, and as she went, she slipped.

She gave a scream of fright as she thought she was going to fall into the water, but something seemed to have caught her and she wavered over the edge for a moment but then settled down on the path once more. She turned to see what had caught her and gave a little gasp of surprise to see that her tail had of its own accord wrapped itself around a nail sticking out of the wall.

She looked at Valarie in surprise.

"Seems you have your animal's instincts, as well as its looks, that's a good thing Losia."

They didn't talk much after that but scurried as fast as they could along the ledge eager to reach the end of the stench filled drain.

At last they arrived at a place where the drains broke into three different tunnels.

"Which do we take do you think?" asked Losia.

Valarie stood on her hind legs and sniffed into the air at the three different tunnels. After a few moments she said, "This way" and led them along a tunnel that quickly started going uphill. It wasn't long before Losia could smell the wonderful smells of cooking and realised that Valarie was leading them towards the kitchens. As the smell of baking bread wafted down the tunnel her stomach rumbled and the desire to dive into cheese filled her senses.

They came to the end of the tunnel without even seeing another mouse, and this fact had been worrying Valarie for quite some time. Where were the rats? Just then a trap door above them was opened and someone threw a bucket of water into the drain. The two of them clung onto the sides of the ledge for dear life as the water splashed by them like a sudden waterfall. When the gush of water had gone they looked up at the trap door, which was closed once more.

After checking all over they finally found a mouse hole that led from the tunnel through the brickwork to the kitchens above. 'Must have taken mice years, to gnaw their way through there', thought Losia.

They squeezed themselves into the opening and both stood there, their noses poking out of the hole; looking into the massive castle kitchens.

It was a hive of activity. Cooks were chopping food and stirring pots and the main cook was yelling orders at everyone else. Footmen and page boys ran around trying to fulfil all the demands that the head cook made of them.

There were young girls at the huge marble sink washing pots and a group of young lads sat around a big wooden table polishing the cutlery.

Besides the aroma of baking bread that was making their mouths water, there was the wonderful smell of roasting pheasants and an odour of garlic.

Valarie was looking at the cold kitchen and all the herbs that hung there when she suddenly spotted a huge ginger cat poised and waiting to pounce on them the moment they came out of the hole. She gave a shriek and yanked Losia back into the tunnel.

"What's there then puss?" asked a maid bending down to give the cat a piece of chicken. "You keep them dirty mice out of the kitchen now you hear, you good cat you." The big ginger cat curled up in a ball next to the opening and started to eat the chicken.

"Now what are we going to do?" asked Losia. They stood there for a moment in the recess of the hole and then Valarie turned to Losia.

"Are you feeling brave Losia?" she asked it gently but Losia snorted her irritation at the question.

"Very, why do you want me to go and kill the cat?" Valarie spluttered and then chuckled.

"No nothing so drastic. My aunt said that when you were in the water you were almost transparent, so I was just thinking, maybe you could make yourself invisible or maybe change colours to blend in with whatever you are next to?"

"I don't think I can be invisible but yes I do change next to my surroundings. Oh." She gave a chuckle and turned herself back into a pixie, her little pointed nose wiggled from side to side as she tried not to laugh. Her eyebrows rose high over her cheekbones but came low over her nose. Her slim pointed ears stuck out from underneath her long black hair, and Valarie wondered again at the fact that most Fairies thought Pixies had faded away.

Before she could say anything Losia had darted out of the hole. She hovered in the air in front of the cat. The cat meowed with a high

185

pitch sound and lunged at her. Losia changed into the colour of the stone floor and darted under the tables and across the room.

The big ginger sprung after her dropping his chicken tea on the floor and skidding on the stone slabs before crashing into the table leg that Losia had just been stood in front of.

"What's up with that cat?" yelled the cook. Most of the kitchen seemed to come to a halt as they watched the cat meow and dart from under the cook's table to kitchen sink. He leapt off the floor and landed on the washed dishes that lay on the wooden worktop. Two of the plates came crashing to the floor. There were many gasps of shock from all who stood around – who, as one, turned to look at the head cook.

The cook seemed to be going redder and redder and her large rotund body swayed slightly.

"Get that cat out of here" she screeched throwing her wooden spoon at him. Then chaos broke out in the kitchen as everyone at once started lunging at the cat. No longer able to see Losia but quite able to see the wooden spoon that barely missed him the cat jumped from the sink onto the cooks table. Cook threw her hands up in the air and started screaming and six servants at once dived onto the table to get the cat off. The big ginger leapt from the table to the floor, darted through everyone's legs and shot out of the back door.

"Oh, oh" cook said, swooning and swaying heavily from side to side. The porters ran to her side and helped her to the tall backed wooden chair next to the hearth. Most of the other staff set about trying to tidy up and straighten every thing whilst trying their hardest not to let cook see them laughing.

Losia landed back inside the hole next to Valarie, folded her arms and leaned back in total smugness. Valarie was smiling.

"That was rather wonderful" she said, "but let's go quick whilst we can." Losia changed herself back into a mouse and the two of them shot out of the hole, raced across the cold kitchen floor and through a door to the castle passageways. One of the girls in the kitchen saw them and pointed at them with her mouth open but she was too surprised to speak and so no one took any notice of her.

Once in the passageway Valarie looked left and right. Which way should they go? Just then they could hear some people coming down from the right and so without hesitation she ran down to the left of the passageway, Losia close on her tail.

Occasional wall mounted lamps lit up the stone passageway and they saw the shadow of someone approaching before they heard him. Just a bit further up the passage was a cupboard. Valarie ran as fast as she could and both her and Losia squeezed behind it just as a soldier came striding by.

Valarie's heart was beating wildly in her chest and she looked at Losia to find she was in the same state.

"I'm not so sure being mice is such a good thing" she whispered to her.

In a flash Losia changed back into a pixie. "Nor do I" she said.

Valarie changed back into a Fairy and the two of them looked at each other. There didn't seem to be anywhere else to go so Valarie flew to the top of the tall cupboard and sat on the top of it, Losia followed her.

"What now" asked Losia?

"I have no idea" answered Valarie. Two more soldiers came stomping down the passageway then on their way to the kitchen for their next meal. Within moments two girls from the kitchen came rushing down the passageway carrying trays laden down with food. Losia's stomach rumbled again.

"Wish I had eaten before we set off" she said.

"So do I" replied Valarie.

The two of them sat on top of the cupboard and watched castle life move to and fro from the kitchen. It would be well after sunset before the kitchen would finally shut down for the night and the traffic coming and going in the kitchen would finally cease. Then, and only then, would Valarie and Losia fly up the passageway in search of the royal chambers.

Chapter Twenty-three ~ Demon Attack

Cassandra paced back and forth and tutted quietly to herself. Turtledoff was taking forever to take his boots off.

"How could you get stones in both boots Turtledoff?" she asked impatiently. Turtledoff peered at Cassandra from under his big bushy eyebrows and his soft felt hat that hung down over half his face.

"A moment or two won't make much difference Casey; we shouldn't even be going to the castle in times like this. What if someone follows us home? Have you thought of that?"

"No one will recognise me Turtledoff." Cassandra came and knelt by Turtledoff as he started re-tying his bootlaces. "I need to go for myself, if my father really is ill I need to be with him and I need to let him know that I am alright; I know he banished me but that won't have stopped him from loving me and worrying about me. Besides I want to tell him about Absalom."

Turtledoff looked at her and pursed his lips tightly together: he had tried for weeks to dissuade her from this trip but when she had shown she would go on her own if he didn't help her, he had finally given in and agreed to take her through the mountains and bring her back to Havenshire.

"If someone recognises you I won't be able to save you and Absalom will grow up Motherless: if you are not recognised the chances that they will let you in to see the King are a million to one, we are on a wasted journey."

"It will be alright Turtledoff I just know it will, trust me." She looked up at him with her soft imploring eyes and he shook his head as he knew she would have her way.

"Besides which, we have come all this way, it would be silly to turn around now don't you think?" She stood up and looked down at the landscape before them. Soft rolling hills; which farmers had cut up into various shapes, each growing different crops, gave the land the appearance of a patchwork quilt, and formed the perfect frame for the city of Havenshire: that lay nestled in the hills, like a heavy crown upon a soft bed. The cold mountain river cascaded down the hills, a deep cut scar of blue across the greens and browns, which split into two as it flowed to either side of the castle before joining and becoming one once more, as it sped south towards the Seas. Cassandra sighed, she had missed her home so much and there was a joy rushing through her at the sight of it.

Turtledoff came and stood beside her.

"There's no place like home, I know lass" he put his hand on her arm and the two stood looking at the peaceful sight. After a moment or two something started to puzzle Cassandra.

"Something's wrong." Turtledoff looked up at Cassandra waiting for her to finish but she had screwed up her eyes and was intently searching the land before them.

"It's almost eventide, farmers should be bringing their cattle in for milking; normally in this season men should be working the land till sunset, tilling it over. Nothing's happening. The land is still, no dogs barking, no children calling out." Cassandra turned and looked down at Turtledoff, "where is everyone?" she asked. Turtledoff shook his head; he couldn't see or hear anyone: it was indeed not a good sign.

Lights suddenly blazed in front of Turtledoffs face and he swooned then fell backwards onto the grass.

"Turtledoff" Cassandra cried and fell on her knees beside him. "Turtledoff?" she whispered stroking his face. Turtledoff moaned and Cassandra gave a sigh of relief.

"Turtledoff are you alright?" He blinked and opened his eyes and Cassandra sat back when she saw the fear in them.

He tried pushing himself up, "Wait a moment" said Cassandra, "go slowly." She helped him so he could sit up.

"We need to go home lass, we need to go now." Cassandra sat back and looked at him in sudden suspicion that he had pretended to faint to persuade her to go home.

"And why's that?" she asked.

"Oh tis bad lass what is happening in these parts" Turtledoff dropped his head his face ashen and Cassandra knew he hadn't pretended.

"What did you see old man?" she asked. Turtledoff looked straight at her.

"There are flying demons Casey, many of them. They come out in the dark, and they kill anything they find. There are other things happening to but I cannot put names or faces to them, all I know is, there is an atmosphere of magic over the place and that it is not good magic: I fear for Martha - I want to go home."

Cassandra looked at Turtledoff, he really was afraid, and maybe it would be good for Absalom if he went home, but how would she find her way back to Tamarind?

"We are so close now Turtledoff, please let's go on. We will spend only one night I promise and we'll leave at first light tomorrow." Turtledoff looked at the scene before him - so peaceful, but over it lying like a shadow, scenes of murder; and he shivered. It would be safer for them to spend the night inside the castle walls, he was sure. He nodded and pushed himself up.

"Come lass let's get there before dark." His first few steps were slightly wobbly but after that he felt normal once more and set off at a pace that was neither running nor walking, but somewhere in-between, so that he could last the pace. His short legs were strong, even for his age, and he could walk for days, but speed was not naturally his – and speed was definitely what they needed right now.

From a height Melanie sat in the branches of a great Oak. Her normal white dress switched today for mottled greens to better hide amongst the trees. She had been on watch now for most of the day and soon someone would be coming to replace her. Three would replace her, for the nights were more dangerous. She couldn't wait for them to come; it was monotonous, waiting. She yawned and stretched and shook her head from side to side endeavouring to stay awake, and just as she was refocusing her vision she saw them: two dots of colours, rushing down the hill, heading for the castle.

How could she have missed them? Moraine will be so cross. She sprung upwards, banging her head on the overhead branch and cursed at the pain. In three agile leaps she was on the ground. She watched them rushing into the valley and wondered what to do. If she went to turn them around she would never get them back to the lakes before dark, but if she left them, anything might happen.

She looked to the west where the sun was slowly slipping over the edge of the world. Her replacements would be here soon, Water Element be praised, let them be early this night.

Both Turtledoff and Cassandra were tiring. Their pace, despite their determination, was slowing, and they both knew it. They didn't have to look behind them to know the sun was beginning to set either and the two of them rushed without words, to what they hoped was safety.

Like some nightmare the castle seemed to be forever a great way off. They crossed over the fields, not bothering with the paths, to take the shortest route to the castle. Normally farmers would have chased them off their crops, but no one was around.

The missing sound of the birds singing before sunset worried them both, were there even no birds around?

A cold wind picked up and initially they were both grateful for it as their pace had left both of them red faced and sweating, but after a while the wind seemed to cut through their clothes and they felt cold to the bone.

Turtledoff stopped and rested his hands on his knees, bent over and puffing in pain. Cassandra stopped next to him, her eyes flying from one part of the field to the next seeking anything unusual. Although she could see no one she had the feeling they were being watched, and the closer they got to the castle the stronger the feeling became. She reached out and pulled gently on his sleeve. He nodded at her and the two set off once more.

The sun was almost gone now, the atmosphere totally cold and unmoving but Cassandra knew they were only a couple of fields away from the castle now and felt her spirits rising.

"Almost there" she panted between breaths. They climbed over a sturdy stile and there was the castle in front of them. One more field and then the road would lead them to the drawbridge in a matter of moments.

At last she could see them flying towards her. Melanie flew into the air and raced to meet the water witches. As the four met in the air the sun finally let go of the day and the night's dark began.

Half way across the final field the dark fell; and with it chills descended down their backs. A thin eerie wail came down the hills. Turtledoff and Cassandra looked at each other and started running through the last section of the field. The gate was almost in reach when suddenly something knocked the pair off their feet and sent them flying to the ground. Neither tried to see what it was, both simply started getting up again. But before they could even get their balance something crashed into them again and they both fell, face down in the dirt. A stench of sulphur hit them and Cassandra heaved under the smell. Something grabbed her hand and she screamed, but it was Turtledoff.

"Here lass" he whispered and pushed a dagger into her hand. She grabbed it tightly and cautiously got to her knees. Turtledoff did the same. They moved until they were back to back and then they stood up.

"He's playing with us or we'd be dead by now," whispered Turtledoff. Cassandra swallowed but that was the only bit of fear she would show. She would not die here: this was not her destiny. The demon came screeching towards them, a large black blob, the only part of him clear to see was the red sparks of his eyes.

They braced themselves and as it flew into them again, this time they tried stabbing it with their daggers. The demon screeched his rage and swirled into the air to come at them again.

"Oh please Elements, please. I want to see Absalom once more" Cassandra whispered. Just as the demon turned to start his descent again, there was a flurry of something in the air. Moments later the blood-curdling scream of the demon was heard and then a moment's silence.

Something landed in front of Cassandra and she screamed.

"Hush child" said a lady and as Cassandra peered into the dark the image of a beautiful woman, dressed in white, appeared before her.

"You must flee, he was not alone and the others are coming. Do not look back as you run, keep focused on the drawbridge, once on it you will be safe: for some reason they cannot enter the castle grounds. Now go, you have no time to waste." With that the woman rose into the air once more and could not be seen.

After the briefest of pauses Turtledoff and Cassandra raced towards the last gate. They didn't wait to open it, but with an agility that neither of them knew they possessed, with the strength that mighty fear gives you, they leapt over the gate and raced towards the drawbridge.

Behind them they could hear the deadliest of screams and screeches, and knew that a battle was being fought.

Neither of them knew who had come to their defence but they cried out to the Elements to help them. The Elements would not respond to their cries this day: and when the morning came the Water Clan would bury four of their own.

As soon as they put a foot on the drawbridge two figures appeared by the gate. They paused only for a moment fearful they would be turned away, but as one of the figures raised his torch she could see it was Sebastian and she sighed in relief, she was home.

Sebastian closed the gate behind them and at last Cassandra could look at him properly. She was shocked at the change in his appearance.

From the draw bridge she had recognised him, but he was so changed the fear inside her turned from herself to her father and the people of the castle.

Sebastian raised his finger to his lips to warn them not to speak and then they rushed down alleyways and side passages for what seemed like forever, before arriving through a servant's entrance into the castle itself. They rushed along the castle passageways and then finally entered the library.

Now Sebastian turned to look at her, he gave her the once-over and then looked at Turtledoff. Shaking his head he turned to his friend.

"How did you know they were coming and why risk everything for a farm lass and her short friend." Turtledoff spluttered at the reference to his being short and raised his shoulders.

"I'm known for my height where I come from if *you don't mind!*"

Sebastian smirked and simply raised one eyebrow at him.

Cassandra was standing, slightly stunned. Sebastian hadn't recognised her: she hadn't changed that much, surely?

Marcus, who stood by the huge fireplace, came towards them. Cassandra raised her eyebrows in surprise to see the purple gown of a magician.

"Sometimes I hear someone speaking in my head, I don't know how or who, but I have grown to trust the voice. I simply heard, two come – hide safe. And here they are, he yawned then turned back to stand in front of the blazing fire.

"Too cold for this time of year" he said poking the fire with the large metal poker. Just then the door opened quietly and a young lad poked his head around the corner.

"'Er mister" he said looking at Marcus, "the healer be wantin' ya mighty quick." The boy didn't wait for an answer but shot away. Marcus picked up his cape and went to Sebastian and placed his hand on the Knights shoulder.

"They'll be safe with you. I'll go and see what Idi wants and then we'll meet in my rooms later for supper, bring them with you; I'll be interested to learn a little about them." Sebastian nodded and Marcus closed the door quietly behind him as he went out. With the door closed, finally alone with Sebastian, Cassandra looked at him and asked,

"Do you not recognise me Sebastian?" Sebastian looked at her in surprise, how did she know his name? The look on his face showed he didn't know who she was.

"It's me, Cassandra."

"No" said Sebastian quickly with scorn on his face.

Turtledoff reached up and ruffled Cassandra's short dark hair and smiled at Sebastian. "Used to be long and fair and wavy" he said. Now Sebastian came close and looked at her face. Her tiny delicate features suddenly seemed to become clear to him and then when he looked into her soft blue eyes he took a sharp intake of breath.

"My lady" he said coming towards her, then suddenly as if yanked by a rope he stopped and reared backwards. There had been too much magic around the castle in the last years and he had begun not to trust his eyes.

"I don't know who you are but my lady is long gone." His mistrust saddened Cassandra but she had come prepared and pulled out a pouch sewn into her cape. She pushed her hand into the soft velvet bag and pulled out a piece of metal. She stretched out her hand to Sebastian to show him the golden half pendant.

"I don't know exactly if this one is yours Sebastian for I was given fifteen on one day." Sebastian took the broken pendant and looked at it in wonder. Could it be? His hand went automatically to his broken pendant that hung from his neck and rested under his shirt. He looked once more at the woman before him and suddenly he saw clearly who she was.

"My lady" he said and fell on one knee, before picking up the hem of her mud stained skirt and kissing it, tears beginning to roll down his cheeks.

"Oh my lady, you have no idea what this will mean that you have returned." Cassandra laid her hand on his head, choked beyond belief that he could still be so devoted to her.

"I cannot stay Sebastian, and no one must know that I am here. I have only come for one night to see my Father; I have heard he is ill." Sebastian rose to his feet and wiped his face on the back of his sleeve.

Turtledoff tutted and raised his eyebrows, "where's your manners boy" he said.

Sebastian looked at Cassandra and was lost for words. If she had come home to stay then the other Kingdoms might stop their allegiances with each other and stand by Havenshire once more. He had to get Myles: Myles would be able to change her mind. Without speaking he marched quickly out of the room and left Cassandra and Turtledoff standing by themselves.

Cassandra began to pace the room; she knew instinctively that Sebastian had gone to fetch Myles. It was the right thing to do, she supposed, as Myles was the head of the Knights and also her Father's right hand man. They didn't have to wait long before the door flew open and in marched Myles. He came right up to Cassandra and peered deeply into her eyes. She saw mistrust and fear and hope all mingled together and her heart leapt as her love for him flooded her.

"Dear old Myles, it really is me." He grasped her hand, held it tight for a moment and then raised it to his lips and kissed them.

"You come home in bad times my lady."

"So I hear; that is why I have come. I need to see him Myles." Myles let go of her hand and started pacing the room.

"It's not safe to see him Cassandra, he is not" Myles paused for a moment and then continued, "he is not, quite, himself these days."

"If he has gone mad then I want to see it for myself." Cassandra squared her shoulders; she had braced herself all the way there to hear the worst.

Sebastian and Myles exchanged glances.

"What, what is it?" demanded Cassandra.

"It's not so much that he has lost his mind, more a case of someone else taking it over." Myles looked at Cassandra meaningfully: would she know enough of the world to understand what he was saying?

Cassandra's heart was beating wildly in her chest, what were they saying? "I want to see him."

"It's not a good idea my lady, no one sees him these days except Norvora, Myles is sometimes called in and given orders but besides that no one sees him. The servants have to leave the room before he enters, and I fear" Sebastian paused, the words painful to say, "I fear he will have you arrested if he sees you." Cassandra was shaking. Unsteady on her feet and finding it too hard to stand up she moved to a chair and sat down.

"Norvora? But why would he only let Norvora see him when no one else can?" Turtledoff decided it was time for him to sit down to and hopped onto a chair by the hearth.

Cassandra remembered Norvora on the night Absalom was born and the memory of him filled her with loathing. Neither Myles nor Sebastian answered and she stared into the fire. Inside she knew the answer but she didn't want to acknowledge it. Slowly though, through a feeling of mist and fog, words began rolling around together until suddenly they made sense and she knew the answer. Magic. Norvora had taken over her Father's mind with magic. Things began to make sense. She had always known deep within her that her Father couldn't have been responsible for the things that people were saying about him.

As Myles watched her he saw the realisation dawn on her face and went to a decanter in the corner of the room and poured her a drink. When offered the glass she simply took it and drowned the contents in one shot, which made her cough and almost choke.

After a while Myles and Sebastian pulled up chairs next to them and the four talked in earnest. Mostly Cassandra asked questions with Myles answering. They didn't know the exact date but they remembered being concerned when her Father had suddenly started listening to Norvora's advice over theirs. Over time though the council meetings had become shorter and shorter until finally, all pretence that the King was in charge, faded. Norvora would meet with the King and then Myles would be called and given orders.

No amount of pleading with Hamish would make him change his mind over his orders and he had threatened to have all the Knights hung before Myles had finally given up all hope and stopped pleading with him.

On top of the insane orders the King had been issuing there were horrors being committed all over the land, and so far, no one had been caught committing them. The most distressing tales were the ones of whole villages being slaughtered.

Norvora had the far left wing of the castle turned into his own private quarters - where only his servants were allowed to enter. It was rumoured that he had turned the entire wing into a place full of black magic. His fires were always burning bright and a range of colours often poured through his windows as the flames burnt in different colours. It was said he killed animals, from rats to cows, and poured their blood down the castles walls: in short everyone feared and hated him, and no one could do anything about it.

"We have brought Idi and Marcus to the castle. We hope that if we can get them to Hamish they will be able to help him, Idi is the greatest healing magician that ever lived: if anyone can save Hamish it is him." Sebastian told them eagerly.

"The trouble is" joined in Myles, "we've heard that Norvora is trying to kill Idi, and so we are careful to keep him hidden from all except a trusted few. And herein lays our hope: if Norvora is afraid that Idi will heal Hamish, then there must be the chance that he can." Cassandra nodded, it seemed there was a glimmer of hope after all.

"I look forward to meeting this Idi."

"My lady I don't think you should meet anyone. Sleep awhile and at first dawn we shall escort you, quickly, out of Havenshire, so that you may return to the place that has kept you safe all these years."

"No, I want to meet him. If I am not to see my Father then I will at least meet the man who may save him." Sebastian and Myles looked at each other.

"You always were as stubborn as a mule" Myles said fondly.

Turtledoff laughed, "Oh I can vouch that she hasn't changed on that score!"

Cassandra pulled a face at them.

"You must promise not to let anyone else know who you are though Cassandra. You already risk much by being here. If Norvora knew you were here his men would have you in his towers in moments. He won't admit it but we know he has been looking for you all these years, we don't know why, but whatever the reason he wants you and I fear tis not for your good." Myles looked at Cassandra and she nodded her agreement.

"That's settled then, we might as well go now." Instead of heading to the main door Myles led them over to the plain stone wall. He reached up and pushed a particular stone and suddenly the stones moved and opened inwards to reveal a tunnel.

Myles turned to Cassandra who was looking at the tunnel in surprise.

"They are kept secret for times such as these," and with that he reached up for a torch on the wall and led the way into the tunnel. Sebastian came last and closed the entrance behind him. They walked along the tunnel for only a short distance before Myles stopped and opened up another secret door. It swung over into a large circular room, and Marcus and Idi both turned to watch them enter their secret rooms.

When the door was closed behind them Cassandra turned to Myles, "Does my Father not know about these places?" she asked.

"He does, but for the time being, his illness seems to prevent him from remembering most things, so we think we are safe, for now anyway." Cassandra was pleased; she hated the thought that there might have been secrets held back from him.

"Arr, our two that came" said Marcus going forward, "come, come and sit down at the table we have supper ready." Everyone gathered around the table and for a while the talk was sociable and pleasant, however, when the food was eaten and they had moved to comfortable chairs by the fire the pretence that all was well, faded away.

"You had an eventful journey here?" asked Marcus.

"I wouldn't say that," growled Turtledoff.

"What happened" Idi asked.

Turtledoff told of their journey, and occasionally Cassandra interjected with odd comments.

"So we don't know who came to our rescue, but we will be eternally grateful to them," Turtledoff concluded.

"I believe it must be the Water Clan Witches," said Marcus thoughtfully, "they fly and wear white clothes mostly, but I am curious as to why they should be flying out over the plains at night when they are sure to know about the demons. And why should they go to the aid of passing strangers. Umm think I shall visit with Moraine soon." Silence fell on the small crowd for a short time.

"I hear you may be able to help the King," said Cassandra looking at Idi to watch his reaction.

"Yes I might" Idi answered a little hesitantly. Cassandra sat back disappointed – he wasn't confident.

"Yesterday I didn't think that I could reach him through this heavy atmosphere of black magic, but today I called out to his mind – and he answered!" Everyone sat up and looked at Idi intently, waiting for him to continue.

"I've been standing in the tunnels that run along side his room, trying to work out a way to go through the magic to reach him: the magic is too strong for me to be able to enter, the smell of it makes me sick and the power of it will crush me. I couldn't find a way and I was beginning to despair when suddenly I called out in my mind to him, pleading with him to help me – and he answered!"

"What did he say?" whispered Cassandra.

"Help me." Everyone looked at Idi trying to work out why this was so good. Idi explained.

"If his soul can hear me, I might be able to persuade him to leave his room and come to us. Once he is here we would have to trap him and keep him long enough for me to be able to fight the magic. I don't think it would be long before Norvora would know what was happening though, so I am not sure I would have long enough. It took me three turns of the hourglass before I could heal someone else who had been touched with black magic. And if it takes that long to reach the King, if I can, then we will surely all be caught."

Sometimes timing can be perfect, and just at that moment the secret door creaked open and the young lad came through. He ran to Sebastian and whispered something in his ear.

"Well done lad" said Sebastian and the lad hurried out down the tunnel again. "It seems we have some good news for once" he said smiling, "It seems that in the morning Norvora is going back to his own towers for a visit, he will return at nightfall, but if we are lucky, that means we will have all day before someone knows the King is not in his chambers." Excitement tingled in the air; it was the best possible stroke of luck. Cassandra sat back in her chair and smiled: Idi would help her Father; she knew it in her bones.

Marcus watched Cassandra. No one had bothered to introduce her, so he knew that they wanted to keep her incognito. He didn't ask but he wondered all the same, something was tugging at the back of his old memory cells.

"Will you stay with us long?" he asked her. She shook her head.

"No, I promised to return home tomorrow so that is what we shall do."

"Where is home?" he continued. She looked at him and answered,

"How long have you been in Havenshire Marcus, I don't remember you?" *So she would not answer any more questions, fair enough.*

"We came seven years ago" answered Idi, unaware of the undercurrent that was building up. Cassandra turned to him and smiled.

"Idi is an unusual name," she said.

"Well it's not really my name; it's just something that people call me."

"Oh, and what's your real name then?"

"Don't know, I want to know with every fibre of my body but as I don't know who my parents are I have to accept that I will never know."

"Myles, tomorrow when," she paused, "when my Father is himself once more. I want you to tell Idi how each of you found your real names."

Idi looked at Myles, sudden eagerness in his eyes, "How did you find your real name?" he asked. Myles smiled and patted him on the shoulder.

"All in good time lad, all in good time. It is time for us to separate now though for it won't be long before the dawn is here. And you especially Idi, need some sleep."

Idi could have burst with frustration but he nodded. Farewells said and expressions to meet again when things were different were exchanged and quite soon Marcus and Idi were left on their own.

"What do you think she meant Marcus?"

"I don't know lad, but don't torture yourself - you will know soon enough." Idi stared into the light of a candle for a while.

"Can you imagine" he said softly, "finding out who I am; wouldn't that be wonderful."

"I already know who you are lad, you are a wonderful person; a new name won't change that." Idi didn't answer, it was no good trying to explain to someone who had always known his name; this was Idi's second favourite day dream, finding out his real name: it would change everything he was sure.

"Come lad, let's to bed and try to sleep." Marcus blew out the candle that Idi had been staring at but Idi didn't mind, he would lie in bed and dream about his real name. The name that would give him a sense of belonging, a sense of being part of someone else, and not just a rejected piece of rubbish that he had always felt himself to be.

Chapter Twenty-four ~ Earth & Water Unite

As the last servants were climbing into their beds, Valarie and Losia went flying down the main corridors in search of the King. They made themselves tiny and flew under doors into each room they passed. Room after room didn't reveal what they were looking for. However, in one room someone had only eaten half of a mini banquet before retiring to the next room to sleep. Losia took one look at the food and darted back out into the corridor to get Valarie.

"Come" she whispered, and Valarie followed her back into the chamber.

"What is it?" Valarie asked.

"Food."

Valarie was about to answer that they didn't have time for food when her stomach grumbled. They should keep up their strength, she thought as she broke a piece of bread off. They didn't stay long, ate quickly and stuffed tiny pieces of cheese into their pockets. They got the giggles. Being mice had turned their senses towards cheese and both were amused that they still fancied some.

They had to twist and turn down many narrow stone corridors before finally coming to a room that they couldn't enter.

Valarie saw the magic over the door and pulled Losia back, who had just been about to fly under the door.

"We can't go in there," whispered Valarie, "the magic is bad." Losia looked at the door but couldn't see anything.

"What do we do now?" she whispered back. Valarie thought for a moment.

"We find somewhere to hide and we wait. Sooner or later someone will come and open the door and we will see whether the King is inside or not, but my feelings are that he must be here."

~~~~~~~~~~

Cassandra stood at the small slatted window and watched as the sun slowly began to creep over the horizon.

"This is a sad visit for you lass, I know that, but I am sure you will return one day in happier times." Cassandra turned slowly and looked at Turtledoff.

"I thought you were still sleeping."

"No lass, been watching you for a while now."

"I would have liked to have seen him."

"I know." There was no more need for words and they washed and put their capes on over the clothes that they had slept in. Shortly there was a gentle tap at the door before being slowly pushed open.

Sebastian stood there. He didn't look like he had slept at all. His face was white and his eyes were lined with dark shadows.

"Good you're up, I have pilfered the kitchens for you," he said with a smile and handed Turtledoff a soft leather bag with the food in.

"We will make for home as quick as we can, we'll stop on the way when hunger overtakes us." Sebastian nodded, he understood, he didn't feel like eating either.

Sebastian led them back down secret passageways, and then outside down tiny alleyways until finally they were on the drawbridge.

Sebastian lifted Cassandra's hand and kissed it gently, but as she looked at him she was overcome by the thought of happier times and threw her arms around him.
Sebastian was surprised and slightly embarrassed and his cheeks flushed with colour.

"Take care of him," she said as she let him go. Sebastian knew she meant the King.

"I promise," he answered. Turtledoff and Cassandra turned and started to walk down the wooden drawbridge.

After a few paces Cassandra stopped and looked back at Sebastian.

"Is Mary well?" she asked.

"She is my lady, she has returned to live with her brother on his farm and the last I heard she was well."

"Should you ever get the chance?" Sebastian cut in,

"I will tell her you are well and asked after her."

"Thank you" Cassandra said with a croak in her voice. Sebastian watched them for a moment as they crossed over the drawbridge, then ran a few steps to catch them up.

"My lady" he said. Cassandra turned to look up at him.

"Sebastian?"

"Did my lady" Sebastian stopped to chew his lower lip momentarily, "did my lady have a child?" Cassandra smiled.

"Yes I did." Sebastian was looking at her and she realised he was waiting for a fuller answer.

"I have a healthy son." Sebastian burst into a grin.

"Oh that is good news my lady, good news indeed."

With that, Turtledoff and Cassandra headed off into the early morning mist, to make their way home as quickly as possible. They opened the gate into the first field with some trepidation. They had no need to talk; they both felt the same fear. They practically ran through it. The morning mist lay over the land and hid from them the sight of the yellow stains left from the slain demons and the red blood from the four who had sacrificed themselves to ensure the King bearer lived.

~~~~~~~~~~

Far to the south of Havenshire lay the Lands of the Lakes: great rolling tree-covered hills, overlooking large pools of water that were the Galayian Lakes. On the crest of the largest lake the Water Clan gathered. A raft was pushed into the lake as the sun rose over the first of the hills. When the raft had gone a short distance into the lake, four Witches raised their bows high and sent four flaming arrows onto the raft. Instantly the dried hay caught fire. The four dead witches would burn and their ashes would dissolve into the Lake, their souls set free to serve the Water Element in her world.

Moraine watched the raft burn. A sadness lay heavy on her shoulders: the Oracle had told her to watch for the King bearer and she had known they risked their lives staying out over the plains but she had asked her Clan for their help and they had responded as one: they would share the responsibility and the risk. Now four lay dead. That the King bearer and her friend lived was good, but she felt the loss of her own friends greatly.

After the rafts had burnt brightly for a while and had drifted far across the lake, Moselle came and gently laid her hand on Moraine's arm.

"Let us go," she said softly. Moraine let Moselle lead her away from the lake's small beach and down the winding path to home.

Their houses were made from wood and stood on stilts in the far corner of the lake. She looked over at the cluster of homes and wondered if they should leave their home for somewhere safer. So far the demons had not ventured to their part of their world; whether that was because they knew the Witches would fight back she did not know, but she did know that sooner or later they would start getting braver. Their numbers seemed to be increasing and with that so did their nerve and daring. If they were led by any one demon and he found out that the Water Clan had slain nine of his own that night, then they would have something to fear. Moraine shivered at the thought.

Just as they were approaching the narrow wooden walkways that led to their homes across the lake, there was a commotion in the air. Looking up, Moraine saw seven Earth Clan Witches flying towards them.

"What does Misha want now?" Moraine moaned under her breath, "I am in no mood to entertain today."

The orange clad Witches came to land gently in front of Moraine, who had stopped by the lakeside to wait for them before crossing the walkways.

"Greetings Moraine" said Misha, nodding her head slightly.

"Good morrow to you Misha, I don't know what brings you to the lakes, but I must warn you, today is not a good day."

"So I have heard, and I am sorry for your loss." Moraine looked at Misha, slightly surprised that she should know of their news already. Misha continued.

"That is the reason I am here Moraine, we have to talk." Moraine sighed, nodded and led the way across the walkways to her home.

Moraine's home, like the rest, was basically one large room. In the centre of the floor was a huge round glass slab, enabling you to see into the waters a short distance below. Misha looked through the glass at the fish swimming below and marvelled at their colours and beauty.

Moselle came quietly into the room and laid a tray of refreshments down on the table.

"Thank you Moselle, will you fetch Silvia, Natasha and Fiona and return with them, I think you should all be present for these talks." Moselle nodded and hurried out of the room to fetch the others. Once they returned Moraine waved her hand towards the chairs to indicate that they should sit.

"Well Misha, what is it you wish to discuss?" asked Moraine, folding her hands sedately in her lap.

"War" answered Misha.

For a while there was silence and Moraine looked resigned.

"Why do you wish to discuss war with me Misha?"

"I believe a great war is coming to Talia."

"The demons do not bother us Misha."

"I do not mean the demons, they are a part of it yes, but they are only pawns to the ones who want to destroy the Earth." Misha shivered: the thought of the Earth being destroyed was too much.

"Sometimes the Earth talks to me Moraine, as I am sure the Waters do to you, the Earth is afraid." Now Misha began to shake and Moraine looked at her, concerned. Through chattering teeth Misha continued.

"A blackness is building in the underworld. They are drawing on the depths of old magic and evil is being leaked into the Earth. It has been happening for years now and no one has noticed for a long time; blackness grew in tiny amounts, seeping into Earth, whispering its innocence and so it was basically ignored. Now we can ignore it only at our peril." Misha was shaking so much that two of the Earth Clan moved to hold her.

Moraine stood up and slowly walked over to Misha, she stood in front of her for a moment and many abstract thoughts raced through her mind; her childhood, discovering she was a Witch, the others coming to follow her and the death of her friends last night. Suddenly she just knew her whole life had been building up to this point. She stood here now at a crossroads - she could choose which path to follow, what kind of person to be, what kind of life to lead. Knowing the power of words, she pulled on her magic, knelt down in front of Misha and declared:

"The Water Clan serve the Light: we will fight for what is right, true and just; we stand besides our sisters the Earth Clan and declare this day, that nothing of the dark shall be safe so long as there is breath in our mortal bodies."

Chapter Twenty-five ~ What's in a name?

"That was it" Marcus jumped out of bed. All night something had been nagging away at his old brain. "Stupid, stupid, stupid," he declared hopping on one leg whilst trying to pull on his trousers.

She said "does my father know" which meant only one thing, she was Cassandra, princess of Havenshire, and if any of the rumours were true then she had been pregnant at the time the prophesied one was to come. How could he have been so stupid as to let her go?

"Idi" he yelled pulling his shirt over his head, "Idi." There was no answer, "Oh damn and blast it" growled Marcus looking everywhere for his belt, "where is that boy when you need him?"

~~~~~~~~~

"If I tell you" said Sebastian, "you must first give me your word that you will not leave the castle until you have at least tried to heal the King." Idi looked at him; that was an easy promise.

"Of course I will, what kind of man do you take me for?" Sebastian nodded.

"Then I shall tell you as we go to fetch Marcus for I have just heard Norvora has left the castle already." Idi nodded in agreement and the two of them set off back into the castle and headed down the long passageways from the garrisons, from where Idi had found Sebastian.

"West of here, twelve sunrises away, there is a huge lake called Dark Pool, in the centre of the lake is an island named Treffernon. At a certain point at the lakes edge a small boat is always moored; nobody knows where it comes from but it is always there. When you reach there you must row to the island; if you are luckily enough to reach it, "*She*" will tell you what to do."

"What do you mean if I am lucky enough?" Sebastian put his hand on Idi's shoulder to stop him for a moment.

"Out of every ten men who try to reach her only one will return alive."

"I don't understand."

"Only someone pure of motive will ever reach her Idi, if there is but a trace of darkness within you then she will destroy you. Many are killed by the lake before even reaching the island; others reach the island but then never return."

"But you went Sebastian and you returned." Sebastian dropped his hand off Idi's shoulder.

"Yes I did" he agreed, "but it was the most frightening thing I have ever faced." Sebastian started walking down the corridors once more.

"I knew ever since I can remember that I was supposed to be a Hadrian Knight, but you cannot become one unless you are given your true name from the lady of Treffernon."

"What was the name you had before?" Sebastian turned and smiled at Idi.

"Sebastian" he answered.

"But I don't understand, you had to go to find out your real name."

"Ay and it turned out that Sebastian is my true name Idi, it means 'entitled to respect due to great age or wisdom'."
Sebastian laughed, "Can you see me gaining respect due to great age or wisdom Idi, I don't think so. The others used to joke about it saying when we go into battle they want me by their side because they are convinced no battle will ever see the end of me." Idi looked sideways at Sebastian as they walked.

"Yes Sebastian I can see you entitled to respect." Sebastian went quiet and looked straight ahead.

"I still don't understand why you were given the name you already had though." Sebastian looked straight ahead as he walked. After a moment he answered Idi.

"I already possessed my name lad, but had no understanding of who I really was, we go to seek the name, but in truth it is not the name that gives us our strength but the knowledge of our own worth." Sebastian paused for a moment and looked at Idi side on.

"The truth is that if you go on this adventure lad you may not return, are you willing to take that chance?"

"Yes, oh yes I am."

"What about Katrina?" Now it was Idi's turn to go quiet, he didn't want to die but he had to know who he was.

"Marcus will always take care of her."

Just then Marcus came charging down the corridor in front of them.

"Idi where have you been I've been looking everywhere for you." Before Idi could answer Sebastian said,

"Norvora has left we have to be quick." Marcus stopped in his tracks, he had momentarily forgotten about the King's plight.

"Yes of course" Marcus said, "Is everything ready?"

"Martin has gone to fetch Miles and a few other Knights; we can't all be here for it would raise suspicion if some of us weren't practicing in the court yard. Myles will meet us outside the royal chambers." They hurried on in silence then, the gravity of their tasks weighing heavy upon them all.

They found Myles and the others outside Hamish's room. All took a step back and let Idi come to the door. He couldn't put his hand on the door. The black magic on it swirled like a thousand snakes, but he reached up with his hand towards the door to have something to focus on.

"Hamish" he called out with his mind. There was no answer so he called again. Again and again he called to the King but no answer came and he was beginning to panic that something had happened to him. Then it occurred to him that part of him was longing to be gone, to go in search of the Dark Lake and discover whom he was. He took a deep breath and calmed his breathing. 'If I do not manage to reach the King' he thought, 'then I will not go to the island.' He took a deep breath and focused all his energy into his mind. Now urgency was within him, not only for the King but also for his dream. He searched deep inside himself for his magic and then sent a wave crying out to the King.

"I'm here" came the reply and Idi sighed in relief.

"You must come out here your Grace."

"Where is here?" came the answer.

"Not far, just outside your door that's all."

"And why must I do that and who are you that can talk to me?"

"My name is Idi and I am your friend, come outside now, you will feel so much better when you do." Something occurred to Idi then, "all your headaches will go away, your Grace. I will be able to help you."

The King moaned and all standing outside the door heard it and looked excitedly towards the door, could Idi persuade the King to come out?

"It hurts to move boy, I don't think I can come."

"You must try, your Grace, you must. It is really a very short distance and once you are here we will be able to help you."

"We" said the King suddenly full of mistrust and Idi could have kicked himself.

"Yes your Grace, your friend Myles is here. He has missed you so much and he longs to see you, won't you come out just for a moment?" The King moaned again and this time the bed could be

215

heard creaking. The Knights looked at each other, the pain of waiting an agony for them.

They could hear the King moan as he tried to move.

"It's hard, so hard. Everything hurts boy."

"I know but I promise I will be able to help you if only you can do this hard thing first and come outside." They could hear the King shuffling along the floor and they could hardly breathe. Then they heard his hand on the handle and one of the Knights reached forward to help open the door.

"No" hissed Myles and grabbed the Knight before he could touch the door.

Painfully slowly the door opened and Myles groaned at the sight of his old friend. Thin beyond belief and his skin the pallor of yellow, the King looked like death. The moment he staggered through the doorway the Knights made a grab for him before he changed his mind and returned to his tomb of magic.

The instant they grabbed him it was as if the King woke up and he began screaming Norvora's name. Myles clamped his hand down heavily over the Kings mouth. Hamish tried to fight and kick at them but within seconds his wasted body was exhausted and he simply collapsed in their arms.

All of them raced down the corridors and into one of the spare royal chambers. Once inside they went to the secret panel and pushed it open. They would take Hamish to the secret rooms. No normal ear would hear should he cry out again; and should Norvora return early it would take him longer to find them.

Just as the door was closing two mice ran across the room and into the tunnel before the panel door swung shut once more.

They lay Hamish, gently as if he were a baby, onto the bed and stood back to allow Idi to get next to him. Idi gave Marcus a nervous look, remembering that his last encounter with black magic had brought him close to death.

"I will not move from your side lad" Marcus said. Idi gave the briefest of smiles and turned to Hamish. He saw and smelt what the others could not; the black oozing seepage from the King's body and the almost unbearable stench: this was worse than what he had had to face with Misha. But he breathed in deeply, he knew better this time what he was facing.

"Light" he demanded and suddenly the room flooded with light that poured from his body. The Knights took a step back.

Light pouring from his every pore, he lowered his hand slowly onto the Kings chest. Suddenly the King sat bolt upright, his face distorted; his eyes burning red.

"How dare you touch me" the voice had come from the Kings body but it was not the King who had spoken. Suddenly, like a demon the King flew off the bed and landed on Idi. The two of them crashed to the floor. Idi was taken completely by surprise and his light flickered off in an instant. The King began ripping at Idi's body and Idi screamed in pain as the King tore at his flesh, leaving deep gashes on his face.

"Enough" yelled Marcus and a bolt of lightning shot from his hand and hit Hamish in the back. The bolt should have taken all the man's strength but Hamish just turned slowly on his heels and looked at Marcus from under his eyebrows, his eyes burning deep red with hate.

"You do not belong in the King's body demon, now be gone." Marcus threw another bolt at the King, which hit him in the shoulder. Hamish jolted backwards slightly but then steadied himself. Hamish saw the indecision on their faces; they should help the magicians, yet how could they fight their King? As they reached for their swords at their sides Marcus put his hand up to signal for them to halt and the Knights, always obedient, stayed their hands and stood still.

In the deepest of voices the King growled at Marcus.

"Is that all you have magician?" and with that the King leapt off the ground, attacking Marcus. But Marcus was more prepared than Idi and instantly shielded himself in magic. Hamish bounced against the Light without being able to reach him. The King growled his frustration and hurled himself at Marcus once more, but Marcus's shield covered him. Idi moaned and tried to sit up. The King smirked.

"I'll take this one first then," he hissed, but as he reached with up his fist to pound down on Idi's chest, Valarie transformed herself from a mouse back into a Fairy, but the size of a human.

"Stop" she said lifting her arms towards Hamish. Light flew from her hands and flowed like a river across the room, when it reached Hamish it started to wrap itself around his body.

"No" he growled tearing at the light as it wrapped itself around and around him. "No" this time the 'no' that came from him was weak and more like Hamish's voice. Valarie walked over to him as he crouched on floor.

"Sleep" she whispered and she leant towards him and blew gently over him. The King slowly fell to the floor in a deep sleep. Valarie went to Idi and helped him to his feet.

"You are badly hurt," she said in a soft voice. Idi was looking at her, puzzled, where had she come from?

"I'll be alright," he said, already healing himself. One gash on his left cheek though seemed to hurt more than the rest and he couldn't quite seal the wound. It would leave a scar on his face, a gentle reminder to him always, that he couldn't heal everything.

Valarie turned to Marcus.

"Hamish sleeps under the spell but I don't know for how long. We must be quick now."

"Who *are* you?" Marcus asked.

"I am Valarie, high Fairy of Hal-Luna-Tania, and this" she paused and pointed to a mouse on the floor, "is Losia." Before them the mouse began to shimmer and then Losia appeared, as herself but like Valarie as large as a human.

"Pleased to meet you" Losia said lifting her right shoulder provocatively and giving Idi the most alluring smile.

"You're Fairies!" said Sebastian, his jaw dropping. Losia giggled.

"Oh wait till I tell them you thought I was a Fairy, oh how funny. Do I *look* like a Fairy?" She bent her waist to the right and rested her hand on her hip. They looked at her black and green striped stockings and her black spiky hair and then looked at Valarie who was in a white and gold dress that hung softly on her body. They were definitely different.

"Well if I had ever seen a Fairy before I might be able to comment" said Sebastian.

"We must hurry," said Valarie, looking back at Marcus.

"I don't know if I can do this," said Idi.

"No, on your own you would not be able to do this sweet Idi, but together we will drive Norvora's demons from Hamish's body."

"And how will you do that?" asked Myles.

"A table with one leg will not stand, nor will another with two legs; but put three legs on a table and you'd be surprised not only will it stand but it will stand strong." She reached out her hands to Marcus and Idi, taking hold of each of them she moved them back to the Kings side, who lay still in a ball on the floor.

"Do you believe in the power of words?" Valarie asked them.

"I do" both Marcus and Idi responded.

"Then we shall tell the demons to leave." She closed her eyes and pulled deep on her old magic. Both Marcus and Idi felt old magic run through their veins for the first time and were thrilled at the touch,

Idi felt his heart would burst with the surge of love for the Elements he felt flooding through his body. Light began to flow from Valarie. It flowed from her to Marcus and then on to Idi and then back into Valarie. She sent it around again; and again until it built in power and speed. Soon the three became a blur of light and the others in the room turned their faces away from the intensity of it.

The King moaned and tried to turn.

"It burns," he cried in a pitiful voice, "stop it, it's killing me."

The three lowered themselves in their hurricane of light, and, still holding hands, reached out and touched the King.

He screamed with the voice of many demons.

"Be gone," sang Valarie's voice in the circle, "be gone and do not return."

Marcus followed her, "Be gone" he declared "and never return." Idi followed. "Be gone," he declared. Now all three took up the cry, "be gone and never return." Over and over they said it picking up in volume and purposefulness.

Hamish screamed and writhed around on the floor. Then there was one last mighty scream and Hamish jerked, then fell silent. The light slowly began to fade and when it had gone Hamish was himself once more.

The Knights reached down and picked up their King, laying him gently on the bed. None of them felt like speaking. Being Knights, they had fought in wars and seen many terrible things but this was something they had never seen before nor ever wanted to witness again.

"It's all gone," said Valarie.

"Will he be alright now?" asked Myles, gently touching his old friend's forehead.

"Yes, the demons have left not only him but the castle as well. This will be good and bad for you from now on." Myles looked up at her.

"Why?"

"Your friend is back with you Myles, but the demons that were embedded deep in the castle stopped the other things of the night from entering. Now that they are gone I fear you will have a war to fight."

"A war I can handle my lady, it is the unseen that drives me to destruction."

"I don't think I can help you any more so we must leave now."

"Our thanks will ever go out to the Hal-Luna-Tania my lady," said Myles.

Valarie smiled back at him. Marcus reached up and took Valarie's hand; he raised it to his lips and kissed it.

"If ever my lady is in need of my help you need only call to me." Valarie smiled and nodded her head, "and I am grateful for your offer good magician, for who knows when I might need it."

Losia moved over to Idi and came to stand very close to him, tilting her pointed little face up to his, she smiled and said "And if *you* ever need me, for anything, just call my name." Idi blushed.

"Losia!" called Valarie and Losia took a few steps back from Idi fluttering her long eyelashes at him as she did so.

Valarie reached out and took Losia by the hand and Losia turned to face her. Valarie gave Losia a little nod of the head and the two of them transformed back to their normal size. They flew in the air and hovered for a moment taking one last look at every one and then made themselves even tinier and flew under the door. With the demons gone there would be no need to go back through the drains and they found the first window they could and flew out of the castle. Both breathed in the fresh air deeply, and then, laughing with joy, headed for home.

Elroy who had sat in the same spot all these hours spotted them instantly and laughed loudly in relief, "Well bless the Elements" he said taking to the air and chasing after them.

Back in the secret room the King opened his eyes. His hand shakily reached up for Myles.

"Myles" he whispered huskily, "what's happened, where am I?"

Myles grinned from ear to ear and leant down over his friend.

"Oh tis mighty good to see you your Grace, you have been ill for quite some time, but you are over it now, you will soon be well." He looked at Marcus, "he will be won't he?" he asked.

"I see no reason why he shouldn't heal quickly. Your soothers will be able to look after him - they will fill him up with good things and get his strength back."

"You are leaving us then?" asked Sebastian.

"Yes we are, but I am sure we will return one day. Shall we go Idi?"

"Shall we ever" declared Idi and Marcus looked at him in surprise as Idi shot out of the door.

"We shall meet you at the gate magician to bid you farewell" said Sebastian. Marcus nodded and went out after Idi who had vanished down the corridors already.

Marcus could hear Idi yelling at Katrina as he approached their rooms.

"But I don't want to leave, I like it here: besides everyone says I am going to be the greatest warrior, I have to stay for my training."

"You can't stay and that is all there is to it young lady, now *pack*." Katrina looked up as Marcus walked in and as soon as she saw him she raced across the room and threw her arms around his waist.

"Oh Marcus you tell him, he won't listen to me. I don't want to leave, can't we stay, please?"

"I'm sorry lass but we need to go north and find Cassandra, and I am afraid we need to go as soon as possible." Katrina ran across the room and flung herself on the bed bursting into tears of frustration.

Idi stopped his packing and turned to look at Marcus.

"I am not going north Marcus; I am going west to Dark Pool."

"But Cassandra must be the mother of the prophesied one Idi, we need to find her when there is still a chance, we must pick up her trail before we lose it once more." Idi turned back to his packing, when he had finished stuffing the bag he pulled the strings tight and picking up his bag turned to Marcus again.

"I understand what you must do Marcus, but that is not my path. I go to seek my name from the lady of Treffernon." They looked at each other in silence for a moment. They had become like father and son, both respected and loved the other: going separate ways now would be hard for both of them. Katrina had listened to all and sat up.

"We're a family," she declared, "we can't separate." Both Marcus and Idi turned to stare at her; neither knew what to say. "We must stay together" she said her lower chin quivering as she held back the tears.

Turning back to each other and both speaking at the same time, Idi said, "I just have to do this Marcus."

"I promised Oleanna," said Marcus. They stared at each, willing a solution to materialise. Then speaking at the same time again: Idi said, "I suppose the lady won't disappear if I go in a few days time."

"I have probably lost her trail already" said Marcus.

The two men grinned at each other, Idi dropped his bag and strode to Marcus and threw his arms around him. Marcus gave a "huff" at the hug but after a moment's pause slapped Idi heartily on the back and then returned the hug briefly.

"Yea!" shouted Katrina bouncing on the bed; once more they turned to look at her.

"Maybe we should leave her here" said Marcus.

"What?" screeched Katrina.

"Yes, maybe you're right, I am sure Sebastian would know a good family to look after her until we return," replied Idi.

Katrina's face was a picture of shock, "You *will not* leave me here" she declared in a most indignant manner. The two men looked at her and both burst out laughing.

"Women are so contradictory," said Idi.

"*I know!*" replied Marcus, "one minute they want this and then the next they want that, and what gets me is that they want both with equal amounts of passion!" The two of them burst out laughing again and Katrina pulled her most sulky face. Idi could bear it no longer and went to the bed, picked her up and swung her around the room.

"We'll all go after Cassandra Katie love, don't you worry; nothing would make us leave you behind." Katrina burst out laughing and the merry sound carried down the hallways of the castle. When Idi had stopped swinging her around Marcus came and touched his arm.

"We go west lad, all these years have passed without us finding 'The One' - a little more time won't make any difference: we will fulfil your dream first." Idi felt his chest fill with love for the old man. Nodding at Marcus, his chin firmly set, in an attempt to contain the emotions he was feeling.

"First west: then north." Marcus nodded in agreement, clasped Idi's outstretched hand and shook it firmly.

Chapter Twenty-six ~ Loyalty

Back in his towers Norvora was staring at his face in the mirror. The light that had radiated through Hamish had burnt his spirit, almost shrivelling it up beyond life, but the Three had caught hold of his soul as it had whirled in the abyss of death and darkness, and yanked him back to the living. He reached up and touched the burn scar that lay angrily down the right side of his face.

Oh he would make them pay for this, he would destroy all of them, and he would do it slowly and cruelly.

"Norvora" sang the Three in his head and he groaned; he just wanted time to recover. "Norvora" they sang again but louder. He put his hands over his ears. "Go away" he hissed.

"Norvora" they called again only this time so loud he thought his head would explode.

"Coming" he moaned in defeat. He went out of his private chamber and down the hall to the special room. Outside the room he put his hand on the door and hesitated. If he had known how much of himself they would demand he might have thought twice before he ever started searching for them.

"Norvora" they snapped.

"I'm here," he said as he pushed open the door. The room was a black box, a cube. No windows and only one door. Each side of the walls and the floor and the ceiling all perfectly matched in size, fashioned in black marble. To the left of the door was a large table with a single chair. The table was full of scrolls and inkpots, quills and maps. Opposite the table was an ornate black marble stand; lay on top of the stand was the glass orb.

"You failed again Norvora" one the Three spoke. He had been waiting for this, planning his response.

"Yes but if you hadn't have called me away from the castle I would have been able to stop them getting him out of the room." Suddenly Norvora moaned in pain and grabbed his heart, doubled over; but just as quickly as it came, the pain went and he stood up straight once more.

"Do not dare to defy us Norvora, you are nothing without us."

"Yes my ladies" said Norvora bowing towards the orb, "I am worthless without your guidance. Forgive me please?"

"We have a little task for you Norvora" they purred, and the image of Megan appeared in the air. Norvora scowled at the image; he would kill the witch if he were given the chance.

"What do you require of me my ladies?" he asked.

Then the three of them whispered in his ears and his scowl faded to be replaced with a smirk. He took a step towards the orb and gave an elaborate bow.

"It will be my pleasure," he said before swirling around and walking out of the room as a man with renewed purpose.

~~~~~~~~~~~

Three sunrises had come since the King had been healed. He stood still at the windows of his day chambers and wondered why they had let him live. After all the things that he had done to Havenshire: he deserved death. It didn't matter that everyone seemed to be loyal to him still, that his precious Knights still swore allegiance to him amazed and humbled him. No matter what they all said to him though, he knew his beloved lands were in grave danger because of him, and his weakness in fighting the darkness: he leaned forward towards the window. He should jump now and be done with it.

At that moment there was a commotion in the hallway. Just as he was about to cross the room to find out what was happening, the doors flew open and his servant John came crashing through, staggering, and fell at his feet.

"Good gracious John what is going on?" Hamish asked.

"Your Grace," Hamish looked up to see Torra bristling with anger.

"He's a traitor," Torra declared. Just then Sebastian and two other Knights also turned up behind Torra, panting as if they had run fast to get there.

"What is going on?" Hamish asked again. Torra turned to Sebastian but Sebastian shook his head, "Nay Torra, tis your tale, tell it now." Torra came a few steps closer to the King and bowed before beginning.

"He is Bluedane your Grace."

"You mean he has been to Bluedane?" replied Hamish.

"No your Grace, I mean he is from Bluedane. I caught him copying your papers in you private rooms. From the moment I caught him he just keeps saying over and over again, 'it's too late he's nearly here'." Hamish's face was pained and he looked down at John questioningly.

"Are you from Bluedane John?" John gave one sharp nod of the head. Hamish shook his head in disbelief, John had worked for him for years; he would have sworn that John was loyal to him. Another reason why he was no longer fit to be King: if a King lost his judgement then he wasn't fit to serve.

"He has worked in the castle for eight summers and seven winters your Grace, I checked with the keeper of keys." Realisation dawned on Hamish and he looked down at John and there was great sorrow on his face.

"So the time has come" he whispered, "I never got away with it John did I?" The others were looking puzzled but John snarled his answer towards Hamish and as he did so all his subservient mannerisms fell away.

"You can't murder King Pedro's only son and expect to live you old fool." He spoke with utter contempt and Torra gave him an almighty thump in the face that sent him flying to the floor.

Hamish raised his hand to stop Torra from hitting him again and shook his head. John got back to his knees.

"For what it is worth John I didn't know who the man was; I thought him a simple sailor who had ruined my daughter and taken away her innocence, and with it the only chance of security for Havenshire." John spat at Hamish's feet and Torra kicked him in the stomach. Hamish put his hand out to stop Torra.

"What else does he know Torra?" Hamish asked, noticing that Myles had now also turned up.

"He says Pedro's army are on the seas and that they will be here in the rising of fourteen more suns." Hamish drew a breath and squared his shoulders, fourteen sunrises wasn't enough to prepare an army that had slowly been dismantled over the last few years.

"It's worse your Grace," Hamish turned his gaze back to Torra's eyes and tried to focus, which was hard because he felt as if the room were spinning.

"Pedro has made alliances with Norvora, William and Henrietta." Now Hamish staggered and Sebastian and Myles rushed to support him.

Myles turned to Torra. "Well done man, now take him to the dungeons. Someone else go sound the drums, we will meet in the great hall." Torra grabbed John by the hair and dragged him to his feet whilst another of the Knights ran to sound the drum that had been silent for the longest time. As Torra marched John from the room, John turned his head and called back at Hamish.

"I've been spying on you for years; he knows your every secret he does. He has plotted his revenge down to the tiniest detail; he will wipe the name of Havenshire from the books of history. Your entire kingdom will suffer for your crime." Torra pulled back his right arm and squarely punched John so hard in the face he knocked him unconscious, he caught the falling servant and flung him over his shoulder to carry him to the dungeons.

Hamish allowed Sebastian and Myles to support him only for a moment before knocking them off. He straightened his back and held his head up as he walked the cold corridors to the great hall.

Two guardsmen leapt to attention as they approached, quickly lifting the heavy metal latch and pushing open the huge ornate doors that opened into the hall. Suddenly, seemingly from nowhere, servants came running; some began to pull back the heavy patterned curtains whilst others set the massive fireplace to burn and yet more ran around lighting the thousands of candles that lined the walls.

Before Hamish had even crossed the great length of the room; a servant arrived beside his throne, a golden tray bearing golden goblets and a glass decanter of the Kings favourite brandy in his hand.

Hamish sat on the throne, took one of the goblets and poured himself a drink: he needed it to steady his hands. He inclined his head towards Myles and Sebastian that they should take one also but both shook their head.

A drum was suddenly beaten in the main courtyard. The large drum, hollow and solemn in sound, was struck to the rhythm: one, one-two, one, one-two. It would continue to beat until someone waved a red cloth from the great hall window to indicate it was time to stop. Over and over the drum was beaten, its boom echoing through the streets of the city. All normal sounds of castle life came to a halt, fading away as everyone froze at the sound that announced war.

"Tis the end Myles" said Hamish staring across the wall to where a painting of his late wife hung. *'Soon to join you my love'* he thought as he stared, longing for the comfort of her arms once more: oh how he missed her counsel and steadfastness.

Myles had been with the King since they were both boys and he looked at him, knowing him as a brother, and he knew what Hamish was thinking.

Myles fell on his knees before Hamish and placed his hands on Hamish's feet.

"No your Grace, *we must not surrender.*"

"Myles you know as I do, that even without the support of Bluedane, if Norvora, William and Henrietta decided to go against us we would be hard pushed to survive. There are other Kingdoms surrounding us but all are smaller and not prepared for war. Norvora to our east, Henrietta to the south and William to the west; with Bluedane's army on their sides we don't stand a chance."

"But we must fight: we must make for ourselves `a chance'. We cannot give up without a fight Hamish."

"Get up from your knees my friend; you are too old to be down there." Myles stood up and Hamish reached out and put his hand on Myles arm.

"If we surrender, my head, and those of the Hadrian Knights, will roll. But, the people will be safe; they will live and carry on with a new master: and who knows Pedro might be a merciful man: I hear he rules Bluedane as a fair and just King. Who is to say he wouldn't rule Havenshire the same way? He would probably do a better job than I have done lately," Hamish finished bitterly.

"The people love you Hamish, they would not stand by and watch you be beheaded. We cannot, must not, surrender." Myles choked on his words and Hamish looked at his faithful friend with love in his heart.

"There is no alternative my friend."

"There is" said Sebastian with his whole being, "We will barricade the city. We have been fortifying the walls for many seasons, excuse me your Grace, even against your knowledge, they will not breach us easily."

"Yet if we surrender only a few must die, if we barricade the walls, thousands may die."

The young servant, who had stood holding the tray without moving since he arrived beside the throne, put the tray down on the floor and turned to Hamish. The young man gave an elaborate bow and Hamish looked at him in surprise.

"If it pleases your Grace, may I speak?" Hamish nodded at him.

"I may only be one, and I may be young, but I am sure I speak for the multitude. We would rather die than surrender. We could never serve a master who had killed our King," he took a deep breath, his nerves obvious to see. Then in a loud voice he proclaimed, "Long live King Hamish, long live the King!"

As soon as the drum had started beating the castle folk had been flooding into the great hall, and when that had become full they remained in the hallways of the castle and spilled over into the courtyard. A red flag was waved from the window just then and the drumbeat came to halt. The silence lay heavy in the atmosphere; and into the silence the young servant boy's cry resounded again, "Long live King Hamish; long live the King." There was just the slightest of pauses and then an eruption of sound flooded the city as every man, woman and child took up the cry `long live the King'. The cry was called again and again and as Hamish stood, to acknowledge their cry, tears rolled down his face. The people of Havenshire began falling to their knees, bowing their heads to show their respect for the man who had cared, above all else, for them.

Chapter Twenty-seven ~ Who Am I?

Somebody had called his name and he sat up in bed with a start.

"Mother?" he said.

"No Absalom it is just I, Tarsin." At first Absalom couldn't see anyone and then there was a faint shimmering of light in front of him, as Tarsin came to rest his feet on his bedroom floor to become solid so that Absalom could see him.

"You're the man from my dreams" Absalom said.

Tarsin smiled at him, "Yes I am."

"Have you come to take me home already?"

"No Absalom you must experience many things yet before you have learnt enough about all true things and can return home."

"Like love?" he asked.

"Yes Absalom, like love."

"Will I be a good man?" Tarsin smiled at him.

"Oh yes, in the end you will be a very good man." Absalom grinned back at him, happy at the thought that he would be good in the end; he wondered briefly how long was left until the end.

"Why have you come?" Absalom asked.

"I have a gift for you."

"Oh" said Absalom sitting up straight, for he loved getting gifts. Tarsin came to the side of the bed and leant towards him. In his hands was a medallion tied to a piece of thin leather. He bent forwards and tied the medallion around Absalom's neck. Absalom lifted the silver medallion up and looked at it. There were funny markings on it and he couldn't see if they made a pattern or not.

"It is old writing; it means `one born'."

"Oh" whispered Absalom slightly bemused but he was sure it was good.

"Can you keep a promise?" asked Tarsin. Absalom sat up straight and squared his shoulders, bristling with earnest pride he declared,

"Yes, I can keep a promise."

"Good, then I will share something really important with you, but you must promise not to tell anyone."

"I promise."

"The pendant is magic."

"Oh" said Absalom, immediately impressed.

"It has a special power."

"What is it?"

"It stops the eye of black magic from finding whoever is wearing it. I need you to make me a promise Absalom." Absalom looked at him with big wide eyes.

"I need you to promise me that you will never; *never,* take the pendant off, will you promise me that?" Absalom nodded vigorously. Tarsin looked at him as if trying to work out whether the boy would keep his promise. After a moment he nodded to himself as if believing he would.

Tarsin took a few steps back getting ready to leave, this felt so insignificant but it was all he could do for the boy for now.

"Can I ask you a question?" Absalom asked. Tarsin nodded.

"I had a dream last night, and in the dream someone told me that I was born to be a King. Is that right? I'm going to be a King one day?" Tarsin was surprised; he thought the boy was born a `normal' without any special powers. He came back to the bed and sat on the edge of it to be at Absalom's level.

"You are only born to be the person you become Absalom. Who can say whether you will be a King or not: that is not important. What is important, is that you grow and become you." Absalom pulled a face; he didn't really understand what Tarsin was telling him. He brightened a bit.

"I have been practicing all the weapons, I am very good with the sword; I would make a great King." Tarsin smiled and ruffled his hair.

"A great King is not made by his sword Absalom, he is made by his mercy and understanding." Absalom's face dropped again, he wanted to fight evil and save people, he wanted to be a hero. Mercy didn't sound very much like a hero to him. Tarsin stood up.

"I have to leave now but you will keep your promise won't you?"

"Yes."

"Good, your mother will return in the morning but you mustn't even tell her, do you understand?" Absalom nodded. He had never kept a secret from his mother and he wasn't too happy about having one now, but he had made a promise to Tarsin so he would keep it. He was just about to ask Tarsin if he would come back and visit him again but as he looked up Tarsin had gone. He clasped his small hand tightly around the pendant and dropped it under his nightshift. A warm feeling came over him and he felt safe.

"I'll never take you off," he said to the pendant as he lay down and pulled the blankets up over him. He gave a big yawn, suddenly tired. A magic medallion! It was the best present he had ever had.

Chapter Twenty-eight ~ Leona Earth Enchantress

Caldwin had been restless and eventually decided to get up and make himself a drink. He sat at the big wooden table in the kitchen and wrapped his cold hands around the hot mug. All day he had felt a build up of pressure in his chest and he just knew something bad was about to happen.

He wished Marcus was still here, he would know what to do; he missed him so much: always calm, always a wise word, he wished he could be more like his mentor. Seven years had passed since Marcus had left the homestead, and it felt like an eternity.

The wind was picking up, sweeping in from across the ocean and bashing four bells out of their home. There was a loud crash as wooden boxes in the yard were sent flying by a sudden ferocious gust. He shuddered. The fires were kept burning all night these days as the weather was the coldest they had ever known, but even with the burning coals he felt chilled to the bone.

Just then the door opened and Leona and Joanna came in. He smiled at them, he wasn't surprised the wind had woken them, what did surprise him was that anyone slept.

"Go sit down child, I'll make us some hot milk." Leona came and sat down next to Cadwin and he lifted his arm so that she could snuggle into his big chest. He laughed softly and pulled the blanket wrapped around his shoulders so that it covered both of them.

Just then the main kitchen door nearly blew off its hinges as Selwin came fighting his way into the kitchen. It took all of Selwin's strength to lean against the door to be able to close it enough to lay the wooden plank across the hinges and close it tightly once more. Caldwin looked at him as if he was mad and shook his head.

"Twas the horses" Selwin said, "They sounded so panicked I had to go and check they were alright."

"And are they?" Joanna asked, fetching another mug from the cupboard to make Selwin a drink.

"Yes they're frightened, but safe. I have locked them down in the inner bays to make sure they can't break out in their fright."

Just then the inner kitchen door opened again and Matthew came in.

"Well hello everyone, looks like we're having a party!" Leona chuckled under Caldwin's blanket.

"You young lady, should definitely be asleep," said Matthew pointing at her, Leona went quiet and snuggled in deeper to Caldwin's shoulder.

"Nar man I tell yea I don't know who can'na sleep in this storm" they turned to look as James came in to join them. "Tis hot milk yer makin' there Joanna, good I'll be havin' a drop of the warming stuff in mine if ya don't mind." Joanna shook her head at him but reached to the high shelf for the bottle of special warming stuff!

Hot milk in everyone's hand they sat around the table, silent for a moment listening as the wind mercilessly hammered their home.

"Shall we play dice then, take our minds off the storm what do ya say?" Everyone nodded at James, it was a good idea. Just as he was standing to get the dice the wind died down, and just like that, it completely stopped. Everyone froze, holding their breath waiting for the storm to start again, for storms did not finish like that.

Suddenly Leona started screaming.

"What is it child" said Joanna rushing to her ward's side.

"Leona stop, stop child tell us what is wrong" urged Caldwin.

Leona stopped screaming but her eyes were wide with fear and she shook from head to toe. The others looked at her not knowing what to do.

Suddenly the inner kitchen door crashed open once more and Anthony stood there, his long white hair falling wildly around his face.

"Oleanna comes, she is in trouble" with that declaration he flew across the kitchen in his bare feet and nightshirt, pulled the plank off the door, and went running outside. The others all looked at each other in surprise but as one they scraped back their chairs and went running outside after him.

Anthony stopped in the centre of the courtyard and looked up at the sky. The others did the same and searched the sky. Suddenly a streak of lightning could be seen tearing across the sky.

"It looks like it's coming this way," said Selwin with a nervous laugh. The others just watched, but after a few moments it was obvious the lightning was indeed heading straight for their yard. Caldwin spun around to Matthew.

"Go fetch the others" he said and Matthew went tearing into the homestead. Caldwin turned around just in time to see that the lightning was about to hit him and jumped back against the wall.

There was a tremendous crash as the lightning hit the ground and everyone cowered as pieces of stone slabs and mud went flying into the air. When the dust had settled, they turned back to the centre of the yard to see a huge shallow hole created by the lightning, and lying in the centre of it was Oleanna.

They gathered around her, fearful that she was dead. She was so still and every so often she shimmered in-between substance and a pale vapour. Caldwin knelt by her side and lifted her hand gently. He sent a wave of healing down his arm and into her arm and she moaned. He looked up at the others. "I think we should take her inside in case the storm comes back."

"No" Oleanna tuned her hand and grabbed Caldwin's wrist. "We don't have time, quickly get into a circle around me and wrap your arms around each other's shoulders." Caldwin looked at her but didn't move.

Oleanna used a large proportion of the strength she had left and sent them all an image as to what she wanted them to do. Antony touched Joanna's arm.

"You sit with Oleanna" he said, "you too Leona."

"No" croaked Oleanna, "Leona must be one with you, twelve for strength."

They moved to form a circle just as Matthew came running into the yard with the others.

"Don't blame me for being so long" said Matthew spotting Caldwin's look, "blame Thomas it took all three of us to wake him!" Having received the same visual as the others the newcomers quickly joined the circle.

"What's going on?" asked Tanner.

"They're coming," whispered Oleanna. She threw another image into their heads and instantly the brothers created a dome of glass that covered them.

It was created only just in time, for just as the magic dome was formed the first of the demons arrived and went crashing into the invisible wall. It screamed in rage, its red eyes blazing, its long claws scratching at the dome as he slid down the outside of it. Then seconds later another crashed into the dome, and then another. Thomas turned his head to see behind him.

"No" cried out Oleanna. "Close your eyes everyone, do not look; do not fear. Concentrate on the dome for yea must hold it until the dawn." They closed their eyes as they were bid and sent their magic, in all its different forms, flowing into the dome. Oleanna leant up slightly on her elbow with Joanna's help.

She had to make sure they were concentrating, if they were to open their eyes and let fear flood their hearts, they would falter and be lost. She collapsed back into Joanna's arms. She threw one last thought into all of their minds.

"Stay focused, keep your hearts pure, believe in safety and do not look upon the evil lest its pure darkness should cut your resolve."

The demons came like a plague of locusts, thousands of them. They battered the dome with their fists. They climbed on top of each other to cover every inch of the dome and en masse, they pounded upon it.

The dome flickered for a moment: the brothers gasped fearing the dome would collapse under the demons' onslaught. On and on the demons battered on the dome, so dense were their bodies that the first to reach it were crushed and their black blood trickled over the clear curved wall of the protective chamber. Joanna began to cry as fear gripped her soul, she hadn't meant to open her eyes but as her lids had fluttered slightly she had caught a sight of the demons, their sharp jagged teeth in huge gaping mouths that saliva drooled and dribbled out of in a constant flow. Their red eyes seemed like a million fires and the very sight of them filled Joanna with sheer terror.

"We must go" she screeched and attempted to stand. Oleanna grasped her wrist tightly and forced Joanna to look into her eyes.

"Be very still woman or you will kill us all. You must not break the dome or disturb the brothers or the demons will break through. Close your eyes and ask the Elements for their mercy." Joanna whimpered but quickly did as she was told, screwing her eyes closed as tight as they could possibly be and then crying out to the Elements for their mercy.

"Leona" Oleanna called.

"I hear you" Leona called back in her mind.

"You must reach down to the Earth Element, you must beseech her help, I fear we will not last long and the dawn is still too far away."

"But I don't know how to talk to an Element" Leona cried back.

239

"Look deep inside you child, there is a way, you must find it. The Elements do not answer the call of men normally but I think if you reach her she will answer you."

"I will try." Leona's soft brown nightdress flowed from her neck down to her ankles. Her tiny bare feet could be seen beneath the hem. Her toes curled under tightly as she began to concentrate.

"Do not break the circle," Oleanna warned all of them before she fainted with exhaustion.

The demons continued slamming their bodies against the dome, screaming in their frustration at not being able to break it. They were relentlessly bashing with their fists and clawing with their nails and talons. After what felt like an eternity the demons seemed to go quiet and then backed away from the dome.

"Do you think they are leaving?" Thomas whispered, his eyes squeezed tightly shut to stop himself from opening them.

"I should think not," answered Damien, "tis still a long way before dawn." He was right, if any of them had opened their eyes they would have seen the Shee-Dragon swaying her way across the yard towards them. The demons shrank back from her and when she was ready she lifted her head and sent fire hurtling through the air at the dome. She pulled back her head and screeched in frustration when the fire did not penetrate the dome.

"What was that?" asked Matthew his voice decidedly shaky.

"I don't know," answered Tanner, "but tis getting mighty hot." The others murmured their agreement. Just then there was an almighty crash as a tree was thrown at the dome. There was a tiny sound that brought fear to the brothers: it was the sound of glass cracking.

"It won't hold much longer" cried Selwin, "we have to concentrate everyone, concentrate: don't think of what is happening outside the dome think of something you love. Concentrate on that, pull your magic from that feeling; concentrate, for our lives are at stake." The brothers fell silent and each searched inside themselves for their own special thing. They couldn't see it but the crack in the dome closed over. Something else was thrown at the dome and this time it felt like a house and the dome shuddered under the attack.

Fire and strength were not going to break the dome and the Shee-Dragon decided to change her line of attack. A flash of light seemed to come from beneath her scales and the demons had to turn their eyes away from its brightness. When they turned back again they smirked. The Shee-Dragon had gone and walking towards the dome was the most beautiful woman the world had ever seen. She smiled sweetly and reached up to gently caress the dome. If she couldn't get in then she would have to get them out. She flicked her long beautiful hair back with a quick toss of her head, then smiling, she began to sing. The demons shrank back slowly, some of them actually turning green, some threw their hands over their ears, others threw up vile liquids that filled the night air with a stench so bad the grass withered and burnt under it.

Her song of sweet love poured from her lips like golden honey, all the previous sounds of terror became silent and only her song pulsated in the cold night air.

"That's me ma" cried Thomas in surprise, "what's me ma doing outside? We have to get her in here quick." He flung back his arm to reach through the dome towards his mother.

"No" screamed Selwin who was next to him and felt it the moment Thomas let go of the circle. He reached up and yanked Thomas backwards into the dome. But in that slight moment when Thomas's hand had reached through the dome the Shee-Dragon had blown fire and Thomas's hand was burnt. He screamed his pain and the brothers all opened their eyes at once to see what was happening.

241

Leona screwed her toes up and as she did so she felt the soil beneath her feet. She decided to concentrate on the soil and tried to block the screams of Thomas from her mind.

"Earth Element" she cried. Then like an in-built reflex she sent her soul flowing from her body and into the soil through her feet. Lower and lower she went, below her feet into the soft soil, further down, through the soil and through the rocks. Deeper and deeper she sent her soul, all the time crying out "Earth Element, Earth Element." Suddenly Leona felt as if she had been gathered into someone's arms. She was filled with a sense of warmth and well-being.

"What are you doing here child?"

"We need your help, Oleanna sent me. Without your help we shall die."

The dome started flickering and the dreadful sound of cracking glass filled the dome.

"Hold the dome" yelled Tanner, "hold the dome or we are all die." The demons, sensing victory close by, began pounding the dome again with all their strength. They threw their bodies at it and the sound of cracking glass grew louder and louder.

"You must resume the circle Thomas" Selwin looked into Thomas's white fear stricken face. Thomas wanted to curl up in a ball because of the intense pain from his hand; but instead he reached up and put his arm around Selwin. He staggered slightly as he did it and Selwin pulled his body as close to him as he could to help support him. The brothers now knew how easy their dome could break, and although they were brave men, fear began to worm its way into their hearts. The brightness of the dome began to pale, and the Shee-Dragon smiled, turning back into her normal dragon form.

Leona began to cry, gentle tears rolling down her cheeks. She loved the Brothers: she did not want them to die.

"Hush now, my sweet, let me see you." Leona couldn't open her eyes but she felt loved; and a feeling of total well being washed over her. She curled up in the arms that held her.

"I mustn't go to sleep" she murmured, "We have to do something."

"Hush my sweet," the voice said and Leona drifted off to sleep.

"Ouch" yelled Tanner.

"What is it?" asked Selwin fearing for a moment the demons had finally penetrated the dome.

"Ouch" yelled Anthony. Both Selwin and Caldwin opened their eyes once more to see what was happening. Neither could speak - they just stared at Leona in amazement. A rose bush was growing around her and completely covered her, you could see the shape of her still but you could see no actual part of her. And not only that, the rose bush was growing at a tremendous speed, across from Leona and to Anthony and Tanner who were on either side of her. As the first thorn dived into their flesh the men felt a stab of pain but after that they fell instantly asleep. Before Selwin or Caldwin could react, the thorns had reached them, plunged into their skin and sent them to sleep.

Joanna had been cradling Oleanna's head in her lap, crying to the Elements for their help, pledging to be a better person should she live and see her family once more. After a while she realised that the brothers had stopped talking and slowly raised her head and ventured a glance of them. She dropped her head instantly and started crying out passionately for help.

The brothers could not be seen; in their place was a thick hedge of rose. Deep green leaves smothered with deep red roses. Their fragrance rose in the air and filled the dome.

There came a tapping on the dome. It went on for some moments, and didn't seem to be stopping. In the end Joanna couldn't any more and sneaked a look from under her hair to see what as causing the noise.

The moment she looked up the Shee-Dragon crashed a huge rock down on the dome; it quivered slightly but did not break. Joanne screamed and buried her head down into Oleanna's hair and started to weep.

Joanna did not know how long she wept but after a while she was aware that all was quiet. She didn't lift her head again; she couldn't bear to see the demons. After a while in the quiet, and being exhausted, she to fell asleep.

The dawn came, and the things of the dark returned to the underworld. As the sunrays crept over the horizon the roses began to fade, then the leaves, and then the thorny stalks began to retreat into the earth once more. As the last of the rose stem was sucked back into the earth the brothers woke and the dome fell away.

Leona yawned and stretched as if she had just woken up from the best sleep she had ever had. She saw Joanna all crumpled up where she had fallen to her slumber and ran to her side.

"Oh child, child" wept Joanna with relief when she realised the dawn had come and they were safe. Leona hugged her tight.

The brothers looked around them in shock. The homestead was no more. Every wall, every building had been crashed to the ground; nothing stood for a good distance all around them, even the trees were uprooted and laying on the ground.

Just then there was a sound like the clap of thunder from a far distance. The brothers jumped in fear that the demons had returned.

But before they could move, another Oracle stood before them. Draconis took in the scene and rushed to Oleanna's side. Joanna and Leona stepped aside as he bent down beside her.

He reached down and put his hand on her chest and after a moment Oleanna gasped and opened her eyes.

"You live" he said, lifting her hand and bringing it softly to his lips.

"And so do you my love" she smiled back at him softly. He bent down and placing his hands under her, lifted her gently up into his arms.

"The others?" she asked.

"Tarsin lives but Baruh is no more."

"Oh no" she said softly and buried her head in his chest.

"There was nothing to be done" Draconis continued, "Never in the history of the Kingdoms have the demons planned such a feat that they should attack each of us at the same time so that we could not help each other."

"And in such numbers" Oleanna shivered, she looked up at Draconis, "I owe these people my life, I was losing and I couldn't reach you so I came here, I risked all their lives Draconis, that was a terrible thing I did."

Draconis looked at the brothers standing before them.

"I owe you a great debt," he said, "for saving Oleanna's life you may ask of me anything you desire and it shall be done."

"There is no debt to repay," said Selwin and the others murmured their approval.

"If Oleanna had not come here and shown us how to defend ourselves we would all be dead this day, the debt then is ours to you." Again the brothers murmured their approval of the comment.

"You must all leave here now," said Oleanna turning her head to face them, "it is not safe for you here anymore. Go find Marcus, he needs you now: the war has begun."

With that Draconis lifted himself and Oleanna into the air and they were no longer visible.

After a moment of silence James turned around and started walking towards the ruins of the homestead.

Well then I not be knowing about any of you's lot like, but I
nd to find me trousers before we set off." The other brothers
looked down at their own nightclothes and then laughed and started
following James across the rubble.

"My bedroom was this way," said Leona skipping across the
fallen stones.

"Does anyone know where Marcus is anyway?" asked Caldwin.
The others stopped for a moment and then each shrugged their
shoulders in a gesture to signal no, not at all.

"Arr well then, tis a mighty fine adventure we be in for" said
James.

"Found them" cried Damien swirling some trousers in the air
with glee.

"Tis sure you are that them not be my trousers now are ya?" said
James.

"Oh I'm sure," answered Damien, "these would never get over
your ever expanding waist."

"Hey you" replied James and sent a mug he had found flying
through the air, which missed James by a great distance.

"I meant to throw it there!" said James when he saw the look on
Damien's face.

A few of the brothers gathered around Thomas who was
crumpled on his knees. Together they wove a healing spell and sent it
flooding through his body. The pain began to ease at once and he
sucked in the air deeply in his instant relief. When they had finished
the spell they looked at him. He lifted his hand before them, the tops
of his fingers had gone and five short snarled stubs were left. The
brothers gasped in shock at the sight.

"It is alright," said Thomas, "the only important thing is that I
didn't kill us all. Let this..." he raised his hand, "always be a reminder
to me to have more faith and strength." Selwin nodded at him and

offered Thomas his hand to pull himself off his knees. Thomas lowered his burnt hand and shakily took Selwin's outstretched hand with his other hand.

For a moment the brothers stood in silence and looked at each other. In the passing of one night their lives had completely changed.

Joanna begged to go home and they let her, they would take care of Leona.

And so it was that the Brothers and Leona embarked on their journey to find Marcus. The twelve of them set off down the little worn path that led away from the ocean and the ruined homestead and forwards to find their mentor.

The night had been horrifying; but with the Earth Elements' intervention they had not only survived but had the best night sleep ever!

Their spirits were high.

"Marcus you old owl, we're coming to find you – ready or not." The cry had come from Tanner and they all laughed, they felt the same excitement. A purpose had been planted in their spirits. All the years of learning and studying suddenly had meaning. Yesterday had come and gone and today was a day full of hope and adventure.

About the Author

Tracy Traynor is an accounts manager and to mother of four sons. Since being very young she has loved fantasy stories and her picture story books by the Brothers Grimm and Hans Christian Anderson are still on her treasured book shelf.

When she was at school she was told that she couldn't learn French because her English was so bad. This and knowing she couldn't read and write like her peers led her to believe she was stupid. It took many years to overcome that feeling of being inferior. Now at the age of 52 she has published her first book and those belittling beliefs about herself have long gone.

Visit Tracy's face book page: http://www.facebook.com/tracytraynor
Or blog http://borntobetracytraynor.wordpress.com